No Fake Dating for a Cowboy

Escape to Cowboy Crossing, Volume 1

Alexa Verde

Published by Alexa Verde, 2023.

No Fake Dating for a Cowboy
Book 1 in the Escape to Cowboy Crossing series
By Alexa Verde

·

·

Editing by Deirdre Lockhart at Brilliant Cut Editing.
Cover by Julia Gussman at https://sweetlibertydesigns.com[1]

---

1. https://sweetlibertydesigns.com/

Dedication

To Jessie Gussman.
Heartfelt thanks for coming up with the idea for the Cowboy Crossing series and for helping me so much on the way. You make me laugh, you make me smile, and you make the world a better place.

Chapter One

Looking out the lodge window where the snow-covered slopes gleamed blindingly white, Jessie Ashford shivered at being in the middle of nowhere. Fine, not quite nowhere. Close to some small town in the Show Me State, so different from the hustle and bustle of Houston, Texas.

She made sure to keep close to the oak-paneled wall and stay invisible from outside. She doubted they'd be ambushed yet, if ever, but one had to be careful. Despite the lodge's heating system kicking in, she shivered.

"You know we could be somewhere in Bermuda right now, wearing flip-flops and aloha shirts. But no, you had to pick this place," she told her friend Paisley as Jessie stepped away from the window.

Paisley flipped back her hair—half of its strands shimmered in sapphire blue and the other strands ruby pink. "Stop whining. And one only wears aloha shirts in Hawaii."

Paisley used her phone to check the security cameras. She was a computer whiz, but no one would guess it based on her spectacular hair, petite size, and annoying optimism.

"What does one wear in Bermuda then?" Jessie asked as they walked the rooms.

Paisley examined the surveillance equipment while Jessie ensured she'd have a clear shot at anyone who decided to scale the hill. As a former cop, she might be seeing danger where there was none, but she'd never risk her friends' safety. Not after that recent obituary set things in motion.

"Considering how many ships disappear in the Bermuda Triangle, my guess would be a tracking device." Paisley's upbeat tone took some of the chill off Jessie.

"We already have one of those. We'd fit right in." The view was clear, but it didn't stop her from longing for sunsets as rosy as Paisley's hair—fine, half of it—and attitude. Jessie's aching knee agreed with her.

"You're forgetting one little detail. This place has a basement that closes off to the world if a shootout happens. I'm not sure a house built on sand could handle the same design." Paisley giggled.

Giggled!

"Right. That *little* detail." Jessie had already memorized the place's layout, but a refresher never hurt. Missing something minor could get one shot. Ask her how she knew.

"Okay, I'll admit." Paisley sighed. "I chose this place because one of my pen pals was born nearby and grew up here. The way he talked about his ranch, the rolling hills, and the friendly community... It sounded like a place where we could not only escape to but also, well, maybe belong to." She paused, her gaze becoming distant. "Even if for a little while."

Belong... What an elusive word! Knowing better, Jessie ached for her friend. They'd wanted to belong somewhere for as long as she could remember.

At least the lodge interior wasn't bad. A far cry from the roach-infested cramped apartment where they'd begun their independent life. Hardwood oak floors spread through the entire single-story lodge with its rustic décor. Rugs and paintings depicted untamed wildlife, cozy fireplaces offered inviting warmth, and queen-size beds boasted chocolate-hued embroidered bedspreads and fluffy pillows.

She nodded to herself. If she had to sleep with a gun under her pillows, they'd better be fluffy pillows.

They moved to the living room where a safe lurked behind a painting of grizzly bears. So unimaginative. Both the painting and the location. She gestured to it. "That's a boring painting. Why couldn't the artist have bears wear, I don't know, overalls?"

Paisley squinted. "I can't believe you just said that. First, it would be disrespectful to the bears. Second, our darling Genevieve likes wearing overalls."

Jessie swallowed fast. She'd never wanted to offend one of her foster sisters, not even in her thoughts. "Never mind. The painting is great as is."

"Don't worry." Paisley smirked. "I'm not going to repeat it to her. Arriving tomorrow. Genevieve, that is. Not bears."

Jessie continued her inspection. "Are you sure this place can't be traced to any one of us?"

Paisley folded her arms across her chest. "I hope that's a rhetorical question. Do you doubt my abilities? It leads to an account in the Canary Islands, then Bermuda, then the Caymans, then Bermuda again."

"See? You did think of Bermuda!"

This time, Paisley just rolled her eyes. Then those same eyes narrowed as she looked at her phone. "We've got a visitor. A green sedan's moving up toward the gate."

Seconds later, a voice came on the intercom from the gate. "I'm Ronan O'Neill, and I work for the Cowboy Crossing Police Department. I'd like to speak to you." The voice sounded rich, masculine, and... uncomfortable?

Jessie flattened her lips and shook her head at Paisley. Why would a police officer want to talk to them? The two of them had kept such a low profile since arriving here. Just a little lower, and they'd be in the basement.

Despite Jessie's warning, Paisley buzzed him through the gate, then smiled. "Go meet him."

"Why me?"

Paisley had an outgoing personality. Jessie's was anything but. But then getting stabbed twice, struck in the face three times, and shot once, not necessarily in that order, could take a skip out of one's step. Plus, being hit with a crowbar in the kneecaps, but who counted?

Paisley fluttered her eyelashes. "Because you have a gun tucked into the back of your jeans and I don't."

"Which is an oversight on your part." Jessie huffed and crossed her arms as the doorbell rang.

"I'll see what I can find out about the visitor in the interim and decide whether you should shoot him or invite him in." Paisley tapped a finger to her chin, raising an eyebrow toward a lock of pink hair. "Um, I was joking about the shooting part."

Jessie studied the man through the peephole. Dressed in the local police uniform, plus a cowboy hat and cowboy boots, he held up a badge. Paisley wouldn't have to search long. But then, the uniform and the badge could be fake. Jessie and her recovering kneecaps knew it too well.

"What can I do for you, Officer?" she asked, hoping it was some weird neighborhood watch. She'd made a thorough search of the house to ensure no bodies had been buried there before they'd bought it. It had been too cold to dig in the yard, though.

Which was another reason she should've worked harder to persuade the others about Bermuda. Hawaii sounded good to her, too. She wasn't picky.

"Could I please come in? It won't take long. I promise." A husky voice filtered through the massive bulletproof door.

Jessie glanced back, and Paisley nodded. Apparently, Officer O'Neill had checked out. She never asked how Paisley did what she did. Better not to know.

"There's no one behind him," Paisley mouthed.

That was Jessie's second question. Thankfully, Paisley understood without Jessie asking. Growing up together and living through a tragedy could do that to people.

She opened the door slightly but didn't invite him.

"Your neighbor reported her cat missing," Officer O'Neill said.

Jessie stared at him, wishing his intense brown gaze didn't make her pulse quicken for some reason. If police officers investigated runaway cats in this town, she should've transferred here a long time ago. Her knees and ribs would've been grateful, and she wouldn't have lost her job in Houston.

Well, she didn't exactly *lose* her job. She'd been put on administrative leave while her superiors were going to make a decision. In a fit of anger and stubbornness, she'd resigned. That wasn't one of her stellar moments.

Pain ripped through her, but she did her best to ignore the regret. Hmm, that would be a cat willing to travel far in the cold because they'd purposefully bought a house without any close neighbors. "I feel her pain, but I don't understand what it has to do with me."

There.

That sounded a lot nicer than "You gotta be kidding me." She could nearly feel Paisley high-five her in approval. Jessie moved the door to close it, unhappy with the warm air escaping as if it were her personal property. Bones, once broken, didn't like the cold.

"The owner suspects the cat might've run into your backyard." He placed his cowboy-boot-clad foot in the slit, preventing her from closing the door.

"You gotta be kidding me." Jessie suppressed a sigh as the words escaped.

There wouldn't be a high-five from Paisley now. Now, Paisley would tell the story to the rest of the girls when they got here—and enjoy it, too.

"No, ma'am. I need your permission to look in the yard and retrieve the cat. I didn't catch your name."

"That's because I didn't introduce myself."

A few beats passed.

She sighed. "Jessie Ashford." At her insistence, their group decided to keep their real identities while moving to the lodge. She didn't offer her hand because she might need her hands free to shoot. Then it dawned on her. "It's all a ruse, isn't it? There's no traveling cat. Someone reported new people at a previously vacant house, and you're checking to make sure it's not a robbery in progress."

He chuckled. "That, too. But unless you intend to have a new pet, I'd like to bring Scratcher home. I also consider it my duty to warn you that he lives up to his name. He's a scratcher *and* a biter." A twinkle lit his brown eyes. The guy was broad-shouldered, muscular, and attractive, but even under different circumstances, Jessie wouldn't be looking for romance.

"A scratcher and a biter. Then maybe the owner *wanted* him to run away." A loud meowing coming from the backyard confirmed his words. A runaway cat did, in fact, exist and somehow made it to the backyard. "Hold on." She closed the door and turned to Paisley, then lowered her voice. "Did we miss a cat getting in our backyard?"

Paisley spread her hands. "Only because he wasn't armed. Not dangerous."

"Didn't you hear? He's a scratcher and a biter." Jessie slipped into a parka over her gray sweater and jeans and fur-lined boots. "I guess I'll have to help reunite Scratcher with his human." And get a few more glances at their visitor, and she didn't mean the cat.

No. Thinking. Like. That.

Paisley snapped her fingers and then pointed at Jessie. "You *do* have a soft spot. Or do you just want to spend more time with the handsome officer?"

Jessie nearly choked on her own saliva. "What? No! Next time *you'll* be going on the animal-rescue mission, and I hope it's a coyote." Wait. Why was she salivating in the first place?

"It's all clear so far. I'll watch your back." Paisley's expression turned serious. Literally.

While Paisley didn't like guns, she knew how to use them. They all had to learn, and not because they'd wanted to. But because they'd needed to survive and protect their secret.

Met by frosty air, Jessie stomped outside to their yard. The only footprints were of the guy and the cat, and she paid attention.

Despite being on high alert and noting his impressive frame, she didn't feel threatened. By now, Paisley would know what kindergarten the guy had attended and who'd been the first girl he'd kissed and at what age, not to mention his credit check and background history and whether indeed he worked for the local police.

Warmth crept up her neck. She didn't need to know what girl he'd kissed. Or whether he was single. Did she?

They found an overweight tabby cat in an oak tree, meowing loudly.

She measured the tree, reluctant to add falling from a branch to her list of injuries. "Now what?"

"I'm going to retrieve the poor animal." He stepped to the tree.

The cat arched his back and hissed. Would he bite or scratch first? Happily, Jessie wouldn't be the one to find out.

But maybe she'd be the one to clean Ronan's scratches. Her insides warmed despite the freezing temperatures. Though Madeline hadn't arrived yet with enough supplies to perform emergency surgery, Jessie and Paisley always traveled with first aid kits. Jessie also made sure to have a shovel in the trunk, but she'd rather not remember the reason for that precaution.

Ronan started climbing while she tore her gaze away and paid attention to her surroundings. And the fact that the cameras probably recorded her blush.

She also made sure she stayed out of the way. While she wasn't petite like Paisley, having two hundred pounds and six feet of pure muscle drop on her wouldn't be fun.

Then she stared at Ronan who made it down the tree with the squirming cat. "No scratches?"

"You sound disappointed."

Hmm. Maybe she'd enjoyed the idea of tending his scratches a little too much. Best to send the guy on his way.

"Mom, I brought Scratcher back." Ronan placed the crate on the floor of his childhood ranch home, ready to bolt to the stable nearby.

He'd executed a conflict of interest to search for his mother's cat. In his defense, his mother had called the dispatcher, and Ronan had received the assignment. Embarrassing.

He did love his mother, and Mom adored Scratcher, so he kissed her cheek.

"Wait. I just made apple cake. Your favorite." Based on how she crooned over the feline, getting it out of the crate and cuddling it, one would think the cat was the one who loved apple cake.

The yummy scent drifted to Ronan, but he resisted. The full name of the dessert was cast iron Irish apple cake, and his mother had perfected the family recipe. This place always smelled like yummy food and love, and the familiarity of it warmed his heart.

"I've got to go." With his spare time, he wanted to dig deeper into the lodge's new inhabitants.

Several things put him on guard. The difficulty tracking down the new owner. Jessie Ashford's clear resistance to opening the door and her not inviting him in. Things didn't run that way in this small town. And when she'd turned her back to get her coat, he'd noted a distinctive bulge, signifying she was armed. She also moved in a quiet, stealthy way she surely hadn't been born with.

Plus, the lack of anything suspicious, even speeding tickets on her record, which he'd checked on the way to his parents' place. What kind of person didn't have traffic tickets? Maybe it was just his gut instinct, but she piqued his curiosity.

She looked athletic, on guard, with raven-black hair framing her pale face where not a muscle seemed to move as if she were trained to control her facial expressions.

Growing up with five brothers, he was used to fights, but lots of laughter, as well. Jessie hadn't smiled once, not even when he'd victoriously brought Scratcher down from the tree. He couldn't decipher the expression in her attentive gray eyes, which seemed to study him as much as he'd studied her, and for some reason, he wanted to discern it.

His mother looked up from her seat as she stroked the cat. "Why such a hurry? It's not like you have a girl to run to." Her eyes, the same warm brown as his, turned compassionate. "I'm sorry about what happened to your Isla. I really am. I know how much you loved her." She paused, and her voice soothed even more. "But it's been three years. The only girls you've dated since were the ones I set up last month. Note, after considerable nagging on my part. And now you're refusing even those."

He groaned. Not again. Pain erupted inside, absorbing a blade of guilt about his fiancée. "Mom, please."

"I'd like grandchildren."

The cat meowed his agreement. Traitor. Who brought him back from the cold? But no, Scratcher sided with his human mama.

Then his mother's face lit up as she stroked Scratcher, causing the cat to purr loudly like a tractor. Uh-oh. She had that expression when scheming a so-called bright idea. "Why don't you take this cake to thank the nice woman who helped get Scratcher back?"

"How do you know it was a woman?" Not to mention Jessie didn't seem all that nice, which made his hastened heartbeat all the more inexplicable.

"Don't you know how well the grapevine works here?" One didn't answer such a rhetorical question. "Who's your best source—unpaid by the way?"

He knew better than to answer that too. Still, he admitted, "You."

She took pity on him. "I saw an unfamiliar woman in her mid-thirties with gray eyes and short-cut black hair buy beef, coffee, rotisserie chicken, and donuts at the grocery store. Then my friend saw the same woman buy dog food at our pet store. She took off her gloves to pay, and she didn't have a wedding ring. Another friend saw that woman drive out to the lodge that used to have a for-sale sign and doesn't any longer." If his mother didn't come from many generations of ranchers, she could've made a good detective. She also had an extremely efficient circle of friends who probably bought binoculars in bulk. "The woman was rather thin, so she *needs* this cake."

His mother loved feeding people, for which everybody on the ranch was grateful. But *he* didn't need a headache, and he was getting one anyway. "I seriously hope you're *not* trying to matchmake me with a new woman in town you've never met. First, we don't know how long she's staying. Second, she might have a horrible character. Third—"

His mother's chin lifted, together with her hand to keep him silent. Even Scratcher stopped purring. "Dog food is a good sign. Anyone who loves animals is a nice person. Your father and I are a prime example of that."

"Of course, you are." He gave her a peck on the cheek again. He was blessed to have great parents like his, and he knew it. "If I see Jessie, I'll make sure to give her your thanks."

Warmth spread through him. He didn't mind seeing Jessie again. Not at all.

Maybe that trace of vulnerability in those hostile stormy eyes drew him in. Or just the hint at a smile that tugged at her lipstick-free lips when she'd talked about his lack of scratches. Or maybe the tiny birthmark above her upper lip.

A jolt surprised him. Seriously? Why would a birthmark make his heart beat faster?

Yes, he was going back to the lodge, not to deliver the apple cake but to watch the place. Some people would call it stalkerish, but he called it protecting the community he served. Why so much secrecy on Jessie's part?

He smelled trouble as clearly as he smelled the apple cake. His stomach grumbled. "Maybe I'll have some cake afterward."

"Nope. It's for Jessie. Besides, I heard the way you said her name." His mother grinned like a cat who'd just caught a canary.

Him being the canary. "The way I said her name? Seriously?"

That was enough for his mom to hear wedding bells. He had plenty of brothers, and he wasn't even the oldest, so why did he have to bear the brunt of his mother's quest for grandchildren? In all fairness, two of them didn't live at the ranch, but still.

About an hour in, his stakeout paid off. No, Jessie didn't leave the lodge, which was a pity, but another car pulled up to the gate, a nondescript Toyota so popular it had become one of the most stolen cars. Not because it brought the most funds but because it was easy to sell for parts. The white car didn't stand out on the snowy background, which might be on purpose.

The window rolled down for the visitor to put in the code and revealed a stunning blonde who looked like a supermodel or an actress or at the very least a brain surgeon. Well, the way the brain surgeons were portrayed in TV series. She didn't stir his blood as Jessie had, but it surprised him enough that he stumbled out of the car to take a better look. After all, dressed in all white, he was also camouflaged like a polar bear in the snow, and he didn't even have to cover his nose.

The beautiful stranger's door opened, and a German shepherd shot out of the car and charged toward him, barking and snarling. The dog must've smelled the cat on him.

Ronan stumbled back and was hit by a tree branch. The world went black.

Chapter Two

Ronan came to his senses but didn't open his eyes, embarrassed to the core. If criminals had been at the lodge, he'd be dead now. Some cop he was.

"Maybe we should do CPR." That was Jessie's voice, laced with concern. Maybe his mother was right, and Jessie *was* a nice woman.

"Are you volunteering?" Must be that stunning blonde. Even her voice sounded like music.

He didn't like the teasing in that musical voice, though.

"He was watching the house. That's suspicious." Blonde again.

Despite all that beauty, he liked her less and less.

"He's a cop, and his story checked out." Jessie checked his pulse. He imagined it quickened at her touch. "And he saved a cat."

"Cops can be bought." What did he do to the blonde woman?

"There was no recent activity on his bank account. I checked a year of his deposits. Cop salary," another, younger and more upbeat, voice chimed in. "And I checked the exterior and interior of his place online. He wasn't bought. Unless he's very, very cheap."

Well, that was downright offensive.

Wait a moment. His insides went cold. How... how could they check his account? Or the exterior and interior of the house? Who were these people?

The German shepherd growled. Ronan was surprised the dog didn't go for his jugular yet. Surprised *and* grateful.

"We know you're conscious. You might as well open your eyes." The blonde's sarcasm made him fling his eyes open. "You're trespassing."

Her icy blue stare sent another shiver through him.

He'd looked down the barrel of a gun before, and he'd felt more comfortable than he did now looking in her eyes. "I brought apple cake from Scratcher's owner to thank Jessie for the cat's rescue."

"Isn't that sweet?" the youngest woman among them chirruped. She either had two-colored hair, blue and pink, or he had a concussion. Possibly both. He'd never seen that kind of hair in Cowboy Crossing before.

"Literally." The blonde's eyes narrowed, and the dog growled—huh, a chain reaction. Any time she narrowed her eyes, her pet growled. They must make a fascinating pair.

"Madeline, can you please check him out?" Jessie asked.

He'd rather Jessie check him out. Waaait! What was he thinking?

"That cake better be good." The blonde sighed and shone something in his eyes, then told him to follow her finger without moving his head, then asked weird questions about who the president was now and what day of the week it was.

She was checking him for a concussion. Which was a good sign because, if she was thinking about shooting him, she wouldn't bother to do that. At least, he hoped not.

Jessie introduced the blue-pink-haired woman as Paisley and the blonde as Madeline.

Minutes later, they walked him to his car where he surrendered the cake. "I'd love to show you around town," he said, looking at Jessie. "Considering you're new in town and all."

It wasn't too suggestive, was it?

Paisley giggled.

Madeline glared. "A welcoming committee, huh?"

The German shepherd growled again, but at Madeline's hand-gesture command, the dog went quiet.

There was a pause. Then Jessie said, "No, thank you."

His heart dropped, but at least some genuine regret deepened her voice.

Later, he watched them in his rearview mirror. He was going to go back. He had to. Mom loved that large plate he'd delivered the apple cake on.

The next morning, Jessie schlepped into the kitchen, wiping cobwebs from her eyes. How did she manage to pull night shifts before? The answer was coffee and lots of it.

On the other hand, Paisley looked as perky as her hair. Talk about rubbing it in.

"I've done my research on everyone in the local police department, and Ronan O'Neill seems like a good guy," Paisley said over a bagel and a cup of coffee.

Coffee! Yay!

Jessie brightened for several reasons as she surveyed the snow-covered grounds from the window—redundant, yes, since Paisley had been watching the cameras. "See, I told you." She poured herself a cup of coffee as the rich aroma of roasted beans spread through a kitchen equipped with pots and pans and anything needed for cooking, the knotty pine cabinets offsetting the oak walls and floors and locking her into the rustic atmosphere.

Jessie didn't care for cooking, and wasn't impressed by the stainless steel appliances. But she'd committed to memory what knife she could pull out fast and which pans would work best as a shield if she didn't have her gun on herself. And she could find her way to coffee with her eyes closed. That had actually happened before.

Madeline marched in with her head high and her long straight chestnut-hued hair impeccable. The luscious blonde wig was gone, but she still looked as if she could do a shampoo commercial in the next second. Even early in the morning after a long and exhausting trip, she could've stepped from the cover of a fashion magazine, wearing eyeliner and lip gloss and a fashionable white dress.

On the other hand, Jessie was dressed in sweats with a coffee stain, her short hair sticking out in all directions, and must look like something a cat—maybe Scratcher?—dragged in, took a closer look at, and lost interest in.

Double not fair.

But Jessie and the rest of the group had bigger things to worry about. Like how they were going to relocate Gold here quietly, quickly, and without the use of much force.

The sound of nails against the hardwood floor announced Rusty's appearance. He seldom strayed far from Madeline, and Jessie was grateful for that. But instead of begging for food—or demanding it—he stretched in the hall close to the kitchen, watching the girls with intelligent eyes, ready to defend Madeline at any moment.

Madeline filled his bowl with kibble and another one with water, then went to her pet, knelt, hugged him, and rubbed behind his ear. Rusty's tail thumped against the hardwood as he licked her hands. Then she walked back, blushing at the unusual-for-her show of affection.

Jessie sipped her hot, flavorful black coffee from a gigantic no-nonsense mug she'd had for years. Madeline had brought the good stuff—she didn't use any other, unlike the stale and/or burned liquid Jessie used to gulp in buckets at her former job.

Her heart contracted. Yet she missed the adrenaline rush and the sense that she was making a difference, being part of something bigger than herself. Her contracted heart twisted. If she hadn't listened to her treacherous heart, she could've still had her job. Falling in love, letting people close, could only bring pain and disappointment.

Madeline washed her hands, spreading the scent of lavender hand soap through the kitchen, adding to the lavender-scented shampoo already emanating from her long hair. Then she poured coffee into a delicate porcelain cup with golden trim, turned around, and leaned against the marbled gray counter. Fixed on Jessie, her gaze cut like the scalpel she was used to holding. "You like that guy, don't you?"

Jessie nearly choked on her coffee. "What? No! Of course not!"

"The lady doth protest too much." Paisley winked.

Was that Shakespeare? Genevieve's literature degree must be rubbing off on Paisley.

"Girls, I gave up on romance. First, my boyfriend took a crowbar to my knees. Then, my fiancé shot at me. With the way things are going, my next love interest will either put a bomb in my car or set my house on fire. And I don't intend to find out which it's going to be."

At the kitchen island—more knotty pine topped with marbled gray and surrounded by tall bar stools—Paisley grimaced but devoured the rest of her bagel. "So sorry. You deserve better."

Madeline cut an apple into slices, the scent vying with the coffee aroma for attention. Madeline preferred fruits over donuts and bagels, which perplexed Jessie no end. "Yes, with the situation we're in, it's best not to get involved with anyone."

Coffee turned bitter in Jessie's mouth. Maybe she did protest too much. But needing to deflect attention from herself, she raised a brow at Madeline. "Are you okay putting your life on hold?"

She didn't ask Paisley because Paisley could work anywhere with an internet connection. And since Jessie had surrendered her badge, she was only too glad to leave her private security gig where she babysat rich people's possessions while they were away.

Yes, she'd enjoyed their Jacuzzi, but who needed five Jacuzzis in different parts of the house, then another with a waterfall for about ten people in the yard? She was surprised they hadn't put one on the roof, but they likely would've if they weren't afraid it interfered with their helicopter pad.

Meanwhile, people died on the streets.

Jessie squeezed her teeth together and helped herself to a glazed donut. Getting addicted to donuts was an occupational hazard. So it was her job now to make sure none of her friends died if...

Best not to think about it.

"It's fine." Madeline's words interrupted Jessie's thoughts as she sat down. If Madeline was an actress, she could be playing a countess right now with the way she held the porcelain cup. But then, she possessed a bred-in elegance that even all they'd gone through in their childhood and teens couldn't erase. "I wanted to take a sabbatical. And it's not like anyone is going to miss me."

Jessie's fingers tightened around her mug while compassion tightened her heart. "Your colleagues respect and admire you. And I'm sure they love you, too."

"Yeah, then why didn't anyone tell me about my husband cheating?"

Paisley got up and hugged Madeline. Unlike Jessie, Paisley never hesitated to express her feelings. She was also the most sociable one of them. "You're better off without him."

"I know." Madeline returned the hug, her twisted smile sad. But it didn't prevent her from getting hurt. How could anyone cheat on gorgeous Madeline?

A memory showed up uninvited. The screech of tires and rupture of shattering glass still sounded in Jessie's ears. Like the rest of their team, she knew the code to the gate and had a key to Madeline's mansion. But Jessie didn't have to use the key. The info that someone was robbing Madeline's house had come from Paisley, who'd invaded Madeline's privacy and hacked into the house camera feed. The worst part, the robbery was happening while the owners were inside the house, bound and gagged.

A shiver ran down Jessie's spine despite the hot mug in her hands as if it was still that off-duty night when she'd received the call from frightened Paisley. Sure, Jessie could go to the chief, and he'd put an operation in motion. But who knew how long that would take, considering she wasn't in favor with him. She'd had to act because her friend's life was on the line.

"I still can't believe you propelled your car through the glass doors." Madeline shook her head. "As much as I'm grateful to you for saving my life."

Jessie smiled. "Good old days. Though I still advise against glass doors and large windows, unless they are bulletproof like here."

"But I don't think they make Jessie-proof windows."

Adrenaline shot through her, giving her a better jolt than coffee, even if it was just a memory.

Paisley turned her compassionate hazel eyes toward Jessie. "You miss being on the force, don't you?"

"I miss being needed," Jessie said.

Paisley leaned toward her. "*We* need you."

And for that, Jessie was grateful.

"I'm sorry you had to quit the job you loved." Madeline frowned at the apple slice in her hand, lowered it to the table, and lifted heavily lashed eyes.

"It wasn't you. Your ex filed the lawsuit." Making Jessie a liability to the force.

Because Jessie's shot at the robber might have hit Madeline's ex, when the robber snatched him and used him as a human shield. The ex had walked away with not a scratch but "with a lot of emotional distress" as the lawyer had stated.

Jessie had proved Madeline's ex sold their pricey possessions and replaced them with replicas, then staged the robbery to cover it up and maybe have Madeline killed. He'd persuaded her to take out an expensive life insurance policy beforehand. He'd even already found a prospective getaway wife.

Once the truth became known, it gave more substance to his claim that Jessie had shot toward him on purpose. It didn't help him much where he was going, but the lawsuit and bad publicity had been the final nail in the coffin of Jessie's career.

Madeline looked calm, but powerful undercurrents ran under that cool-as-marble surface. Considering her profession and how deep those undercurrents ran, Jessie and the rest of the girls had spent a long time with

Madeline after she'd found out about the betrayal, reminding her they were in essence good people who didn't go around killing people. And anyway, the soil was too frozen to bury a body.

Since then, no matter how many advances men had made at her everywhere she went, she'd stayed single. She'd gotten a dog from a shelter instead and fell in love with the sad-eyed German shepherd at first sight.

"It wasn't your fault. I was on the bad list long before that mess," Jessie said. "Chief told me I was giving him acid reflux and about to give him a heart attack. When he placed me on administrative leave while deciding what to do with me, I decided to resign." In a moment of anger she regretted.

But no matter how much Jessie missed her job, what was done was done.

Jessie drained her coffee and finished her donut. She drank coffee without sugar or creamer, so that should cancel the calorie intake in the donut, right?

"I told you to go into my profession. Unlike yours, my customers never complain." Madeline delicately nibbled on the apple slice.

"No kidding." Paisley snorted, then covered her mouth. "Oops. I know it's not a laughing matter."

Jessie straightened her back. She didn't like to think about regrets. She had more pressing things right now. "Well, Madeline, we need you to memorize the layout of the house so you can run through it half asleep. I'll explain where the weapons are and every escape route. I hope we won't need either, but it's better to be safe than sorry."

Paisley pulled up something on her phone. "Then study the layout of the nearest town. You can pull it up on the map, but I'll send you detailed photos of the establishments' plans with exits marked. The chances of a car chase or any other chase through it are small but worth spending time on."

Jessie nodded. "All ammunition has been placed. I tried to go with your tastes." Which meant an assortment of the knives Madeline was so accustomed to and a small gun for Paisley to cause lesser recoil to her petite stature. "Each of us has a Kevlar vest in our closet, several, actually."

Madeline sighed. "What a fashion statement. And they are uncomfortable."

"Excuse me." Jessie pinned her with a stare. "Not as uncomfortable as a bullet accessory in your chest. Kevlar vests saved my life several times. We might never have to wear them, but one never knows."

Madeline lifted her hands in mock surrender. She'd seen the results of what a bullet could do to a body. "Fine."

Paisley's sparkling eyes became haunted. "Do you really think Wyatt's death wasn't an accident?"

"I don't know." Jessie itched to stay and investigate it back in Texas, but she was needed more here. "Either way, our Gold is in more danger now."

"I could do a little digging online." The sparkle returned to Paisley's hazel eyes. Of all of them, she'd seemed to recover from their horrible upbringing the best, but sometimes Jessie wasn't so sure.

"There's nothing little about the digging you do." Madeline finished her plate of apples and peeled an orange, sending the tangy aroma skittering across the kitchen island.

There was a moment of silence.

"It's scary, isn't it?" Paisley asked the question they all thought.

A shiver traveled down Jessie's spine. "Yes. Precautions might not be necessary, but still wise. If someone connects all the dots, they might come after our Gold. We're talking about rich, powerful people who can hire the best in the business. And if they find out about our Gold, they'll be motivated. I still don't think that the private plane crash was an accident, either."

If the assault happened, she'd be the one to stay behind while others tried to escape with Gold. Her rib cage constricted. But she'd always stood for what she believed in, and she wasn't going to stop now. Well, she might as well have a slice of that delicious apple cake Ronan had brought. Tomorrow was never guaranteed.

The thought of the handsome officer brought a jolt to her heart. Weird.

Paisley rolled her eyes and helped herself to some cake. "Well, I meant it was scary that Genevieve was dieting again. The thought of eating this yummy cake reminded me. But that, too."

Right. For most of her life, Genevieve was comfortable in her skin. It took Jessie's and Paisley's combined weights to make one Genevieve, and she seemed fine with that.

But once in a blue moon, she'd go on a diet. The last time it happened, she'd growled at everyone for a week, then locked the refrigerator and handcuffed herself to the door to keep from eating anything besides disgusting herbal cocktails. Jessie had the key to the lock, but she was forbidden to enter until two days later.

When she'd entered Genevieve's place then, she found the refrigerator empty and the door taken off the hinges. There was no food in sight, and even the toothpaste tubes were empty. That blue moon was yesterday because Genevieve had decided to diet again.

Jessie reached for another slice of the cake while she had the chance. "Paisley, remember, when she gets here, you're not going to tell Genevieve what I said about suggesting a bear wear overalls, right?"

Paisley shook her head, sending blue and pink strands flying in a fascinating effect. "Of course not. Otherwise, *you* might be wearing that painting, as unimaginative as it is."

Jessie rolled her eyes, then pulled up the cameras on her phone. "We need to watch our surroundings. You missed the cat getting into our yard yesterday."

Paisley helped herself to another cup of coffee. "I didn't *miss* him. I just didn't do anything about a roaming cat. I mean, he couldn't have hidden guns and knives under that fur, so how much damage could he have done?"

"He was a biter and a scratcher," Jessie said, then realized she sounded ridiculous. "Next time, we need to know if even a mouse crosses our yard."

"There's a raccoon there right now." Paisley tilted her head, strands of pink hair flowing into her eyes. "Wanna go say hi?"

"You know what I mean," Jessie muttered.

Madeline laughed, then plucked one orange slice from her plate and plopped it in her mouth, somehow not smearing her lipstick.

Good, she wasn't thinking any longer about that night when she'd been on the hard cold marble floor, bruised and hurt, the gag shoved so deep down her throat she couldn't breathe, her arms bleeding on her silk pajamas. Thinking those might be her last minutes. Having flashbacks to the most horrifying night of her childhood.

And all the pain, all the suffering was because of a man she'd loved, a man who'd vowed to love her and cherish her forever.

Jessie knew the feeling. And who was to say Ronan would be any different from the other men in their lives?

Paisley's phone beeped, and she fished it out of her checkered pink and white pants and answered a text. Work, most likely. Because Paisley looked younger than her age and sported such funky hair, clothes, and shoes—her current shoes had large pom-poms to match her hair—people often patronized and underestimated her.

But Paisley had single-handedly created a profitable and surprisingly law-abiding business, and her mind was razor-sharp. Her funds, plus Madeline's, funded this lodge and its expensive renovations as well as a chateau in France, Genevieve's suggestion, and another, smaller and more rustic lodge in the Canadian wilderness, shockingly, Madeline's suggestion. Who was going to do Madeline's manicure in that wilderness? Grizzly bears or an occasional moose?

Breakfast finished, Jessie cleared the table and gestured to the hall. "Let's go see our fleet."

As the one not tied to a job these last months, Jessie was also responsible for getting their transportation. It started with a Harley Davidson for herself. Though Madeline had driven here in a car that would go under the radar, her real love was Ferraris. Which was fine because they needed a fast car, and Jessie had some alterations done to make it even faster. Genevieve loved SUVs.

That left Paisley whose taste in cars changed as often as her taste in hair color. But they needed a truck, so Paisley was getting one. Which wasn't right, considering she was paying for all this.

"You can paint it pink if you'd like?" Jessie said hopefully.

"Oh, I love it as is." Paisley grinned.

Jessie released a sigh of relief.

It might be for a tragic reason, but it was good to be together again. They understood each other and cared about each other. While they weren't sisters by birth, they were foster sisters who'd grown up together and been bound by a closer sisterhood.

Not just because they shared the same trauma.

But because they shared the same important secret for which Jessie would risk her life in a heartbeat.

Chapter Three

Ronan asked around about the newcomers in the lodge, and nobody knew anything. Even his mother had nothing more to add, which was highly unusual.

He slipped into his car in the police department parking lot and started the engine, letting the car warm. He'd found out some things about the lodge, though. It was still difficult to track down the new owner or the person who'd paid for renovations. Finding companies that had done the renovations was a challenge, too. But once he had, the nature of them was interesting. Why would someone need a bulletproof front door, bulletproof windows and glass patio doors, that high fence, and a hidden safe?

Especially near a sleepy town like his.

That probably wasn't all, just the few things he'd discovered after calling in too many favors. Jessie and her friends had converted the lodge into a fortress, and nobody did that unless they were waiting for an ambush. His fingers tightened around the steering wheel. In his experience, if people felt themselves in danger, real or imaginary, they went to the police. Jessie and the others hadn't.

He'd done his shift, which included two lost and recovered cows, three teenagers breaking a window at the school, and one elderly lady mistaking a raccoon for her cat and being assaulted by the said raccoon. Raccoons could carry rabies, so it was serious and not a laughing matter, unlike the time he'd received a call to remove a skunk that made a nest in someone's garage. Neither the skunk nor Ronan were happy about it, and it had taken days and many showers before people allowed Ronan to approach them.

Including his parents and brothers.

He frowned at the memory. This wasn't what he dreamed of when he'd gone to the police academy, breaking the family tradition of cowboys and ranchers. And in his job in nearby Springfield, which was much bigger than his hometown, he'd apprehended violent criminals and helped solve murders. But after Isla's death, he couldn't stay with the Springfield Police Department. He just couldn't.

A knife turned in his heart. Springfield was her hometown, and everything about that city reminded him of their time together there and her stubborn determination to protect others. The words he'd said the last time he'd seen her stabbed him again. Yes, he'd said them because he'd worried about her being a firefighter and risking her life at her job every day, but how he wished he could take them back, dial back his angry tone.

Returning to his hometown and hard work on the family ranch had saved his sanity then. His parents and his brothers had been there for him, their silent support meaning the world. As soon as there'd been an opening at the local police department, he'd joined it, while still helping at the ranch as often as he could.

He slowed to avoid a pothole.

Really, he shouldn't lament the low crime level in his hometown. It was a good thing people trusted the police with any issues and often met him on the porch with hot chocolate. But it was a while since the town had a murder or any other serious case, an opportunity to prove himself again.

Because he wanted to serve and protect in the full sense of the words. He'd have asked to transfer somewhere he could make a difference, but then who'd protect the citizens of this hometown he loved so much? Maybe God had brought him here for a reason, though that reason still grated like crushed glass traveling through his veins.

He made a turn on the road leading to the lodge, his heart beating faster since he'd see Jessie soon. Did that vulnerability in her gray eyes, well hidden as it was behind an off-putting attitude, draw him in? Or the clean, fresh, slightly citrus scent of her perfume that reminded him of snow and waterfalls, though, of course, not together? Or the mystery surrounding their group like morning mist?

He shook his head to shake off the memory of those large expressive eyes as he sped up. Though Isla was a tall blue-eyed blonde with hair that covered her back when she wasn't on duty and Jessie had short raven-black hair and gray eyes, each had a similar stubborn tilt to their chins and the same determination in the roll of their shoulders.

Either way, getting attracted to Jessie was a no-no. Not until he knew more about her, anyway, and probably not even then. Based on the changes around the lodge, once he did, she'd become an even bigger no-no. The group was hiding something. And that didn't sit well at all.

After what he'd gone through losing Isla, he'd sworn off romance for good—or at least, for a long time. One crippling heartache stirred with regrets and guilt was enough.

So he was pulling up to the gate, not because he wanted to see Jessie again but because he needed to pick up Mom's plate, which she'd already asked for three times. She must've been restraining herself.

His phone pinged with an incoming text as he pressed on the intercom. He checked his screen while he waited for someone to let him through the gate. Then he resisted the urge to roll his eyes at his mother's text. Correction, *four* times now.

"What can I do for you, Officer?" Jessie's voice came on the line.

"I'm here to pick up the dish. From the apple cake." He cringed. Did he sound stingy?

"You are?" A slight tease lilted her voice. "Come on in and have some peach cobbler with us."

Huh. Was it some weird dessert exchange? He drove through the gate as if it were Ali Baba's cave hiding mysterious treasures.

Jessie waited for him on the porch. Her cheeks were rosy, and her posture more hospitable than yesterday.

His insides warmed, and then he tensed. Huh. Could this be a trap?

No, most likely, only his cholesterol level was in danger.

Curiosity picked up as he stepped inside. He didn't know what to expect. The interior was surprisingly simple, with oak hardwood floors and wildlife-themed rugs. And cameras he was sure weren't there before.

Barking made him freeze and reach for his gun.

The German shepherd shot out and dropped near him, scowling. He had a lot of teeth. Very sharp teeth. This time, Ronan didn't back off but held the canine's gaze. The dog was protective and might smell a cat on him. Again.

"Rusty, heel! Stay!" Madeline strode to him, rich chestnut-brown hair swirling around her. The hair seemed different somehow, as if she'd worn a blonde wig yesterday, not just dyed it now. With her hourglass figure and high cheekbones, she could wear a potato sack and still be a knockout. But she wore a beautiful white knit dress and diamond earrings with a choker. At home.

The dog followed her commands, and Ronan had a feeling a lot of men did the same. But she attracted him as much as the beautiful statue in their school—not at all. Though he did wonder whether she was famous and he should remember her from a movie or social media.

"Good morning," Madeline said as coldly as a statue ought if they could speak.

"Good morning." He responded to her, but his gaze switched to Jessie.

Now that woman could make his blood run faster.

"The apple cake was awesome. Thanks for bringing it." Paisley grinned at him from the kitchen. She wore a wildly multi-colored sweater, checkered pink and white pants, and slippers with different-colored pom-poms. Funky triangle earrings and a woven bracelet that looked handmade—by a kindergartner—completed her ensemble.

She winked at him, then took Madeline, who was a full head taller, by an elbow, and led her away. The dog scowled one more time as an added warning and trudged behind.

Ronan turned to Jessie, who thankfully stayed. "I'm here to pick up the dish. Ah, um..." His tongue stumbled. Right, "pick up the dish" could sound totally wrong! "From the cake." Wow. That sounded romantic. Not!

Well, it wasn't like he wanted to romance her, and her exasperated look said it wouldn't be welcome, anyway.

"Invite him to have the peach cobbler, again!" Paisley yelled from the hall.

Jessie rolled her eyes, but her lips tugged up a little. "Care to stay for some cobbler?"

By the way his heart tumbled at that hint of a smile, not only his cholesterol levels were in trouble.

Decades ago...

Jessie's lower lip trembled as her new foster mom showed her to a tiny room, painted white, probably to fit either a girl or boy. She pressed her lips together to stop them trembling. Though she was only seven, her previous foster homes taught her she shouldn't show fear.

A little scar on her elbow attested to that.

A sob rose, but she pushed it down. Nobody liked a crying child. Well, maybe her grandma would've comforted her. But Grandma died when Jessie was three, and Jessie barely remembered her, though she tried hard. Even now, her forehead wrinkled, and her lips pressed together as she tried so badly to remember. But only a faint scent of lemon zest floated in the memory, probably from when Grandma had baked a pie.

This place smelled like fried chicken and bread, which must be a good sign. But, just because the house smelled like food, it didn't mean she was going to be fed. Her stomach reminded her.

She stole a glance at Mrs. Finch. Another thing she'd learned was never to stare into people's eyes. Not that she could see Mrs. Finch's eyes from her height.

Maybe if she climbed a ladder.

As if understanding Jessie's dilemma, Mrs. Finch stopped and leaned to her. "Two more girls are here already." Her lips stretched in a smile, but no wrinkles crinkled around her eyes, which made something in Jessie's empty belly tighten. The eyes were brown. Hard. "They are asleep, but you'll see them tomorrow. Be good to them."

Jessie nodded as if she had a choice. Being good to other girls wasn't a problem. The question was whether they'd be good to her. Her empty belly tightened further. It was bad they were already here. Whoever arrived first could consider the place hers. Not that anything in the house belonged to foster children. Or anywhere for that matter.

The backs of her eyes prickled, but she didn't cry. Not yet, anyway.

Mrs. Finch looked at Jessie's backpack, which had been blue once but was now faded like her hopes. The woman's nose wrinkled as if she smelled something bad. Was it because Jessie was sweating? "That's all you have?"

"Yes, ma'am." Her scalp prickled. Maybe she was supposed to bring something to share with Mrs. Finch. But Jessie doubted the woman with cold eyes would want her teddy bear whose ear was torn and left eye was missing. Or her worn-out clothes. She nearly giggled as she imagined Mrs. Finch trying to fit the pink T-shirt, pale from many washes, on her large arm.

Mrs. Finch pinned her with a stare, making the nervous giggles disappear before they arrived. "The bathroom is down the hall. But you're not allowed to enter our bedroom. Do you understand?"

Jessie nodded, though she wasn't sure she'd be able to keep the promise. The nod wasn't enough, apparently.

"Do you understand?" Mrs. Finch's tone sharpened.

"Yes, ma'am," Jessie squeaked. Her stomach grumbled.

"Go to sleep. Don't walk around the house. You'll wake up the others. Or Mr. Finch." Mrs. Finch paused for a minute, then left.

So no dinner. Disappointment hit like the punch Jessie'd received in the previous foster home.

Her tummy grumbled again, but complaining wouldn't help. She looked around the musty room, shivering at the spider waiting for prey in a cobweb on the ceiling. The brown bed offered a thin gray blanket that matched the carpet. A small desk leaned on the wall as if its legs couldn't support its weight. Would the chair support her or fall as soon as she sat down?

At least the bed looked sturdy enough.

She didn't change clothes but took out her teddy bear, turned off the light, and slipped under the cover. The bed squeaked, and she froze, afraid she might've woken someone up. With her heart beating so loud, she wanted to turn on the light again, but she didn't want to upset Mrs. Finch.

Then she turned on her side, curled up into herself, and let hot tears slip from her eyes as she hugged Teddy. She tried to pray, the way Grandma taught her, but the whisper stuck in her throat.

Then the door squeaked open, and she held her breath. The footfalls were light, so it wasn't Mrs. Finch or the husband Jessie hadn't seen yet.

Her insides trembled. Was it those other girls who were here first to show who was the boss? To take whatever she had? Would she have to take a beating? She wouldn't be able to complain. Nobody liked a snitch, and Mrs. Finch didn't look like she wanted to be bothered anyway.

"Are you asleep?" A whisper reached her.

Would they leave if she pretended to be asleep? Jessie doubted it.

"No," she whispered back, her little fingers fisting.

Rebellion seethed. Maybe they wouldn't want a one-eyed teddy bear, but if they did, she wasn't going to give him up. He was Grandma's present, the only one she'd managed to keep from being taken away. Bruises and the scar on her elbow were a small price to pay for that. He was her only friend during the last three years. That was as long as she could remember.

Her bed shifted as someone slipped up there. No, *someones*. Two people.

"It's best not to turn on the light." The same voice whispered in her ear. "They don't like it. And they don't like us leaving our rooms."

And that was going to be a problem. Her heart felt like someone took it and squeezed it. Hard.

"Are you the new girl?" A different voice. Stronger. Older. Weird, she smelled bread and chicken?

Jessie would need to look out for that one.

"Yes," she said.

"I'm Genevieve and this is Paisley. One more girl should be coming soon, and that's it. It's hard to eat in the dark. But you must be hungry."

Something was placed in her hand. A sandwich? They must've known she'd be hungry. They probably hadn't gotten food when they arrived, either.

"Don't leave crumbs, please," the younger voice said. Paisley.

Jessie practically inhaled the sandwich, perking up. "Are we allowed in the kitchen?"

"Only to pick up dishes and wash them." Genevieve kept her voice low.

"Not at night, then."

"No," Genevieve said.

So they'd either stashed it in the day or broken the rules for her. That required giving something in return.

She hugged Teddy tighter. A lump grew in her throat. "You can have Teddy. Just not, not forever, please."

"It's okay." The bigger girl hugged her.

Jessie could see better in the darkness now, enough to distinguish long hair and chubby arms.

The second girl hugged her, too. Paisley's bangs were cut unevenly. Did someone do that to her when she was asleep? Compassion stirred. It had happened to Jessie before.

"Your bangs..." Jessie whispered.

"I cut them myself." Paisley puffed up. "How do they look?"

Jessie thought for a moment. "They look great."

She was much warmer now, and the pleasant heaviness in her belly made her relax a bit. Her eyelids grew heavy, as well, but she couldn't sleep. If she did, she might get kicked out of this house and into the next one. While Jessie didn't like Mrs. Finch, the girls didn't seem so bad.

"They shouldn't find us in each other's rooms. It's against the rules," Genevieve whispered. "I'll leave now so you'll have more space. Paisley will leave in the morning. We'll oil the door hinges tomorrow, so it doesn't squeak." The bed shifted, and then there was a movement of air.

Jessie's tummy rolled weirdly as if she were sorry to have the older girl go. But she was grateful Paisley stayed. Not leaving the room might be a problem, though.

Jessie had stolen some rope to resolve that problem before, but she didn't want to use it yet. If someone decided to beat her up, she wouldn't be able to move. She knew it all too well.

Could she trust Paisley with her secret? She'd just met the girl.

"I sleepwalk," she blurted out. Would she have to explain it?

"It's okay. Stay near the wall on the bed. If you're gonna sleepwalk, you gotta move over me. I'll wake up and wake you up."

Air whooshed out of Jessie. That sounded much better than tying herself to the bed. "Thank you."

"You gotta sleep. They make us do chores in the morning." Paisley sighed. "Evenings, too. But don't you worry. Things are gonna be okay."

Jessie shouldn't argue. But the words escaped her mouth. "It's never gonna be okay."

Paisley kept quiet, making something in Jessie tighten. Finally, Paisley said, "Right. Things are never gonna be okay. But they're gonna get better."

That Jessie could believe. She curled up like a kitten and fell asleep.

Chapter Four

Present time...

Well, this was awkward.

This wasn't a date. It was a friendly dinner in the barbecue restaurant with a newcomer in town Ronan was curious about. Like he was some kind of a welcoming committee. That role was assigned to his mother, but somehow he or one of his brothers always got dragged into it.

Okay, this time he walked into it all on his own.

He pulled out a chair for Jessie, aware of the curious glances around him. He gave waves and nods, rumors brewing already. He hadn't voluntarily dated since Isla died.

Not... that this was a date.

Still, he couldn't help noticing she'd chosen the table as far away from the rest of the people as possible—and one from which she could see the exit. She also chose the seat where her back would be to the wall.

So she was law enforcement. She'd told him so over the peach cobbler, and it had rubbed him the wrong way. He had huge respect for women in law enforcement, worked side by side with several, and admired them. He really did. He just couldn't survive another loss. It had hurt too much the first time around.

He winced. Why was he even thinking that? He'd just met Jessie.

She sat down, and he took a seat. The waitress, Makenzie, appeared right away, curiosity gleaming in eyes generously outlined by eyeliner. His heart softened. Makenzie used to be a troubled kid, had gotten into bad company, but had now turned her life around. He made a mental note to leave a big tip. She was going away to college next year on a scholarship, no less, and her tips were for the college dorm fund. She was a good teen, and her appearance with five rings in one ear and two in the nose was deceptive.

She took their drink orders with a smirk, then left. He bristled at the smirk. Couldn't a guy take a gal out to dinner?

Jessie glanced around. "Everyone is staring at us. Huh."

Did all that make it uncomfortable? She'd said it without irritation, as a simple observation, but he suspected she didn't like being the center of attention.

"Because you're beautiful," he said.

That was true, too. Not in a conventional sense, no.

But something about her demanded attention and didn't let go. Short black hair accentuated her prominent facial features, and golden earring studs underscored her delicate earlobes. Unlike Makenzie, Jessie only sported the one piece of jewelry. She wore her simple clothes somewhat baggy as if she wanted to appear bigger and tougher than she was. She didn't add any makeup, and her hair didn't look styled, just brushed through. But she had the kind of understated beauty that took a while to notice, but once it drew you in, it took a hold of you. Most of the women he'd met had done their best to enhance their beauty while she'd done her best to hide it, to blend into the background.

Why?

The aura of secrecy around this group of friends crystallized the most around her. His gut warned him again he'd be better off staying away from her. Or was it his heart?

One thing was clear—it was his *stomach* that growled now.

Just great.

She leaned forward. "Beautiful, huh? You don't have to give me compliments. It's not like this is a date or we are a couple."

His empty, but thankfully no longer growling, stomach sank. Somehow after she said this wasn't a date, which before he'd been totally fine with—totally!—a part of him wished it could be. Even a fake date with her would be better than none at all.

It wasn't male pride, though no man wanted to be friend-zoned. But then, nobody wanted to have their heart broken, either, by a stranger who wasn't keen on staying in his beloved town. By a stranger who held perilous secrets.

"People tell other people they are beautiful all the time. And something about you draws people in. It did with me." He swallowed hard. Did he reveal too much?

Her gray eyes widened. Tiny dark specks were sprinkled in them, and when she was surprised like now, they turned a brighter color like a creek basked in sunlight.

Before she had a chance to reply, Makenzie appeared with their drinks, the same smirk on those blue-lipsticked lips, and took their orders. He ordered a steak with baby potatoes, and Jessie ordered barbecue wings and fries. No wilted salad for this woman, and he took satisfaction in that.

He'd thought before about taking her to Springfield to some fancy restaurant where they could also avoid all this attention and rumors. But he'd been selfish. Isla was from Springfield, and he still didn't like to put a foot in that city unless he had no choice. Besides, he wanted Jessie to see him in his element, in a simple barbecue place where one didn't need to learn which fork to use for what dish, somewhere comfortable, cozy, and homey. He was comfortable in this place with local wildflowers—dried this season—on rustic tables, open beams along the ceiling, and barnwood walls decorated with ranch gear, and he'd hoped she might like the same place and be comfortable here.

At heart, he was still a cowboy, simple, down to earth, and honest to a fault. But who was she, really?

They found common ground in talking about police work, whatever they could disclose. Both of them being cops, though she was a former one, created a bond. Her eyes lit up as if she missed being on the force.

Then why did she leave? He doubted it was because another job paid higher. She seemed a dedicated cop, one who cared about justice or had once. There was something real and solid about her, despite all the secrets.

She must've sensed his question because she then told him how she'd left her job.

Heat flared in him, and his gut tightened as he almost slapped the rustic table, rocking the wildflowers in his knee-jerk reaction. "That's unfair!"

She shrugged as she sipped her black coffee. "Worse things can happen. But thank you."

Her slight bitterness suggested worse things had indeed happened to her. Compassion unraveled, and with it came the desire to know more about her story. It wasn't just because of curiosity or professional obligation to keep peace in town. When did he start caring about someone he barely knew?

Their food arrived with mouthwatering scents, halting the conversation.

Once Makenzie left, he said grace. Jessie's muttered amen hardly sounded convincing.

His heart shifted. Was she an unbeliever? Or, more likely, had she lost her faith? Silently, he added a prayer for her to return to God. Maybe, he could help her believe in a loving God again.

But it was one more thing to add to the reasons he shouldn't be attracted to her. Why was he drawn to strong-willed, stubborn women who lived to protect others, even if it meant putting their lives on the line?

He did his best to mind his manners and even cut the steak carefully. To his surprise and inner approval, she dug into her wings with gusto.

Then he said, "Tell me about your family, please." He truly wanted to know. His family meant the world to him, and his parents and brothers had helped shape the man he'd become now.

Her eyes shadowed. "I've never met my father, and don't know where my mom is. Grandma took me in, but she died when I was three. I grew up in foster care."

His fork with a bite of steak halted halfway to his mouth, and his appetite diminished. He shouldn't have asked. "I'm sorry."

"The people at the lodge... They're the only family I know. Us girls met while being fostered by the same foster parents." Her lips twisted when she said *parents*, hinting not much good parenting had happened.

Genuine affection warmed the rest of her sentence. Now he could better understand the group's close dynamics. They had a bond much stronger than family.

Shared pain could bind people as much as shared blood. Probably more.

His hand shifted to reach for hers, though barbecue sauce glossed her fingers, but he stopped himself from touching her.

Yet he couldn't stop himself from saying, "I shouldn't have been prying. And I'm sorry about your loss." He said a prayer for her.

Her gaze turned thoughtful as she munched on her fries dripping with ketchup. "You see, I don't know whether that was a loss. I never knew my parents' love. My mother was a junkie and likely had no clue who my father was. She left me in the hospital shortly after I was born. I found out later I had a few health issues that required surgeries, but thankfully, the latter were successful. It could've been worse. And I could've grown up with her and the many men who visited her. I was better off growing up with some of the best people on the planet."

He drank some of his coffee, studying her. Her gaze was open. She'd gone through traumatic experiences, but she wasn't bitter. She'd made the best of a horrible situation. He respected that. He could also better understand now why she was so rough around the edges.

The wings on her plate were disappearing fast, and so were the ketchup-drenched fries. She was someone who enjoyed her food—or someone who'd gone hungry in the past and learned to eat fast and as much as possible because of uncertainty over when and if she'd get food next.

Then her hand with a fry stalled. "Well, except..."

"Except what?"

Her expression hardened. "Never mind. How about you tell me about your family?"

He loved that topic, and a part of him relaxed. "My parents were high school sweethearts. They have been married since they were eighteen and still adore each other. Fair warning—Mom can be a nosybody sometimes, but she means well. She still cooks up a storm for all our ranch hands. Both my parents have Irish blood in them."

Jessie took a sip of her tea. "Hence cast iron Irish apple cake."

"Yes. I have five brothers, none married yet, to Mom's great lament, and we all grew up on the family ranch. I'm the middle child. Three of my brothers work at our family ranch, including the oldest who took the role of manager after Dad semi-retired. The youngest is a reporter, always chasing the next big story around the world. He's our wildest one and got into the most trouble as a kid. The second-born joined the military. He's a silent, protective kind of guy who always stood up to the school bullies. Mom worries about those two and doesn't lose hope they'll return sometime soon."

"I don't blame her. It's good to have the family close." Jessie's lips curved up. "I like your mom already, even though we haven't met."

That warmed his heart. He took no shame in loving his mother and caring for her. "She likes you, too." Hence, the matchmaking efforts that tripled since Jessie had appeared in town. But no need to mention *that*.

"Really?" She wiped her hands on a napkin. "When she meets me, she'll know better. I'm not very likable."

"Why would you say that?" His heart shifted, telling him *he* liked her plenty. No need to mention that, either.

"Oh, come on. I'm rough around the edges and don't pretend to be warm and soft. I tell things as they are."

"Just because you constructed walls around yourself doesn't mean people can't see through them." And now he saw her as a brave, strong-willed, and hurting woman. Or was he kidding himself?

"Am I that transparent?" She frowned but then broke into a smile as she helped herself to more fries. A drop more, and they'd be swimming in a ketchup sea. Her entire face lit up when she smiled.

It brightened something inside him, as well. She didn't smile often, but when she did... Wow.

"The opposite. I had difficulty reading you at first." Now he could understand why she was so guarded, though. Or he hoped he did. Because his gut hinted she wasn't telling him a lot.

She'd eaten the wings with such abandonment and enjoyment that sauce smeared not just her fingers.

A smear of it landed on her cheek, close to the corner of her mouth. Not far from the birthmark that drove him crazy. Her plump and kissable mouth... He shifted back. He shouldn't be thinking things like that! Maybe it wasn't his best idea to take her to a barbecue place for this so-called nondate.

A small ball of fire ignited somewhere inside him. He moved his gaze from her lips to her eyes fast and wished he'd asked for iced tea instead of coffee. Winter or not, it felt too hot in the room already.

"Um, you have a little sauce right here." He pointed at the corresponding place on his face.

"Here?" Her tongue flicked out of her mouth.

For crying out loud! Did she forget about the existence of napkins? She used them for her hands. A family of fireballs cavorted in his stomach now, and it seemed they were inviting their friends for the party, too.

"No." His voice was unusually husky even to his ears.

"There?" Her tongue moved further, her expression serious.

"No, the other side." Okay, he knew she wasn't teasing him. She'd insisted this wasn't a date and shot down his compliment. She didn't even try to flirt, which was a shame.

Yet those fireballs were having a dance party now. He suppressed a groan when her pink tongue flicked again. Enough was enough.

He snatched a napkin, leaned over the table, and swiped the corner of her mouth. "Here. All gone."

But his attraction wasn't. He sank back in his chair, watching her pick up another wing with even more barbecue sauce on it.

"Thanks." She reached for one of the barbecue sauce bottles on the table and added it, oblivious to the torture inside him.

Seriously? He couldn't go through that again. "Don't mention it," he said with all the nonchalance he could muster, which wasn't much.

Their gazes met and held, and heat churned in the pit of his stomach, expanding more and more with every second.

"Oh, just kiss the girl already." Makenzie showed up and refilled his coffee cup without asking.

Heat reached his face, probably scorching it the color of ketchup. "Excuse me?"

"Never mind." The waitress grinned. "I don't want to jeopardize my big tip." She snickered and moved on to other patrons before he could say anything.

Jessie quirked an eyebrow as the pile of bones in front of her grew. "What was that about?"

He shrugged. "No clue."

Not true, but he didn't need to scare Jessie off. For her, this was a friendly dinner. But the rest of the town would be discussing their wedding by now.

He grimaced. "Okay, fine, I *do* have a clue. People in town might have some, well, matchmaking ideas. My mother most likely is already thinking about the story she's going to tell her grandchildren about us while she strokes her pet. 'It all started with a cat. His name was Scratcher.'" He cut his steak furiously. How did he get himself into this mess?

To Jessie's credit, she laughed. "A cat, not a kiss?"

He froze. Did she flirt with him? Finally? And why did that send a pleasant wave through him?

"How is Scratcher doing, by the way? No more running away?" Her voice turned teasing.

He loved those teasing notes. "No. Staying nice and warm inside." If he didn't know better, he'd think his mother had driven to the lodge with the cat and released Scratcher.

Ronan was extremely warm inside now as her mention of the kiss had him fixated on her lips.

His phone rang in his pocket, and he ignored it. It must be one of his siblings or their mom curious how his date—ahem, not a date!—went. Ronan had put the volume on low. He should've turned it off completely. But with the local police force so small, people called him sometimes even when he was off duty. He took that trust seriously.

She drained her coffee and waved toward his pocket. "Please feel free to pick up your phone, don't ignore it on my account. Could be something important."

His shoulders sloped. It *could* be an emergency. As much as he didn't want this date to end—nondate, really!—when he'd become a police officer, he'd known he could be called to duty at any time. He'd gladly taken that responsibility, as well as the chance that, between him and Isla, he might be the one to die first. And yet...

The memories were sharp, but not razor sharp any longer. Was he betraying her memory by being attracted to someone else?

"Your phone," Jessie reminded him, her voice amused as he stared at her.

"Right." He swiped the screen to answer.

Once he finished the call, his frown deepened, and he shot to his feet. "There was an accident close to our ranch, and the officer on duty is down with a nasty bug right now. I'm sorry. I have to go." He pulled several bills from his wallet. Enough to cover the bill and a 50 percent tip.

She nodded. "I understand. I've been in the same situation plenty of times. Anything I can do to help?"

"I appreciate the offer, but no thank you." He rushed toward the exit.

He nearly slapped his forehead. He didn't even ask if he could call her again. Didn't walk her to the car and didn't accompany her home. What an awkward ending even to a nondate. His manners were beyond rusty.

Would Jessie understand his hastiness?

Then it registered. The reason the license plate and the vehicle description sounded familiar on the phone. The white Toyota. A shiver traveled down his spine, and not because of the frosty air.

He called the dispatcher back as he hurried to his car, snow crunching under his cowboy boots. "Was the victim's first name Madeline?"

At the footfalls behind him, he whirled around.

Based on the worry in her widened eyes, Jessie had heard him. She reached for his arm. "If this concerns Madeline, may I follow you, please?"

Her gray eyes were pleading. He found out today that group was like sisters. And if one of his brothers got hurt, Ronan would want to be there to help. So as he received the affirmative answer about the vehicle's owner, he nodded to Jessie before sliding into his vehicle.

As he drove off, a more frightening thought appeared. These women had taken a lot of precautions while arriving here as if they were trying to escape.

Was Madeline's accident really an accident?

Chapter Five

They got to our Madeline.

Jessie's heart was pounding as she paced the ER waiting room. The antiseptic scent reminded her of the time she'd been shot. Madeline's face was one of the first Jessie had seen when she'd come to her senses after surgery. Together with the rest of the girls.

A fist tightened around her heart and squeezed. She'd already completed whatever she could on medical forms and now didn't know what to do with herself.

How badly was Madeline injured? Had they been discovered because Jessie was selfish and went to dinner with Ronan? Pain knifed her stomach. She couldn't afford to repeat such a mistake.

Ronan and she had to stop seeing each other.

He'd gone to process the accident scene and write reports, while she'd driven to the hospital where the paramedics took Madeline. Somehow, she missed his silent strength already. Today, he'd had the ability to calm down the restlessness in her, and she craved it now like she'd craved the painkillers after surgery. Not that she'd allowed herself many painkillers, considering her heritage.

She gave a mental headshake. Her foster sisters should be here soon. She'd asked him to help with transportation, but she should've known better than to rely on an outsider, especially now.

Trusting outsiders had never led to anything good, as each of them had discovered. She'd have to hush the longing in her heart. Madeline was more important. A lick of heat in her belly was unwelcome as she remembered his gaze on her lips. As if he'd wanted to kiss her in the restaurant.

The last man who'd kissed her had put a bullet in her later. It turned out her fiancé only dated her to ferret out information about an ongoing investigation. It should be easy to walk away from a new attraction after that.

It wasn't. Regret shot through her.

How could this happen? Ronan and she only had one date—no, not really a date even. Okay, so she'd miss seeing Ronan.

So what?

It was for the better, and her heart would understand it eventually. Her entire concentration should be on Madeline getting better and finding out whether anything sinister lurked behind the accident. Her blood rushed faster, as it always did during an investigation. She'd investigate the events in Texas, as well. She should've done it already. The trail might be cold, but better late than never.

Hurried footfalls announced her friend's arrival. She didn't expect to see Genevieve, and she didn't. Someone had to stay with Gold. Always.

Paisley hugged her. Tears welled in Paisley's eyes, so rare for her, but she lifted her chin. "She's going to be alright. You'll see."

Oh, the eternal optimist.

When Paisley reached her, Jessie glanced toward the ER. "Just how long will it take them to give us some information?"

Paisley gestured to the navy-blue plastic chairs that must be as uncomfortable as they looked. "Let's sit down. They'll let us know as soon as they know."

Jessie's teeth set on edge. Sometimes Paisley's positivity could be annoying. But she did sit. She was wrong. The chairs were even more uncomfortable than they looked.

"I can't even imagine Madeline on the other end of the scalpel," Paisley whispered.

Jessie flinched. "Don't even kid like that. I'm sure it won't come to that."

"While we're waiting, how about you tell me about your date?" Paisley asked, probably to take their minds off the gruesome possibilities.

"That's what you want to talk about when Madeline has just been in an accident?"

Paisley shrugged. "Well, we can talk about all the accident reports you wrote in your life, work ourselves into a frenzy, and—"

"Got it." Jessie lifted her hand to stop the tirade. "For your information, it wasn't a real date. I didn't get any hand-holding out of it or a kiss good night...."

So her heart had fluttered when he'd wiped that barbecue sauce from her cheek, but it was a cleaning activity, not a romantic one. Her shoulders sloped as she slumped forward in her chair and kicked an idle foot against the coffee table before them.

Paisley studied her. "Did you, um, tell Ronan it wasn't a date?"

"Well, duh. And when he told me I was beautiful, I said he didn't have to compliment me."

"You're even more hopeless than we thought." Paisley rolled her eyes. "And that's saying something."

"Nice to meet you, kettle. Anyway, we should be talking about Madeline and not me and Ronan."

Paisley's hazel eyes widened. "Oh, so there's a you *and* Ronan?"

As if conjured by the question, he strode into the room, accompanied by a broad-shouldered bearded man even taller than Ronan was, and that was saying something. Unlike Ronan, who was clean-shaven, this guy had a walnut-hued beard, but they shared attentive brown eyes as well as an impressive physique chiseled by outdoor labor.

Ronan introduced the guy as his older brother, Brandon. A poster cowboy with scuffed brown cowboy boots, the newcomer worried a once-white cowboy hat between his hands, and his shoulders hunched up by his ears even as guilt creased both men's faces.

Okaaay, Jessie didn't like it at all. Her gut tightened as she sat up ramrod straight. What was going on?

"I want you all to hear from us what happened. One of our horses jumped over the fence and into the road. Your friend swerved to avoid hitting the horse and ended up going off the road."

Jessie's eyes narrowed. "Wait a moment. So, right now, Madeline is in the ER because..."

Brandon hung his head. "Because of my mistake. I should've discovered the mare gone sooner. Usually, horses respect our fences, so this doesn't happen often."

Paisley's fingers fisted, fire in her eyes, as she leaped to her feet. "That's a costly mistake to make!"

Huh. Where was Paisley's positivity now? But then Jessie should be on her friends' side and not Ronan's family's.

"This shouldn't have happened!" Considering Paisley's petite size, this scene looked like a Chihuahua barking at a bear, though Jessie would never say so.

Nor should she ever compare her friend to a small dog. What was wrong with her? These weird feelings were affecting her judgment like they had before. Yep, before she'd been shot.

Before Paisley could start pounding on the guy's chest, the doctor appeared. It turned out Madeline had lots of bruises and a broken right wrist.

Jessie flinched. "That's her cutting hand." At the flicker of surprise on the doctor's face, she covered her mouth. "Um, never mind."

Paisley stepped forward, looking calmer now. "Thank you, doctor. None of this is life-threatening, correct?"

"There's always the risk of infection and complications. But currently, I foresee no risk to her life or permanent damage. It could've ended much worse."

Relief whooshed out of their lungs.

"I want to see Madeline," Jessie said. And stop seeing Ronan. One should be much easier than the other.

"Oh, just shoot me!"

As Brandon groaned, Ronan straightened his back the next day. Mucking stables wasn't his favorite job, either. But he'd never complained before, and neither had his older brother. "You're scaring the horses. And if it's that bad, I can do your part, no problem."

Brandon brightened as he wiped his hands. "You could do my part?" Then he groaned again. "You didn't hear it yet, then."

"Hear what?" Ronan finished cleaning and refilling the water buckets and moved closer. It must be something bad to cause such a reaction in his hardworking and usually satisfied-with-life brother.

"After what happened to your *girlfriend's* friend, Mom roped me in to be Madeline's helper while that high-maintenance princess recovers. Because Madeline can't use her right hand, and it's all our fault."

Aha. That explained Brandon's long-suffering look, so unusual for him. Ronan's taut muscles loosened as he moved to scrub the stalls. "First, you don't know she's a high-maintenance princess. Second, aren't you the one who usually does the roping?"

Roping, like many other activities with cattle and horses, was a regular part of their adolescence.

"Very funny. As for the woman, didn't you tell me how gorgeous she was and how she wore expensive clothes *at home*?"

Man, he needed to learn not to share so much with his brothers. "Well, those clothes might not be expensive. Come on. It might not be that bad. Madeline needs help. Tell you what. I work tomorrow, but I can go to the lodge in the afternoon and relieve you."

His heart skipped a beat. Fine, he had a selfish motive, too. He'd have a chance to see Jessie at the lodge. She couldn't be holding a grudge since their horse caused her friend's accident, could she?

"So you could see beautiful but rough-around-the-edges Jessie, right? Mom wouldn't go for it. She wants me to fall in love and marry this new woman in town, never mind how wrong Madeline is for me. Couldn't she at least set me up with a local girl?" He lowered his tone, mindful of the horses.

Ronan started filling feeders with alfalfa hay. "She tried to do that, remember? You refused all her attempts."

"Good thing I don't believe in conspiracy theories with horses. Or I could think..."

Ronan chuckled and patted him on the back. He didn't believe in cats being matchmakers, either. But to think about it, he might bring Scratcher some fancy cat food. "It's going to be fine."

With that frown, Brandon didn't look convinced. "She'd better not send me to fetch her some crème brûlée or something. They don't even have crème brûlée in Cowboy Crossing."

"I'm impressed. You know what crème brûlée is."

Brandon shrugged as he helped Ronan dole out flakes of hay. They were used to working together since they were children. "Mom gave one of our horses that name and said it was because of the color. I looked it up. On a different topic, how is it going with *your girlfriend*?"

This time, Ronan groaned, causing the horses to neigh. "She's not my girlfriend."

Brandon winked at him. "Would you like her to be?"

Ronan took too long to answer, which was an answer in itself. "It doesn't matter. Neither of us is looking for romance." The words hurt, and he needed to cover that hurt before his brother picked up on it. He turned his tone light. "But you'd better look up how to make lobster soup. Oh, and buy some fancy flowers on the way to the lodge. I wonder if our florist has orchids?" He ducked as his brother pretended to deck him.

They said doctors made the worst patients. Jessie wasn't sure whether the same applied to medical examiners, and she wasn't enjoying finding out.

Madeline was cranky and in pain. And having her striking face bruised seemed to make her even more irritable.

They'd all debated whether to allow Brandon in the lodge, but since they didn't want to hire a stranger as a sitter—and Paisley had vetted Brandon as trustworthy from her research online—they agreed to accept the gracious offer. Jessie's vote was the most enthusiastic one.

Fine, maybe their main reason was because Madeline had started grating on their nerves, but Jessie doubted any one of them would admit it. Even Rusty seemed eager to escape into the yard when Jessie took him outside to do his business, and he hadn't left Madeline's sight voluntarily before. Jessie breathed in the frosty air as she stared at the tree where Scratcher had climbed that day, and a smile tugged at her lips.

Then she reminded herself she wasn't supposed to see Ronan again, and the smile slipped. Rusty whined, which was unusual for him. He must be worried about Madeline.

Jessie sighed. "I know, buddy. I know exactly how you feel. Don't we all wish things could be different?"

But they weren't. *She* wasn't different. Even if her exes hadn't done enough damage to her body and her heart, she'd had abandonment issues from the get-go. While her grandmother hadn't left her of her own will, Jessie wasn't enough for her mother to kick the habit or for her father to stick around. Was it any wonder the men in her life hadn't cared for her, either, only pretended to? She'd have been better off sticking to her rule of going it solo in the romance department, and her battered body would've thanked her for it.

"Then why does it hurt so much inside to let Ronan go?" she asked Rusty.

The dog barked, which must mean he didn't know. He was magnificent, his black fur with tan and rusty undertones shining, taut muscles lining his lean body. So different from the starved puppy a passerby had picked up on the street and taken to the animal shelter. She could relate all too well to his sense of betrayal and would've adopted him or one of his buddies from the shelter in a heartbeat. Only the long, grueling hours she'd worked didn't allow much time for a pet. It wouldn't be fair to the poor animal to be mostly neglected again.

Madeline, as cold as she seemed to other people, adored Rusty.

Would Ronan be able to relate to Jessie? Of course not. Her heart shifted as she and the German shepherd rushed back into the warmth of the house. A guy from a happy family like his would never be able to relate to a scruff like her. Plus, he was clearly a believer, and her faith was—rusty wasn't exactly the word. Past events had smashed it into a million pieces.

Rusty seemed to sigh when he trudged back toward Madeline's room after Jessie had cleaned his paws.

"It's my wrist that is broken, not my legs!" Madeline's shout interrupted Jessie's thoughts as she stopped in the hall.

Growling, Rusty stared at the couple before Madeline issued a command for him to sit in a tone that gave even Jessie an inexplicable urge to plop her behind on the floor. Well, well, well. Jessie needed to get her phone to take a photo of this. She hid a smile.

Brandon was walking, carrying Madeline in his arms. As slim as she was, that still took some serious muscle. "You told me you wanted to sit near the fireplace in the living room. And considering you had me do everything else for you, I figured I'd serve as transportation to the living room for you, as well."

Jessie snorted. She should've recorded this.

Then the doorbell made her tense. Paisley was supposed to watch the cameras. Why didn't she give a warning? And anytime any stranger approached this territory, they all had to be prepared. To think about it, why hadn't Rusty barked, either?

"That must be my brother. He promised to relieve me," Brandon said.

"*Relieve* you? I'm not a burden!" Madeline's voice rose an octave.

Jessie didn't listen to the rest of the bickering as she rushed to the door, her heart beating faster. She shouldn't be this excited about him. He was here to help Madeline. That was all. This was worse than a fake date. This was babysitting Jessie's friend, not that Madeline would ever look at it that way.

Paisley appeared in the hall. "Go ahead. Open up. It's Ronan." As she moved closer, she whispered to Jessie. "The area is secure."

Just the same, there had to be a reason Paisley wore a jacket in the house, and the reason was the gun underneath. One of them always had to be packing, and having Madeline out of commission made things more difficult. Probably also why Madeline was so cranky. They all valued their independence and their ability to contribute to their common goal. While Jessie had assumed the role of Defender early on, the other girls hadn't slacked, either.

Jessie didn't need any more encouragement as she checked the peephole, then flung the door open, and waved Ronan inside.

He walked in and opened his arms for a hug, then seemed to remember something and shook her hand. Her spine sagged as she locked the door. Obviously, he was here out of family obligations. Not because he wanted to see her as much as she wanted to see him. Not that... she should want to see him.

It had to be for the better. Seriously.

Rusty greeted Ronan with a bark, but a friendly one. How about that? Madeline gave the dog a nod, and Rusty rushed to Ronan and placed thankfully freshly cleaned paws on him. Ronan staggered a bit but stood his ground as Rusty licked his face.

Huh. Jessie's eyes widened. Rusty appeared to consider Ronan part of his pack already, and only their group had that honorable title before. And then her belly flamed up at the thought of Ronan carrying *her* in his arms.

Rusty stopped his enthusiastic greeting and returned to Brandon with Madeline in his arms and bared his teeth again. But with a wave of her hand, Madeline made the dog sit and stay quiet.

Ronan's gaze lingered on Jessie, causing warmth to rise to the surface before he switched his focus to his brother with Madeline. "So carrying a patient is now on the list of duties. Got it."

Unwelcome jealousy flared up. They'd all gotten used to Madeline always being the center of male attention. They'd even utilized it to their advantage. It had never bothered Jessie before. So what was this inexplicable white-hot jealousy now?

Brandon marched to the living room with Madeline still in his arms. That was a shocker, especially on Madeline's part. Like Rusty, after her marriage fiasco, she didn't let men close to her without growling.

"Thanks for coming, bro, but I can stick around for a few more hours," Brandon said.

Ronan's, Paisley's, and Jessie's jaws nearly hit the floor. Well, well, well.

Then inexplicable panic rose inside Jessie. She didn't want Ronan to leave, and without helping Madeline, what other reason could he have to stay?

Paisley looked at Ronan, then back at her. Amusement flashed in Paisley's eyes as she smiled sweetly at Ronan. "Today's Jessie's turn to cook. Well, it was Madeline's, but she can't do much with her right wrist in a cast. Ronan, I can speak for all of us as I say we'd appreciate it if you could help Jessie in the kitchen."

Chapter Six

Jessie's heart fluttered. On the one hand, she didn't want him to see what a disaster she was in the kitchen. On the other hand, she was loath to let him go, despite all her careful reasoning on why she shouldn't spend time with him.

"I'd love to." Ronan brightened as if he found the prospect of spending time in her company much more pleasant than in Madeline's, and Jessie took some satisfaction in that.

Fine, she took lots of satisfaction in that.

"Awesome. Jessie will show you where the fire extinguisher is." Paisley's lips widened.

Jessie gave her friend a stern look. She wasn't *that* bad. Accidents happened. A few times.

He blinked. "I know how to cook."

"Even better." Paisley nodded to herself, then went toward the watch room, no doubt not only to pay attention to the cameras but also to work on one of her assignments.

A sting replaced Jessie's excitement as she led him to the kitchen. Paisley could work remotely, but it wasn't fair that they mooched off her hard work.

"Great idea!" Madeline called from the living room, somewhat more cheerful than before.

"I second that!" Genevieve's voice came from the room adjacent to the one where Gold was placed.

Jessie sighed at her friends' enthusiasm as she shuffled into the kitchen. "They are scared for me to cook by myself. Apparently, I can't be trusted in the kitchen."

He grinned. "And I thought they were all happy to have me here."

She handed him an apron, earth brown with a gray pocket. "Well, they *are* happy for you to be here. They like you. And they are grateful for your brother bearing the brunt of Madeline's irritation." Oops. She winced. She shouldn't have said that. After all... "Normally, deep inside, she's a sweetheart."

The memory of her panic when she'd learned about Madeline's accident squeezed Jessie's rib cage. They'd made her car bulletproof, but no one had thought to make it horse-proof, if that was even possible.

Instead of being jealous, she should be grateful to God for sparing Madeline's life. Not that she'd thought about God all that often. Her already fragile faith had leaked out the hole made by the bullet her ex put into her.

The thought hadn't brought the familiar ache. The hole had healed. Maybe her faith could, too. One thing for sure—she missed God far more than her ex.

After putting on her apron she tied the strings, then regretted not asking Ronan to do it.

He tipped an imaginary cowboy hat. "I aim to please. As for Brandon, he can be a grouch. But usually, deep inside, he's a sweetheart."

That made her laugh, spreading a pleasant feeling through her. She'd taken him for a tough cop—and he was. But this fun side of him appealed to her. She was serious and focused enough for them both. She needed someone who could make her laugh to counterbalance that.

Hmm.

After the fiascoes with their exes, the girls hadn't let outsiders into their small group, especially when they'd realized their secret might be in danger. So how come they let Ronan and Brandon visit them at the lodge? A mystery. Well, Paisley's vote could be explained somewhat. Apparently, Ronan and Brandon were the brothers of the guy she'd communicated with online for months, her army pen pal. And she was known for doing her research thoroughly.

Jessie pulled out her phone. "Let's see what kind of recipes we can find."

He covered her hand, sending pleasant tingles through her, then removed it fast. She wished he didn't. "What would they think about Irish beef stew?"

"Perfect for a cold winter day." She studied him, the five-o'clock shadow and the crinkles around his eyes as he smiled more appealing than they should be.

A joyful wave spread through her.

Concentrate! She was known to ruin dinners, even without being this distracted. "So you really know how to cook?"

"Well, I couldn't work as a chef in a French restaurant, but I can make simple Irish dishes." He opened the fridge, then the freezer, and studied their contents. "We were raised that way. Mom and Dad didn't distinguish work as women's and men's. My brothers and I helped out in the stables and the fields—and in the kitchen."

"Hmm. You don't look Irish to me." No matter how hard she looked, she couldn't find a speck of red in his brown hair, but the more she looked at it, the more she wanted to run her fingers through it.

So. Not. A good. Idea.

He closed the fridge. "Why? Because I don't have red hair? Or because I don't wear green? Or because I don't say *lass* and *lad* in every sentence?"

She lifted her hands in a mocking surrender. "Okay, I see your point. Um, do we have everything necessary for a stew?"

"No, but it's okay. You already have potatoes and carrots. Irish stew calls for lamb, but we can substitute it with beef."

Jessie braced herself for a trip to the grocery store. "We've got minced beef, but it's a frozen lump in the freezer." She knew because she'd gotten a TV dinner out for lunch. Someone should've started cooking earlier, but she couldn't complain out loud because that someone was her.

His lips pulled to one side. "Mom's recipe calls for chunks of meat, anyway. Okay to go to the store?"

She dragged her gaze off his lips, told the girls where she was going, then shrugged into the parka he held for her. His fingers brushed against her neck, and another pleasant wave rushed through her.

That was well-worth venturing out into the cold. In fact, maybe they could forget to buy something and go to the grocery store again.

"We need a well-marbled chuck roast." He put his coat, his cowboy boots, and his cowboy hat on. He wore all three well, and she was from the state where cowboy gear could be common street attire.

She nodded. "Got it. And our beef isn't well marbled." She slipped on her low-heeled boots. Or should she have borrowed Madeline's fashionable red boots on impossibly high heels?

"Not even close. Too lean." He wrapped the white scarf around her.

And he wasn't too lean. He was perfectly lean and muscled, and... She barely resisted the urge to scoot into his large frame, breathe his enticing scent of—what, pine needles? Having his arms around her was so... comfortable.

She straightened her back. She couldn't afford to get comfortable. Comfortable could get her killed. Nearly had.

She rushed into her room and placed the holster underneath her parka, then took out the gun from the safe and secured it inside the holster. She'd bought a parka a size larger than needed, so it was loose enough to hide the gun. But maybe she should've bought a fashionable white form-fitting coat with a wide belt like Madeline, who carried her weapon in her purse. Jessie's fingers stilled on the zipper. Did this large parka make her look frumpy?

What a ridiculous thought. She shouldn't worry about being appealing. She hadn't before. She couldn't afford to become attached, either.

"So does your family have a castle in Ireland or something?" she asked half-jokingly as they drove to the grocery store. His car smelled of leather and his signature scent of pine needles, and she took a few deep breaths as if to carry those scents with her forever. Carry part of him.

"My distant relatives do. My ancestors on my father's side came to America first. Mom's immigrated more recently, by which I mean several generations ago.... I'm about a quarter Irish."

Envy stabbed her, then shame. It wasn't Ronan's fault that, unlike him, she couldn't trace her history. She had no clue who her father was, and her drug-addict mother was the only child of a woman who'd raised her alone. Grandma was a foster child left near the hospital. Jessie was a flake in the wind without known origins. A plant without roots, if such existed.

She sure hoped she wouldn't continue that family tradition. "I'd love to know if I have some distant relatives on the other side of the ocean. Or even in the same town."

Who was she, really? What kind of identity could she and her friends base their lives on? Well, Madeline knew who her parents were. A prominent well-respected doctor and his beautiful stay-at-home wife, whose adorable child was long awaited and very much wanted, unlike the rest of their group. But Madeline's loss and trauma were so huge Jessie wasn't sure there was any consolation in that.

His fingers left the steering wheel and brushed Jessie's hand, making her grateful she'd taken off her gloves in the car, where the heater was working overtime. "I didn't mean to be insensitive."

"You weren't." Somehow, it didn't bother her as much when she was among the girls. They were all in the same situation there. Well, except Madeline. But Madeline's family history was even more terrifying than theirs.

Now the door inside Jessie she'd kept shut opened, and she wanted to know whether she was one-quarter German, for example. Her ex had asked about her medical history, because "who knew what kind of diseases you might have?"

Her gut churned. She now knew he was wrong for her, but maybe he had a point in those questions? What man would take the risk of marrying her? His questions had fed her abandonment issues like snowflakes built into an avalanche, until they'd smashed her hope of finding romantic love.

Something dimmed inside her.

She glanced in the rearview mirror. She didn't expect a tail, but one couldn't be too careful. There were no car lights behind them.

Silence stretched until Ronan asked, "Have you ever considered submitting a DNA test to one of those ancestry sites?"

"I have. Then I figured it was best not to know. I guess I was too scared to find out. This way I can at least pretend some of my ancestors were nice."

"If you ever change your mind, I'll support you in your search." His voice was firm above the motor's growl. "I'll stand by you."

Something changed inside her. No man had stood by her before.

But she had to continue to be strong. And for that, she had to stay alone. The previous times she'd let attraction blind her, she'd become vulnerable to assault, and a nagging pain in her leg reminded her of that. A lump grew in her throat, but she lifted her chin with her usual defiance. "I have no right to complain. I've seen firsthand the bloody results of sibling rivalry. I've witnessed how parents abused their children. And here, I've got the best family in the world."

"You made the best from what you were given. You're amazing." He parked his green sedan in the grocery store parking lot and turned off the engine but didn't get out. The color, along with his scent of pine needles, was fresh and promising and had no place in the winter of her soul.

She stayed, as well, partly because she always observed her surroundings before leaving a vehicle or a building, partly because the dynamics between them shifted.

It was almost... almost as if she were important to him. As if he understood her. But how could he? He had a happy childhood with parents who adored their children. He knew where he'd come from.

Well, she and her foster sisters had been close to being happy, until...

Best not to think about it.

He reached for her hand, held on a few precious seconds, then let it go. That would have to be enough. She'd learned the hard way she couldn't ask for much.

About forty minutes later, they were back at the lodge with beef that was *very* well-marbled, olive oil that was extra virgin, Worcestershire sauce that was necessary because no other sauce would do—Jessie couldn't pronounce the name even after five tries—thyme, and other necessities she'd been surprised the small-town store carried.

They unloaded groceries onto the kitchen counters, then washed their hands. He took off his jacket and rolled up the sleeves of his Wrangler's shirt, exposing nice muscles. Not that she stared. Much.

They changed into aprons again, and this time, she asked him to retie the strings at her neck because they needed to be adjusted. Well, fine, they probably didn't need to be adjusted, but him touching her neck again as he carefully and slowly tied the strings was so worth the request. A pleasant wave spread through her at his touch.

"Could you please heat some olive oil on medium heat in a large pot?" he said. "Meanwhile, I'll mince the garlic, then prep the beef."

Yep. She didn't think she should be trusted with meat, either. She found a pot in one of the knotty pine kitchen cabinets, placed it on the stove, and poured olive oil.

Watching it heat up was as much fun as watching paint dry. Watching Ronan was a different case altogether, and her heart perked up. In fact, a whole gamut of feelings woke up and simmered like that olive oil. She couldn't believe she used to dislike cooking.

He minced garlic cloves, his hands flying. His large, capable hands that could work a tractor... or hug a girl gently. Or trace the outline of her neck. More heat pooled in the pit of her stomach. Then he sprinkled salt over the beef pieces and dried them with a paper towel. Oh yes. Those rough, callused hands of his could sure be gentle... with chunks of beef. The beef browned, and he turned it over with tongs.

"Could you sauté onions and carrots?" he asked.

"What?" Did she look like she spoke French?

"Never mind." He added garlic to the beef. "I'm sautéing garlic right now."

"Ah." She inhaled the mouthwatering scent, her appetite increasing. Now she understood why people watched cooking shows. If Ronan was cooking with his sleeves rolled up on the show, she'd take a rare day off and watch all day, too.

He opened a can of beef stock and added it to the pan. "Look at that beauty!"

Jessie bristled. Hadn't she told him not to call her beautiful? She was well aware of the fact she didn't have Madeline's looks. She was a tomboy and fine with it.

Well, until now.

Oh, he was talking about the stew. The *stew* was the beauty. Good thing she didn't say anything. Her cheeks flamed up.

Soft footfalls announced Paisley before she wandered into the kitchen. By now, they'd learned to distinguish each other by the sound of their footsteps, and by scent. For example, Madeline favored lavender. Paisley usually smelled like her peach lotion, the scent as sweet and lovely as Paisley herself.

She poked her pink-blue-haired head inside. "Something smells good." Then the rest of her petite body moved in. "Looks good, too."

Jessie gave her friend a pointed look. "Don't you have some computer... thingy to solve?"

Paisley grinned, unoffended. "I already solved the computer *thingy*. Genevieve sent me on fire patrol. I'll be glad to report something is on fire here—but not the food. Oh, and that more than food is cooking."

Seriously?

"Paisley!" Jessie groaned.

"I'll leave you two to have fun. And please remember, a man who can cook is worth his weight in go—platinum—five times over. Especially considering your friends are starving." Paisley sauntered out of the kitchen.

Jessie's cheeks flared up more, and she sent Ronan an apologetic glance. "Please forgive my friends. They mean well—I think."

His brown eyes gleamed. "Your friends are fabulous. But you're the most fabulous one. By far."

"Nice save."

She let him do the rest of the cooking and just enjoyed the view. Maybe she should get hair extensions so he could enjoy the view, too. Athletic and protective, she'd slid into the stereotype of a rough-around-the-edges tomboy early on, not minding a bit while Paisley had rebelled against the stereotype of a computer geek with glasses and social awkwardness early on, too.

Meanwhile, Madeline had accepted the way men had stereotyped her only after a while, mostly after her disastrous divorce. With her model-like beauty, people expected her to be spoiled, high-maintenance, and selfish. So she hid her vulnerability and broken heart behind that perception with a standoffish attitude and designer outfits.

She'd never considered herself too good for an average guy, but she'd accepted that label to keep eager men away and wore it like a bandage over her wounds. Her carefully constructed arrogance and coldness had put off a lot of men, but unexpectedly, it also made others try harder, as if she were a prized trophy to win where others failed. But even the stubborn ones gave up without ever learning who she truly was.

Only her friends knew.

Would Brandon see beyond the flawless skin and cold attitude?

Jessie shook her head. Madeline would play her role well, aided by natural crankiness at being helpless. Brandon would be getting out of here as soon as he could, and Jessie was surprised he hadn't already.

But Ronan... Ronan was here and in no hurry to leave so far. That warmed her better than the best stew in the world ever could.

She and the girls didn't trust other people, and the few times they'd lifted their guard and fallen in love, they'd all been betrayed. Could Ronan be any different? Could he be trusted with her secrets?

The biggest secret wasn't hers alone to share, so there was that.

He added carrots and potatoes and stirred not just the veggies but also new feelings inside her. He was a cop, just like she'd been, but unlike her, he was still on the force.

She'd been itching to investigate the plane crash of Wyatt's mistress in the Dominican Republic and his recent death since she'd read about it. Was it by natural causes, or did it only appear that way? She was needed at the lodge, so she couldn't travel back to Texas. But what if, with Ronan's help, she could do something? At her urging, their small group had already taken the first step.

She perched against the gray marbled counter. "Tell me about your day at work. I'll live vicariously through you."

He did as he added spices to the stew. Then his gaze raked over her face. "You miss being a cop, don't you?"

"I miss being part of the action. I miss making a difference, though I didn't make as much of a difference as I hoped to. I don't miss seeing horrible, gut-wrenching things." Shuddering, she rubbed at the goose bumps rising with the memories.

But Madeline had far more horrifying memories. Those first months, they'd all been woken up to her bloodcurdling screams from nightmares. Then she learned to sleep less because the screams irritated their foster parents. Part of the reason Jessie had gone to the police academy had been an overwhelming need to prevent what had happened to Madeline from happening to other children. Or at least give them closure. Madeline had never gotten hers.

They'd all been damaged in some way. But Jessie had no doubt Madeline, so perfect on the outside, had been hurt more than all of them, and that was saying something.

The haunted look appeared less in her gorgeous baby blues now than in childhood. And Jessie would trust Madeline with her life without a second thought. But if Jessie had to pinpoint one of them who might end up on the other side of the law, it would be Madeline. To prevent that, Jessie even tried to talk Madeline into joining the police academy once they graduated—and fine, it wouldn't have hurt to have a friend training with her.

But Madeline wasn't athletic, and the concept of exercise-released endorphins was foreign to her. Although mildly interested in forensic psychology, she decided digging into people's bodies was more fascinating than digging into their minds. "To help them," she'd once added as an afterthought and before Jessie had a chance to shudder.

"If we had a vacancy, I'd put in a good word with our chief for you. We'd make great partners." His hand stirring the stew stilled. "I mean—"

"I know what you meant." She didn't need a reminder that he didn't see her in a romantic light. But something had to be said about him trusting her enough to cover his back. "Thank you."

"Frankly, I'm being selfish. That would allow me to see you more."

Her heart skipped a beat. "And you'd like that?"

He held her gaze. "I'd like that very much."

Her wonkily beating heart lodged in her throat as his gaze lingered on her. Maybe Paisley was right and something more than the food *was* cooking here.

And maybe Jessie didn't need hair extensions, fake nails, or high heels to be attractive to him. She'd been herself with him from day one, tomboyish, rough, and unapologetic. Yet heat simmered in his eyes when he looked at her. He didn't treat her like one of the guys, though he respected her as an equal.

Could he like her for who she was?

She stepped closer, and a delicious shiver went through her as the back of his palm brushed against her cheek.

Sadly, the selfish stew chose to bubble to the top of the pan, and he hurried to reduce the heat on the stove. If only someone could do the same with the heat spreading inside her.

"By the way, you still make a difference. I'm sorry you lost your job. But I can see you make a difference to your friends. I can't know God's will, but I believe He often puts us in places where we're needed the most."

Then why did God put her in that bullet's path? Or more importantly, why didn't God send someone to protect her friends when they'd been little, helpless, and hurt? Why had God allowed Wyatt to do that terrible thing?

Of course, she didn't ask those questions. She doubted Ronan had answers to them, either.

But thinking about it, she was grudgingly grateful for the opportunity to reunite with the girls. They'd all stayed in Houston, but they'd led busy lives. They weren't as close as they'd once been, and she missed that. Maybe God had brought them together again for a reason.

Besides the shared secret that reunited them once again.

But the same secret would keep her away from Ronan, and her heart ached at the thought.

Chapter Seven

Decades ago...

Jessie didn't know how she'd be able to navigate school without her foster sisters. It was time to do homework after all the chores their dear foster parents assigned to them, besides washing dishes at the café Mr. Finch ran. Jessie was ready to howl. Math wasn't her strong suit. Neither was chemistry. She had a good memory, so history and geography were okay, and she excelled in physical education.

"I wish we had more PE and way, way less math." She opened her textbook and groaned.

"I beg to differ." Paisley rolled her eyes.

"Easy for you to say. You're brilliant at math and computer science. In fact, I heard several teachers calling you a genius." Despite Jessie's grumbling, she was happy for her friend.

Nobody had any doubt Paisley would go to college on a scholarship, except Paisley herself. She wasn't so sure she needed to waste valuable time on college. Or on school, for that matter, but she had no choice there so far.

While the other girls worked for free waitressing and washing dishes in the Finchs' café, Paisley had made way more doing mysterious assignments online. Most of the income she'd had to surrender to Mr. Finch. Whatever she'd managed to hide went into their future house or apartment fund. A place where no one would yell at them or threaten to separate them. Their dream place.

Jessie's heart constricted. As much as she disliked math, she could barely imagine going her separate way from the girls after high school. She'd do a few courses at the local college, then go to the police academy, hence her running track and being part of a volleyball team, then taking up boxing, too. Ever since she'd learned Madeline's story, Jessie had wanted to help people like her.

"Come on. You know I'll help you with math," Paisley said without looking up from the old computer one of their friends had given her because it didn't work any longer. It worked for Paisley.

Jessie smiled her gratitude. "You always do. And I appreciate it. Without you, I'd flunk my grade."

Paisley beamed from her seat at the table and ran her fingers through her pink hair. "And without you, I'd be stuck in a locker every day. Considering I'm one of the shortest girls my age in school."

"Please. With your sunshine attitude, everyone loves you."

Paisley looked away as she touched the scar on her arm absentmindedly. "Not everyone."

Heat flared through Jessie at the memory of Paisley being kicked around during recess. Jessie took a deep breath to calm herself. The kids in school had found out soon that if they offended one girl from this foster family they offended all of them, and her boxing lessons came in handy. Even more so her tenacity. Several bullies had learned the hard way that they'd have to beat her to a pulp before she'd give up, and meanwhile, she'd throw punches, too. She'd a high tolerance for pain and an extremely low one for her friends being hurt.

Madeline walked into their study room and flipped her long hair back, then poured herself a glass of water and took a seat graciously. She didn't try to be appealing on purpose. It came naturally to her, and many boys vied for her attention. Being a late bloomer and a tomboy, Jessie never had that kind of problem.

But Madeline wasn't interested in dating, which earned her the reputation of being hard to get. As if in compensation for her horrible childhood, she'd received not only beauty but also brains and studied a lot. She had to because her dream was to go to med school, and she had to do it on a scholarship. Her favorite occupation was cutting frogs and crustaceans, and she couldn't wait to move to "more complicated matters." Thankfully, she stopped discussing such details at the dinner table, mainly because Mrs. Finch ordered her to stop after turning slightly green.

Madeline was getting great with a scalpel. Great enough that it could be scary.

Jessie pushed that thought out of her mind and buried her nose in equations she'd never have to use in real life. Ridiculous, really. She'd love to meet and have a few words with the person who'd decided these things had to be part of the school curriculum. Her hand fisted. Maybe more than a few words.

"I have some news." Madeline sipped her water. "Someone asked me out."

Jessie chuckled. "How is that news? Tons of guys constantly ask you out."

"It was Timothy Dean."

Jessie looked up, and so did Paisley. "The school quarterback? Wasn't he dating the lead cheerleader? The most popular girl in school?"

The one who'd had some boys gang up on Paisley a week after Jessie had arrived, as Jessie had found out. Finding out people's secrets was as meaningful to her as dissecting frogs was to Madeline. They all had their talents, and they didn't have the luxury to waste them.

"You didn't say yes, right?" Genevieve walked into the room.

As the oldest of their group, she worried about them, and the girls loved her for that. She'd often cooked for them, and the girls loved her for that even more. If Jessie assumed the role of Defender, Paisley was Encourager, and Genevieve was Nurturer.

Something flashed in Madeline's beautiful blue eyes, something Jessie couldn't decipher. And if she wanted to make it as a police officer, she needed to learn to read people. But while Paisley's thoughts were usually on the surface, Madeline's thoughts were a bigger mystery than math equations.

Madeline's jaw set in a stubborn line. "Why not?"

Jessie's heart sank.

"Hello? Because she'll sic the entire cheerleading squad on you, plus their boyfriends. That's why." Genevieve sat down, a frown marring her forehead. "And let me remind you most of those guys are football players."

"Who are best friends with Timothy."

Of all her friends, Madeline caused Jessie the most concern. They all had difficult childhoods and their own ways to deal with it. The beautiful and brainy girl, who was the envy of many girls, used to be a cutter. Somehow, it had helped to diminish her nightmares. She didn't slice her own skin any longer, but that didn't mean it wouldn't start again.

Based on Genevieve's deepening frown, Madeline's propensity for self-destruction worried her, too. Madeline also had a great memory, which was useful not only in remembering what every tiny bone and muscle in the human body was called but also what that lead cheerleader had tried to do to Paisley. And while Madeline had seemed cold to others, she was fiercely protective of her friends.

Even Paisley seemed to lose her eternal optimism. "If you think to avenge me, it's not worth it."

"Relax. I said no to Timothy asking me out, to his utmost shock. Besides, I haven't heard of him breaking up with his current girlfriend yet. But don't you think it's unfair that some people never pay for what they've done?"

Silence ensued. Madeline wasn't talking about the lead cheerleader, was she?

"I'm going to chop up some salad for dinner before I do everyone's chemistry homework." Madeline glanced at Genevieve. "Care to join me? Our fosters want baked salmon and rice for dinner."

Genevieve brightened as she got up. "Sure."

After Madeline and Genevieve started on the food, Paisley explained how to solve the math problem, but Jessie didn't hear her. Yet she could hear the chopping sounds in the kitchen.

Yes, Madeline was good with anything that she could cut. Too good.

Dinner would've been uneventful, if not for their foster father throwing a few glances at Genevieve—the missus had a headache again and took food to her room.

It could be natural as he praised her cooking. But something about the way he smiled as he looked at Genevieve bothered Jessie. Normally, Madeline attracted all the male attention. But by now, he must know enough about Madeline that she scared him.

Warmhearted and gentle Genevieve, who was also well-developed for her age, was totally different.

Jessie had learned to be a light sleeper in her second foster home. It helped her here because when a nightmare caught up with Madeline, she'd whimper before screaming. Jessie could rock Madeline and prevent her from screaming and, therefore, being punished by the Finchs and cutting herself the next day.

So Jessie woke up when she heard footfalls in the hall. She tensed because the footfalls were too heavy for one of the girls. Alarmed, she leaped out of her bed and rushed to the hall barefoot. She found her foster father lingering near Genevieve's room.

He glared at her. "What are you doing here?"

She glared back. "Going to the bathroom. What are *you* doing here?"

"It's my house, and I can do whatever I want." He kept his voice low, though. Probably wouldn't want to wake up the missus. He towered over Jessie, but she didn't back off.

"Not in Genevieve's bedroom." She folded her arms on her chest.

He deflated. "I was getting a glass of water."

"The kitchen is that way." She gestured in the opposite direction.

"And there's a bathroom close to your bedroom." He growled, but again in a low tone.

For some time, he stared at her, but she didn't move, anger seething inside her.

Finally, he stomped away.

Only then did she notice how cold the floor was against her bare feet. Yet she lingered near Genevieve's room while her gut tightened. Jessie had bought Genevieve some time. But she didn't know how long.

Present time...

"You want me to do what?" Ronan's voice rose. His hand froze on the kitchen counter. The beef stew was such a success he'd gotten voluntold to cook the next evening, as well. He didn't mind. He loved spending time with Jessie. Even if that time was finite and she still had way more secrets than he could even begin to guess.

But did he hear her right?

"You sound like I asked you to swim to Ireland." She shrugged but didn't meet his gaze. "I just asked you to help in a small investigation."

He lifted his hand, its warm smudgy imprint fading fast on the marbled counter. He wanted to return to making shepherd's pie, a traditional Irish staple, but he had difficulty concentrating. "Nope. You just implied one of the richest men in Texas got murdered and you want me to figure out who did that."

She sighed. "First of all, that was a compliment. It means I trust you enough to involve you in this. I trust very few people, and nearly all of them live in this house."

He stood taller. "Well, when you put it like that..."

"Besides, it's not something you have to solve. His death *might've* been from normal causes. There was no autopsy. No suspicions. No investigation. I realize this is like finding a snowflake in a field of snow. But I feel a nudge."

He returned to peeling potatoes. "Are you going to tell me everything you know?" He suspected the answer but needed to ask. Her keeping secrets from him bugged him more and more.

He was a simple cowboy and a simple cop. He didn't like things hidden. In his field of work, hidden things could hurt or even kill.

"No. It's not my secret to share." Her voice dipped. "Maybe someday the girls will agree to it. Until then, I'm asking you to..." She ducked her head, falling silent.

Yes, what was she asking him, exactly? And what kind of danger surrounded these foster sisters? His muscles tensed, and his insides burned. How was he supposed to help her if he didn't know any of the details?

Isla had kept a secret from him, too. She'd promised to quit her dangerous job. But she'd only said it to placate him. He'd found out the day before that horrible fire and confronted her. He'd never had a temper, and shame stabbed him over the way he'd raised his voice at her.

Was Jessie part of something dangerous, as well, though in a different sense? His instincts had been right, and he should've walked away from her. Yet he couldn't. And not only because his mother constantly nudged him to date.

"We're not involved in anything illegal. Well, not yet," Jessie said quietly.

He nearly snorted as the pile of potatoes in front of him grew. Yeah, that calmed him a lot.

"I don't think we'll ever cross the line, but if things look that bad, we'll disappear before it happens. We, um, have getaway locations abroad."

He groaned. "Well, this just gets better and better."

And not that he'd think his brother would ever get involved with beautiful, cold, and spoiled Madeline. But Brandon had been spending all the time he wasn't at the ranch with her the last two days, and Ronan started to have a heavy feeling it wasn't out of obligation any longer. Brandon and Madeline were opposites and didn't seem to have anything in common, in either appearance or personalities. But didn't they say opposites attract?

Ronan's rib cage constricted.

"Just think about it." Jessie placed her fingers on his forearm. Moments later, she removed them as if thinking better of it.

But as fleeting as the moment was, he felt it to his very core.

Jessie was wrong for him. Very wrong. He'd never betray his principles if he found out she and her friends had been up to no good. She'd made it clear she wasn't going to stay. And she'd reminded him way too much of all the heartache he'd gone through with Isla and had no intention of repeating.

So why couldn't he walk away? Was it that vulnerability in Jessie's stormy eyes? Or the fact that she'd been wronged many times in her life and he wanted things to go right for her? She clearly could take care of herself, so he shouldn't be feeling this protective toward her.

Shouldn't want to take her in his arms and hold her for a long time.

"How about, for now, you tell me about this thing you're making and how I can help?" Her voice softened.

You could help me by telling me what really happened to you.

He didn't say the words out loud because it was useless. Yes, talking about food was a safer territory.

"This thing is called shepherd's pie. Or cottage pie. Or hachis Parmentier. It has minced meat, onions in gravy, and is topped with mashed potatoes. My family likes to add cheese and a few more veggies." Remembering the familiar story his mother told him did calm him down somewhat. Though after he took one look at Jessie, his heart raced again. That wasn't right.

She moved by his side to peel potatoes, which gave him a whiff of her perfume. Light and citrusy and exquisite.

"People called it cottage pie by 1791. Then shepherd's pie by 1854." He was going to bore her to death with these details.

"Hachis Parmentier sounds French." She'd paid attention.

While he couldn't help paying attention to the graceful outline of her neck, exposed by her short hair, and the tiny birthmark above her upper lip that he desperately wanted to kiss.

He nearly nicked his finger. Served him right. What was she saying?

"That's correct, and it was documented in France in 1900."

"What does it mean?" She looked up from the pile of peeled potatoes.

That I'm attracted to you.

He cleared his throat. "*Hachis* means finely chopped. *Parmentier* was the guy who promoted potatoes in France in the eighteenth century. Generally, this dish was a way to use leftover meat. There are similar dishes in other countries, like Argentina, Brazil, Canada, Indonesia, Uruguay, and others. The Irish call it *piog an aoire*."

"And I guess you cook it American style?"

"You can say that." He made the mistake of looking into her bottomless eyes and nearly drowned there. "Traditionally, it was made with mutton or lamb, but we'll go with beef."

"That I remembered to get out of the freezer last night."

"Correct." Good thing, or they'd have to go grocery shopping. And he'd been too distracted by her eyes to focus on the food they bought last time.

He placed a large pot with water on the stove while she finished washing potatoes. He cut them in quarters and slipped them into the pot, then added a teaspoon of salt. "We'll bring them to a boil, then cook until tender for about twenty minutes."

Tender like his heart was getting around Jessie. He flinched. Why was he thinking like that? He'd never waxed poetic before. He'd been a ranch boy through and through.

"What are we going to do for twenty minutes while the potatoes are cooking?" She cleaned the counter, her dishcloth streaking the marbled gray countertop, then leaned against it.

How about kissing?

Seriously, what was wrong with him? "We'll..." What was the word? "Sauté the vegetables."

"Lead the way."

Oh, he'd love to. His gaze slid to her luscious lips, pink without any lipstick. He stepped toward her. She lifted the onions.

He stopped in his tracks. "The vegetables. Right."

Her brow quirked as she peeled the first onion. "Did you have anything else in mind?"

"What else could be on my mind besides onions?" Okay, that didn't sound right. He started chopping furiously, the knife tapping against the cutting board. At least, if he cried from frustration, he could blame it on onions.

She turned the stove on and placed a large pan on the stove top. "Now what?"

Now I draw you near....

Okay, he needed to snap out of it. "Now you're going to melt"—*my heart*—"the butter."

She did both, and her eyes lit up. "Oh, I know. Now we add onions and saw–*tay* them."

"You're a fast learner." If only his heart learned as fast.

"What about other veggies?" She stirred onions with a wooden spatula.

"Would you like to add peas, carrots, or corn?"

She wrinkled her nose in an adorable way. "Peas, I think."

He turned on the oven to preheat it. "They take less time cooking, so we'll add them right before the onions are done."

They did so, and then he added ground beef. The enticing aromas spread in the cozy kitchen, but the woman in front of him was even more enticing. Her cheeks pinked, probably from the heat, and she licked her lips as if in anticipation.

The fire inside him spread further. Who'd think a man could fall in love over making shepherd's pie? Thankfully, she watched the meat because he'd watched her and would likely burn the meat.

"Looks like it's done." She added salt and pepper. "Now that sauce I can't pronounce, right?"

"Worcestershire. And beef broth." Kinda surprising he found his voice and even pronounced the name of the sauce right. He reduced the heat on the stove, but not inside him. "Let it simmer. We can add more broth if the meat becomes dry."

His mouth was getting dry in her presence. He should do something with this attraction. But he couldn't.

Lord, what am I supposed to do?

Ronan looked into her gray eyes again, and she didn't look away. Instead, her breathing went shallow. Could it be that his attraction was reciprocated? But either way, he'd have no right to act on it. It was one thing to be attracted to a woman who was still a stranger to him. It was a totally different thing to fall for her.

Yet he ran his fingers along her jawline. "Jessie…"

Longing appeared in her gray eyes, but soon regret joined in. "Potatoes… must be… done."

That was what she was thinking about? Disappointment ripped through him, and embarrassment flushed his cheeks. But it might be for the better that at least one of them had some presence of mind.

He checked the potatoes with a fork, and she was right. They were done.

He drained them carefully to make sure the steam wouldn't hit his already hot face, added butter, and searched for a potato masher. Finding none, he used a fork to mash them and, once done, added salt and spices.

"Now we'll spread the meat with veggies in the baking dish. Some people make potatoes the first layer, but I don't. Then we'll spread mashed potatoes over ground beef. And I like to add shredded cheese over the top."

They cooked in silence. He placed the baking dish in the oven, then set up the timer for half an hour. It was a simple and hearty fare, but there was nothing simple about his budding relationship with Jessie.

And that was even before he heard about the case important to her and her friends that might or might not be murder.

Chapter Eight

The next day, Jessie taped Wyatt's photo on the whiteboard in the dark-paneled soundproofed safe room she called the incident room. Her heart was beating faster, and she told herself it was from the investigation—which could be true.

But having Ronan in the enclosed windowless room was another valid reason for her rapid heartbeat. She took a deep breath of air filled with his signature pine-needle scent that teased her senses. At least she could keep the conference table between them, but she needed to pull herself together. Bad enough that she'd nearly succumbed to the attraction that simmered with those vegetables and had been about to kiss him in the kitchen yesterday.

"Thank you for agreeing to help me." Wow. Her voice sounded even. Not bad.

"I keep asking myself what I got into." Apprehension flexed his jaw, but his lips twitched up.

She really shouldn't be looking at his lips. More warmth pooled in the pit of her stomach. Turning away, she braced a hip against the walnut table. A burl on the table's edge pushed against her jeans as she faced the board that was sadly way too empty save for a few photos.

"Wyatt died of a heart attack. Which wasn't surprising, considering he had a heart condition and took medication for it."

"But for a reason you're not willing to disclose to me, you have your suspicions." His voice hit her in the back when he came around to her side of the conference table. "Okay, let's look for a motive. Who benefitted from his death?"

We did.

She didn't say it out loud because then she'd have to reveal the secret.

"The inheritance was divided between his children." She added two more photos, then stepped away from the whiteboard, the plush brown carpet squishy beneath her running shoes. "Wyatt had two offspring he acknowledged, Marshall and Hayden. Both live in the mansion he lived in, though in a different wing."

"There's a child he didn't acknowledge?"

She'd realized her mistake the moment she said the words. Her back still to him, she forced herself to keep her posture neutral. "We'll talk about that later." Maybe. "Marshall seemed to take after his father. Ruthless and dedicated to the family business, but unlike his father, Marshall never married. He lived and breathed the company and moved up in it fast."

Arms crossed, she studied the photo. Immaculate in his grooming and attire, Marshall looked like his father, only his hair was dark brown while Wyatt's was white, and Wyatt stooped and seemed to rely on his cane. But the way the man was, Jessie suspected he might be hiding a blade in the latter. They weren't traditionally handsome, and there was something... hawkish about both men, maybe because of their large aquiline noses and small eyes.

Even in the photo of a man who no longer existed, his hard hazel eyes made her shiver.

Ronan moved beside her and leaned against the end of the table before the whiteboard, his scent closing in on her. Ignoring it—*trying* to ignore it—she focused on the photo of a younger guy with a defiant, slightly amused gaze and a hint of red in the long hair he wore in a low ponytail. A five-o'clock shadow added to his insolent look. Unlike Marshall, who wore a suit in every photo she'd uncovered until she even wondered whether he wore one as pajamas, Hayden usually sported a leather blazer and designer jeans, more of a bad-boy look. Now, this movie-star handsome man took after his mother, whose photo Jessie placed next, both in appearance and character.

"On the contrary"—she uncapped a black marker, releasing its pungent odor—"Wyatt had a strained relationship with his youngest son, Hayden. Wyatt nearly removed him from the family business. Hayden preferred spending his father's funds on his alcohol and adrenaline addictions rather than expanding the operations. His mother, Emberlynn, stood up for him again and again, but their employees had the impression Wyatt was getting fed up over the years." She wrote the name under Suspects, then braved facing Ronan.

He'd pushed the sleeves of his green sweater up to his elbows, exposing the veins tracing their way up his muscled forearms. Now he braced his hands on either side of him as he leaned back against the table, flexing them in evident frustration and frowning at the board. "So you think one of his sons, most likely the youngest one, switched the pills in his bottle to let's say, a placebo."

Good. He was taking this and her seriously. "It's a possibility. Or switched it to something that interacted in a bad way with his other medicines." She jiggled the large marker between her fingers, letting it blur as it vibrated. "Rumor was Marshall was tired of working eighty-hour weeks and still playing second fiddle. He sacrificed a lot to please his father, but Wyatt never seemed to publicly acknowledge it. In the latest meetings, Wyatt had shot down innovations Marshall proposed. Despite his age, he didn't show any inclination of retiring."

Ronan nodded. "What about Emberlynn? The spouse—or an ex-spouse—is usually the first suspect."

"True." Needing the excuse to turn away from Ronan and the way he made her heart race, Jessie underlined the name on the whiteboard and tapped the marker against the photo of a woman with shoulder-length red hair styled in an expensive cut. The diamond earrings sparkling in her ears matched her large diamond pendant. Plastic surgery clearly enhanced her features and made them ageless, but her light-blue eyes held an unforgiving stare. Most of the photos Jessie had seen of her portrayed Emberlynn in an evening gown, each one more beautiful than the previous one.

"She used to be a model, but once she married Wyatt, he put a stop to her career. He was wealthy at that time already, though not nearly as wealthy as now. She seemed to be his arm candy, and he paid little attention to her outside of social functions. She signed a prenup before marrying him, but he still was more generous to her during their divorce than during their marriage. Wyatt wasn't faithful while they were married. Yet the divorce wasn't her idea, hence the generous compensation. By the time they divorced, it was too late for her to return to the runway. Lately, she spends her days organizing parties for different charities—and doting on her youngest son, whom she adores no matter what he does."

"She might still be bitter over the divorce. I imagine she doesn't live in the same mansion Wyatt lived in, correct?"

Automatic alibi.

"Correct." Jessie's shoulders pulled down. "But a few of the servants have been with Wyatt for a long time. They could've maintained loyalty to Emberlynn and considered his treatment of her unfair. Wyatt mostly looked at his household staff as essential equipment, not human beings, and that might've rubbed someone the wrong way. Plus"—she eyed Ronan to catch his reaction—"there might've been a good payout for them from Emberlynn, as well."

A muscle moved in his jaw. "How would they get access to the safe with his pills?"

Right. "I don't know. But one of them could've put something in his food." She suppressed a grimace. They had their work cut out for them.

Then she opened the file and copied a long row of names to the whiteboard. "Wyatt was a tough man, one some could consider ruthless. To succeed, he drove several competitors out of business. Some of them hold grudges. Wyatt received phone threats before his death. The most recent one was from Huxley."

Coming to stand beside her at the board, Ronan raised an eyebrow. "How do you know all this?"

"You'd be surprised how many things one can find online these days. Plus, Wyatt hired a PI to investigate the threats." She couldn't tell him about Paisley's spectacular skills because hacking was illegal. Or that Arianna, the foster sibling who joined their foster family at fourteen, had been hired as a maid at Wyatt's mansion and provided them with additional information.

Jessie pressed a hand over the stabbing pain in her gut. She wasn't just a law-abiding citizen—she used to enforce the law. She'd never do something illegal or immoral. The system was set up the way it was for a reason. Yet she'd looked the other way when Paisley presented her findings, as much as Jessie had protested at first. Paisley didn't do it for personal gain but to help them survive. But that didn't make Jessie's moral battle less severe.

The pause stretched. Well, she could trust him with the rest. "We have a mole in his household."

"Wow." His brown eyes narrowed on her, the sweater bringing out flecks of green in them. "You're invested in this, aren't you? I still can't understand why you're so interested."

Because we have to protect our own. An heir to such an enormous inheritance would have a target on their back. The only protection was that nobody besides their small group knew about the extra heir's existence. At least, she hoped no one else alive knew.

"Let's say, it's important. You need to know something else. Four years ago, Wyatt's mistress Mylah, a beautiful model, was flying in his private plane to his villa in the Dominican Republic. The private plane never made it there.

The bodies of the pilot and mistress were burned beyond recognition. She was identified by the one-of-a-kind pendant he'd given her."

Those narrowed eyes widened. "You think... it was deliberate?"

Jessie clenched her grip on the marker. "The local authorities assumed the small plane had a mechanical failure. Wyatt didn't push for further investigation. Mylah's family tried to complain at first but didn't get far. The plane was in perfect condition before takeoff."

"If these suspicions have grounds, then Wyatt's oldest son's life is in danger." Ronan massaged his temples as if combating a headache.

"Or..." She held up the marker to emphasize her point. "Or he orchestrated it all. Though the youngest son had a stronger motive. Marshall was pretty set and the classic example of a responsible son, his father's favorite, even if Wyatt didn't show it much. Wyatt had already cut off much of his youngest son's income. So Hayden could be on the verge of losing it all, and he had a son to think about. He was separated from his wife, but I imagine he was getting some pressure there, as well." She flicked through the file for what she was looking for, then added a fifth photo to the new lineup, his wedding picture, him in a tuxedo, his long reddish hair swiped back, his face clean-shaven. His bride was beside him, a stunning blonde in an exquisite white dress and sparkling diamond necklace, her eyes dull.

The men in that family married gorgeous women, but did that make them happy? But then, Jessie hadn't seen a single successful marriage. Which made her attraction to Ronan even more inexplicable. Her heart jolted. Not that... not that she'd ever consider marrying him.

"I take it that's him and his wife?"

"Yes." Jessie eyed the photo where two people smiled but neither looked happy. "Also a former model. Dating models must be a family tradition for them. She rose to prosperity as much as Hayden did once Wyatt died. So she also had a motive."

Then she studied the names of the people Wyatt had wronged. The long list still missed a name. Or two. Names that were familiar to Jessie's lips since childhood. Heat flared, and she drew a calming breath of recycled air tinted with Ronan's scent of pine needles. She stiffened at the surprising urge to lean into him for support. She'd made it a point to stand on her own two feet. So why this need for him to hold her?

Calmer now, she consulted with the file and crossed out the names of those who left the country—or left this world.

"What happens if Hayden dies?" Ronan asked.

"Word is, since his inheritance, he's drafting a new will so it all goes to his son, Braxton, who seems to be as rebellious as his father. Braxton is only eighteen, but has already had three stints in rehab and more than a few scandals with famous models and singers around the globe." She pinned a photo of a strikingly handsome teen in a tuxedo who collected the model looks from his mother and grandmother and the arrogance of his grandfather. Despite his youth and those looks, something about his long nose or posture gave off the vibe of a vulture. Diamonds sparkled in his cufflinks and left ear, and another glared from his pinkie.

Ronan shook his head. This must be as far from the quiet life in Cowboy Crossing as it could get. "Looks like Hayden got a taste of his own medicine with his son."

"Yes. Though Braxton seems to take it to the next level. For starters, he crashed a Ferrari in Monaco and was arrested for debauchery at a high-level party in France. Wyatt wasn't happy as it affected investments in his company. Another reason Wyatt wanted to cut off Hayden and his offspring."

Hands on his hips, Ronan rocked back on his heels. "Frankly, without an autopsy or getting our hands on the pill bottle, not much can be done. And even if we had that bottle, it could've been switched to the regular one."

Paisley had tried to get camera recordings from Wyatt's room from the day he died, but security was strong there. Her stomach twinging, Jessie slouched. Disappointment because Paisley didn't find anything. Guilt because Paisley had looked in the first place. Once a cop, always a cop.

"There still should be something we can do." Jessie lifted her head.

"I take it your mole interviewed the household staff?"

That she couldn't do it herself made her purse her lips. She'd read the interviews five times, but nonverbal cues were more important than words. She needed those. "In an unofficial capacity, yes. No one reported anything suspicious. Nobody saw anyone going to Wyatt's bedroom, except for Wyatt himself. And even if someone did go there, Wyatt kept his pills and his gun in a safe."

"Who knew the combination?"

A heavy stone pressed on her chest. "His oldest son." Which was why she put him on the top of the list. "What I am wondering..." She swallowed, clamped her teeth shut.

"Yes?" Ronan's body posture showed attention, and his eyes flashed with something. Worry for her?

His protectiveness touched her. No guy had ever behaved that way, not even her ex. Especially not her ex.

This protectiveness and wholesomeness drew her in. Ronan did seem to be as wholesome as that apple cake he'd brought, a stunning difference from the men in her life. Granted, his great physique didn't hurt, but what she ached to see in a guy were the qualities she hoped she exhibited herself—loyalty, protectiveness, trustworthiness. Had she found a guy who had them, who wanted to protect her, be loyal to her?

Guilt stung. What did it matter? All of the girls, including her, had abandonment issues. One didn't need a child psychologist to figure that out. Not that any of them had gotten to see a child psychologist, and they should have. Instead, they had to comfort each other.

Betrayals in the romance department later in life solidified their childhood assumption—leave before you're abandoned again. Run if you have to. It hurt less that way. It didn't apply to their small circle, but to everyone outside it.

"Are you okay?" Ronan interrupted her musings.

She blinked. Her words from childhood rang in her soul—*It's never gonna be okay.*

Walking away before hadn't been difficult, even from her first love, because she hadn't met men like Ronan before. Or was she creating another illusion? Was she projecting her qualities on him because she got lost so easily in his deep brown eyes?

She shook her head to shake off the feeling. She needed to get back to her ideas as preposterous as they might sound. "I'm wondering whether someone's behind all these events, orchestrating them. Amplifying the sibling rivalry. Or using the younger son's rebellion to stoke anger at the father. Using Marshall's ambitions. Throwing shade on the people Wyatt harmed." She stared at the long row of names on the whiteboard.

"Someone with a grudge against Wyatt? Seems like way too much effort for revenge."

She kept staring at the names, familiar heat brewing in her gut. What Wyatt had done over a decade ago was unforgivable. The fact that he wasn't punished for it sliced her insides. But it hadn't been her decision to make. "Revenge can be a powerful motivator. Especially when coupled with greed."

He leaned forward. "Let me summarize then. We don't know whether Wyatt's or his mistress's deaths were murders. There's no sign of foul play, at least not in his case. There was no autopsy, no tox screen done. No evidence to request exhumation. His bedroom, the crime scene—if it was a crime scene—was never processed. The food he ate that evening can't be checked now. The murder weapon or the pills were tossed away and impossible to retrieve. There are about..." He counted something on the board. "Forty suspects with motives to kill him. But it might be pointless to check their alibis because they could've hired someone from the household staff to do the dirty deed."

Forty-five, but she'd best not mention *that*.

"That about sums it up." Frustration came from him in waves, and she shared it. Shared it for much longer than he'd experienced it.

That they had to do it long distance with crumbs of information tightened her gut. She was used to knocking on the doors, watching people's nonverbal cues as she spoke to them, examining evidence, and so much more. Here, she could do none of that, and it set her stomach on edge.

Just when her skills could be useful to the girls, she felt helpless. It was like she poked into the sky and hoped to touch a star.

That didn't mean she was going to give up.

On the spare part of the whiteboard, she wrote down the household staff, how long they'd worked for Wyatt's family, and what occupation they held.

"Anything interesting in their backgrounds? Probably not, as I'm sure they were all vetted before getting the job."

"Their histories are squeaky clean." She circled the ones who had access to the kitchen and dining room. For one of them, the cook who'd been with him when he'd still been married, she taped up the photo of a plump, white-haired man with a kind smile.

"He had access to Wyatt's food, which moves him higher on the list."

Ronan's gaze seemed to absorb all the info on the whiteboard. "I'll need more info on him and everyone else you mentioned."

"Sure. It's all in the files." She gestured at the stack on the walnut conference table.

"Walk me through what happened that day. Especially in the evening. What was for dinner. When it was served. Who was present. The household staff within proximity."

Jessie wrote the word *Timeline* on the whiteboard. She would've asked the same questions. "Wyatt had half-an-hour cardio at six in the morning with his personal trainer, whose background Paisley and I checked thoroughly. He then took a shower and had his usual breakfast of orange juice and organic free-range eggs with a fruit salad, plus an organic shake."

"Watching his health?"

She nodded. "Very much so. The grandson joked that Wyatt would live a hundred years, and there might've been some bitterness in his remarks. Wyatt's heart issue had improved in recent years. Oh, and he only drank coffee occasionally, but it's some imported organic stuff that tastes like coffee beans but is anything but." She grimaced. She couldn't imagine how someone could live without real coffee. She used to run on coffee.

"Was he alone at breakfast?"

She nodded again. She needed to cut out nodding. And staring at Ronan. It muddled her brain. And put a rush in her blood. But that wasn't the point. What was she talking about? Oh, right. "Yes. Unlike the other family members, he was an early riser. Besides, he wasn't very loved. He had a rule that every family member living in the house had to be present at dinner if he was there. But rules for breakfast and lunch were lax. Therefore, he often spent those meals alone, catching up on business communication. I imagine what happened after breakfast that day wasn't good for his digestion."

"Let me guess. He talked to his youngest son."

"Grandson. Wyatt accused Braxton of stealing from the company and threatened to cut him off if he didn't return what he stole."

This time, it was Ronan who nodded. "A powerful motive."

"Yes. Before you ask, both Hayden and Braxton were at dinner like nothing ever happened. And despite his partying and the recent accusations, Braxton is well loved by the household staff. He was an adorable, spoiled child who grew up to be a charmer."

"But it's all hearsay." He shoved his sweater sleeves up over his elbows again as if impatient to get to work, even though neither of them knew where to start. "This is frustrating."

She sighed, trying not to focus on his arms and wondering what they'd feel like around her. "Tell me about it." It was frustrating to be so close to him and unable to do anything about it. Her face heated. Oh, he meant the case.

Wyatt usually followed a routine, what he did in his daily activities, so everyone in the household knew what Wyatt was going to do at a certain time. That predictability might've been his undoing. Just as looking into Ronan's mesmerizing eyes could be hers...

"What happened after breakfast?" Ronan's voice brought her back.

She wrote Wyatt's business meetings on the whiteboard and the time corresponding with each and who attended them. "He had lunch in his office at twelve while working on his computer, then two more meetings online. Then at two p.m., Huxley tried to get into the building, but the guards stopped him. Huxley left, screaming profanities. Nobody seemed to raise an eyebrow. He was the most recent person Wyatt put out of business."

Ronan crossed his arms over his chest, drawing her gaze to the sweater spread taut over his shoulders. "It's a surprise nobody took Wyatt out before."

"A bulletproof car, a large fence with tight security, and two bulky bodyguards might've helped with that. Wyatt conducted nearly all his meetings online. There's also an unconfirmed rumor that he had a double."

"A double?" Ronan echoed.

"A man who looked exactly like him." Oops, that probably was self-explanatory. "The rumor is unsubstantiated, to my knowledge."

Ronan studied the whiteboard. "So while Huxley had a motive, he didn't have the means."

"Several people from the companies Wyatt put out of business and their relatives tried to get employment at his mansion, possibly to get the opportunity for revenge. But his vetting system was pretty good." It was a miracle Arianna had slipped through it, especially with her past. But then Paisley had turned out to be good at creating a false identity and a false history. Frighteningly good. Also worrying how easy it turned out to be. Jessie suppressed a grimace.

"It had to be, for someone who made as many enemies as he did." His gaze moved from the whiteboard to her and lingered.

She swallowed. How was she supposed to avoid getting distracted when he looked at her like that? "Moving forward. He had a meeting with his chief accountant. My guess was to follow up on his grandson's transgression and the company earnings. It lasted an hour and a half. Then fifteen minutes of meditation on Wyatt's part. Then about fifteen minutes of watching the news. Then meditation again."

"I guess one does need meditation after watching the news."

She suppressed a chuckle, then switched back to serious mode. "Another hour of work, and his chauffeur drove him home in the bulletproof limousine. His chauffeur had been with him for twenty years. They didn't stop anywhere. Half an hour in the greenhouse near his mansion. Then dinner."

"The menu?"

"Organic salad, white rice, wild salmon. The chef had been with the family for a while, as well." Something about that statement bothered her. She'd think about it later.

"If someone orchestrated this and you need to know who that person is, I have a gut feeling it's not only to bring that person to justice."

She wasn't as straitlaced as she wanted to be. Would he think less of her because of that? "Well, there's that. But you're right. There's more." A few heartbeats passed before she could continue. "That person doesn't know about my foster sisters. And we need to keep it that way."

Otherwise, one of them might end up dead, and Jessie would die herself before she'd let that happen.

Chapter Nine

Decades ago...

Arianna appeared in their lives when they were already in their teenage years. She'd come from a troubled background, but in a different way from the rest of the girls. Her home circumstances were so bad she'd run away several times. The last time, she'd been caught stealing from a farm market stand. The details weren't shared with the girls, but the home situation was bad enough that her father and stepmother had lost parental rights and Arianna had been placed in foster care.

Jessie was surprised the Finchs had taken on another child. They weren't exactly a loving couple and were as stingy with smiles as with food. But given the additional income and free labor for their café, it made sense. Besides, Mrs. Finch wouldn't have to mother the teen with a rebellious spirit—they already had Genevieve for that. Genevieve and Madeline would take care of any extra cooking.

The Finchs were cautious, of course, considering Arianna's reputation, and so were the girls. But unlike the Finchs, who hid the valuables, the girls told the newcomer she was welcome to all they had—well, most of it.

Arianna arrived with dirty tattered clothes and a deep-seated look of distrust. She was gaunt, with bones protruding, and one could count her ribs, not that Jessie would try.

"Smile to the girls," Mrs. Finch said.

The girl bared teeth, one of which was chipped.

Appearing as feral as a wolf cub, she took a lot of warmth—and Genevieve's yummy food—before she'd even let the girls approach her.

From the start, Jessie expected Arianna to run away. So Jessie staked out outside the girl's bedroom window. The first two nights nothing happened.

Jessie nearly fell asleep on the third night.

Once she heard a soft thud, she said, "You might need this. There are granola bars, a flashlight, a T-shirt and jeans I think will fit you, and a blanket there." She put a backpack on the ground and stepped away. It was dark, and the Finchs didn't believe in spending on electricity outside at night.

For a few beats, only silence responded. Then like a breeze came, "No pocketknife?"

Jessie winced. "No."

"Pity."

For some time, nothing happened. Jessie strained her ears but didn't hear footfalls. The air nearby didn't seem to move, either.

"It's not bad here," she said as if to herself. "Safe. Not much food in the fridge. But Genevieve and Madeline are great cooks, so they can make a meal from whatever's available. Then there are leftovers from the café. Lots of work there, but we help each other."

Silence.

"And nobody will pick on you," Jessie whispered.

"Right." Arianna snorted. "Look at me. I'm an easy target for popular girls."

"People here know if they touch one of us, I'll beat them up."

Silence again. Arianna obviously didn't believe her.

So Jessie added, "I box and know a few techniques. I could show you. If you stick around. Well, gotta go." She yawned. Three nights without sleep were taking their toll on her, and she'd nearly fallen asleep at school yesterday. "At least one of us needs to get some sleep." She waited for a few heartbeats, then took some steps away.

A single word hit her in the back. "Why?"

She shrugged. "Because you're one of us now. Well, if you want to be."

Then she climbed into her own window because the front door had to remain locked at all times.

The next day, Arianna showed up at breakfast for the first time. She wore the jeans and the white T-shirt Jessie had given her. Even though the clothes hung on her emaciated frame and the T-shirt was a bit short because Arianna was taller than Jessie, at least they were clean. Her hair was washed—apparently, her natural color was chestnut brown.

Days later, when Arianna was reaching for a can on the top shelf in the kitchen, her T-shirt rode up and exposed several long jagged scars. Too deep to be self-inflicted like Madeline's. Jessie, who'd looked inside the kitchen for a glass of water, retreated fast. But not before Arianna glanced back, and their eyes met. Jessie didn't look away, but she didn't ask anything, either.

"Thirsty?" Arianna said finally.

Jessie paused, then nodded. Arianna filled a glass with water from the tap since the Finchs weren't big on buying juices or sodas because, of course, water was the healthiest for the girls. Jessie blinked fast since she'd never let Arianna see tears of compassion.

When Arianna handed Jessie the glass, Arianna's eyes were dry and expressionless. So were Jessie's.

Several months later, the girls still didn't know much about her. But she'd started talking to them in one-word sentences, so that was progress. At Mr. Finch's order, she joined them at the café as a dishwasher. The Finchs didn't ask her to wait on customers because clearly, they didn't want to scare away said customers. She worked fast and ate faster. Any food she'd been given, she inhaled, which the girls decided made sense because Arianna lived for years unsure when or if she'd get a chance to eat again.

True to her word, Jessie showed the newcomer some defense techniques, though the results weren't stellar. Arianna barely had any muscles. So Jessie took Arianna to work out at the school gym. Besides Jessie giving instructions, they didn't talk. Jessie was fine with that.

Two weeks later, when they walked home, Arianna asked, "Wanna know how to pick a lock?"

Jessie blinked and stopped. This was the first she or any of the girls heard Arianna say so many words at once. "Excuse me?"

"You wanna be a police officer. You need to know how a criminal thinks."

Huh. Arianna had paid attention.

Jessie resumed her pace. "Do you know how to hot-wire a car, too?"

"Of course."

Jessie took a long breath before asking the next question. The pocketknife Arianna had mentioned bothered Jessie. There were a few sharp knives at the café. "Have you killed anyone?"

"Not yet. But if I did, do you think I would've told you?" Arianna looked at Jessie with bottomless eyes.

Jessie shrugged. "Probably. You like to impress people."

"You aren't scared?"

Jessie slowed her step. She could see the Finchs' one-story wood-frame house from here. It seemed for most of Arianna's short life, people abused her and blamed her for the results. "No. You survived so far, but you have to realize you need friends to keep on surviving. It's easy to give up. It's much more difficult to go on."

Arianna snorted. "Please. Now you're gonna say you and your buddies are gonna make it easier for me to go on."

Jessie shook her head. "No."

Arianna's step wobbled. "No?"

"But we'll do everything to make survival possible."

Present time...

It took Ronan a while to talk Jessie into joining him for a horse ride on his parents' ranch. He figured, if he couldn't join her world, only glimpse through windows when she opened the curtains for him, maybe he could get her to be part of his world.

They'd already bonded based on their passion for justice and protecting others. And he'd enjoyed introducing her to Irish cuisine, though resisting his attraction to her in a small kitchen where their breath mixed as often as the ingredients hadn't been easy. But while he'd become a cop, he'd never forgotten his cowboy roots—or boots, for that matter. Not that his parents would let him, but that was a different story. His mother, of course, was thrilled he was going on this date with Jessie, no matter how many times he'd tried to explain this wasn't a date. He didn't want to give her false hope.

He breathed in the fresh, crisp air. The sun shining and reflecting off the snow in a myriad of diamonds created an illusion of warmth. But frost nipped at his skin, and their breath fogged in little puffs.

He glanced at his beautiful companion, though one couldn't see much behind her knit hat and the gigantic gray scarf she'd wrapped around her neck and covered her mouth and nose with—likely as much to protect her identity as her skin. As if one could do the former for long in Cowboy Crossing.

She was athletic, but she'd seemed reluctant to venture outdoors, especially somewhere in the open. An alarm rang through him, but he pressed the stop button on it. She'd admitted she shouldn't be in danger. At least not yet.

That not-yet part tasted sharply like blood.

His horse neighed as if sensing his distress. Time to concentrate on the good. The day was bright and beautiful. The company was awesome. His parents and his brothers were alive and well, and his family ranch was prospering.

Thank You, Lord, for these blessings.

What more could one ask for?

How about for Jessie to open her heart to him and maybe even stay here? He sent up a heartfelt prayer.

Jessie tugged at her scarf. Concern stirred him, and with it came the desire to take her hands and warm them up. To take her heart and warm it up. From what he'd understood, no man had ever done so before, and each year froze another layer to the icy fortress around her heart.

"Are you cold?" he asked, questioning his insistence to ride in this wonderland.

Yes, God's creation was gorgeous with each snowflake unique, with trees dressed in white like brides in embroidered dresses—now he didn't need the image of Jessie in a white dress walking down the aisle to him. Most likely, she'd skip embroidery and pearls but have something simple yet elegant.

"I'm fine." Her eyes smiled at him as she looked up. "I forgot how beautiful winter could be. How pristine and innocent-looking. Maybe I concentrated on crimes and violence for too long. As much as I miss my work, I needed this break without realizing it."

"But God realized it."

Her eyes hardened, and her legs moved, prodding her horse faster.

How could he bring her closer to God?

Lord, please guide me.

Ronan kept up with her easily. He was an experienced rider while she wasn't, so for her, he'd chosen a calm mare, a gorgeous Appaloosa named Speckles with a leopard-spot pattern, a white horse with brown spots over her body and a quiet personality. For himself, he took one of his favorites, also an Appaloosa, but with a snowflake pattern, a bay with white spots or flakes. The mare was young, so her flecks were small, but they would increase in size over time.

Granted, even such a calm horse as Speckles could get spooked and bolt, but Ronan hoped it wouldn't happen. So far, Jessie was doing better than he'd expected. She had confidence and inner strength, and Speckles felt it.

He kept paying attention to his surroundings, and he knew she did too. But everything was quiet except for the occasional neighing of horses and chirruping of birds.

With a jolt, he spotted red-winged blackbirds among the white-clad branches against the backdrop of the cerulean sky. They looked like they carried precious rubies on their shoulders. Then a purple finch, close to the color of amethyst, attracted his attention, and further down the trail, an indigo bunting flashed rich blue like lapis lazuli.

What kind of gemstone would Jessie want in an engagement ring? A classic brilliant-cut diamond? Or something else?

Why was he even thinking that? Attraction swirled around them like snowflakes. But he couldn't bring danger to his family—well, maybe he should've chosen a different profession then. And he knew Jessie wouldn't want him to put them at risk. Maybe she and her friends weren't in danger now, but too many unknowns lurked in their story. And he had a gut feeling she had commitment issues, not that it would be surprising with her history.

A guilty sting reminded him he shouldn't be thinking about commitment to Jessie. His experience with Isla proved he wasn't a good partner for someone with a dangerous profession. And besides, seemed she wasn't on good terms with God.

The files Jessie had given him also left an uneasy feeling in his stomach. Two deaths in one family that looked like accidents. But were they?

He halted, and so did his horse. He prompted her to move forward.

Jessie squinted. "Are those bird feeders?"

"Yes." He'd put up feeders with his father since he'd been a little boy.

It had become his tradition. These days, his father spent way more time inside near the fireplace than outside, and Ronan's heart squeezed at seeing his once strong, always-working father weak and quiet. However, the tradition remained. And one day, he could see himself setting up bird feeders with his own son. Would the boy have gray eyes like Jessie?

Whoa. Why did these thoughts keep coming to him?

At least, this time he didn't halt himself and the horse.

He told Jessie about his father before he remembered that she had zero experiences like that. And while his family had many traditions, she had none.

He barely resisted the urge to reach out to her gloved hand. "That was probably insensitive of me."

"Because I don't have any family traditions? Well, if one day I start my own family, the traditions will start with me." She kept her chin high and her voice determined. "Besides, I like learning more about you and your family. How long have your parents been married?"

"Forty-two years. And believe it or not, they are still very much in love. They smile at each other, hold hands, and hug all the time, and there's genuine warmth coming from their union." He swallowed hard. Dare he say the rest?

She said it for him. "Is that why you and your brothers are single? You don't want to settle, right? You want to have what your parents have, and it's difficult to find."

"I thought it was close to impossible."

Until he met his fiancée. And until he met Jessie.

He didn't say the words out loud and even pulled his gaze away from her with an effort, cautious of his surroundings. The sky was clear, but his thoughts weren't.

How long were they going to prance around their real feelings? But she was obviously commitment-shy and could spook more than a horse would spook at a bag flapping in the wind.

A purple finch took off in flight, and her Appaloosa neighed, nostrils flaring. Jessie's head flipped as she scanned the field with scattered trees, and her hand moved to her holster and stayed there. He paid attention to his surroundings as he reached to Speckles and patted the mare's long neck reassuringly. No need for Speckles to take off in fright. The horse calmed, and birds chirruped again, so there shouldn't be any real danger around them.

Yet he took the trail to the nearby forest. Without leaves, the trees didn't provide much coverage, but it was better than nothing.

As selfish as it was, he didn't want to end his time with Jessie.

Silence passed, interrupted only by snow crunching and birds singing. Then she asked, "Did you have a chance to look through the files?"

His shoulders slumped. Was that the reason she'd agreed to this ride? "Read them several times."

"Did anything jump out at you?" Her scarf slid down, revealing the generous mouth he so wanted to kiss and that birthmark above her upper lip that drove him crazy.

Exactly what he should be thinking now. Not!

"I'm still going through the files and doing additional research on my own. I wish a tox screen was done in Wyatt's case, as well as a postmortem."

She sighed. "Me, too. Believe me, me, too."

He wanted to help her. He really did. But he doubted he could be more thorough than she'd already been.

He swallowed hard. Until she felt safe to reveal her secret, until they could solve the mystery, there was no future for them, was there? And even then, there were too many obstacles between them. Just like with Isla, the urge to protect Jessie at all costs unraveled inside, blinding like a blizzard. But just like Isla, Jessie wouldn't let him, and knowing it crushed more than the snow crushed under the Appaloosas' signature striped hooves.

He said a prayer and hoped it was God's will to bring Jessie into his life. God had answered his prayers before, but not with Isla.

Jessie's lips turned down, and he ached to put a smile back on her lovely face. He looked around, aware of his surroundings. Then they dismounted again and tied the horses to a shivering aspen, and she stroked the curling bark on the tree. With her cheeks rosy from the frost when she looked up at him, he saw the same longing in her gray eyes that had consumed him since they'd met.

"I'm not a man of big words, so I don't know how to say it. But you mean a lot to me."

"You mean a lot to me, too." She lifted on her tiptoes and kissed his cheek. Fleeting like the touch of a snowflake before it melted, it still shot awareness to his very core.

A man could only have so much willpower. He dipped his head slowly to give her the chance to pull away. His pulse went into overdrive, and his breathing, visible in the frosty air, went shallow. Her breathing seemed to match his.

He encircled her waist, drawing her close, and she leaned into him, sending a wave of awareness through him. Just when his lips were about to touch hers, her cell phone rang. He groaned.

"Sorry," she whispered. "I'll ignore it." The ringing stopped, then started again. And again.

He missed the time when landlines were the only phones available. "Might be important."

She fished out her phone and swiped to answer. "Hi, Madeline." Then her eyes widened, and she blanched. "Okay, I'll be back as soon as I can."

Concern overrode his irritation. "What happened?"

"Hayden just died in a climbing accident. The girls think he might've been killed."

Chapter Ten

The next day, Jessie did her best not to be irritated with her friends for interrupting her near-kiss with Ronan. As she stared at the way-busier-than-before whiteboard in the incident room, her hand flew to her lips several times before she even noticed she was doing it.

No need to be moody. Ronan was at work, hopefully doing nothing more dangerous than finding a runaway cow or a cat, and she should be working, as well. They'd talked on the phone in the evening, and he told her about his work in Springfield. A part of her, a selfish one, was relieved he didn't work there any longer. Just the thought of him possibly being in danger made her shudder.

She was getting in deep, and she knew it. He'd also told her about Isla, and Jessie didn't know what to make of it yet. On the one hand, compassion had made her want to talk to him in person and hug him and make it better for him. On the other hand, she'd sensed more than grief. There had been guilt there, too. He'd worried about Isla so much that he wanted her to give up being a firefighter, had told her as much many times. Now it weighed on him.

Her gut tightened. If Jessie tried to get work with the police department again—possible since her former buddies said the chief who'd disliked her was retiring and the rumored replacement was one of her friends—wouldn't it be selfish to pursue a relationship with Ronan and risk putting him through the same agony again? Not that she could pursue a relationship in the first place, considering her history with men and the fact she might be leaving this place as soon as she knew it was okay to do so.

Earth to Jessie. She needed to return to her investigation instead of thinking of the handsome cowboy turned cop.

Since she and the girls had been children, they depended on each other for survival, and they'd proven it many times. Her friends had been there for her when she'd been hungry, sad, frustrated, or when her career on the force had ended in disaster and her heart had been crushed—at the same time.

As much as they'd been shattered in pieces individually, together they'd made something whole, and they all knew it.

Painstakingly, she'd managed to cross out more names from the second list of suspects, the ones who'd had a grudge against Wyatt. But one more name in the main list was circled now. Hmm.

Paisley poked her tousled pink-blue head inside. "You have a visitor." She must've been watching the road. Her wide grin suggested the said visitor might be Ronan. As tight as their circle was, the girls playing matchmakers—especially Paisley—surprised Jessie, and her increased heartbeat hinted she didn't mind in the least.

She smoothed her short hair. "How do I look?"

Paisley tilted her head, then crossed the room and fluffed Jessie's hair. "Better now."

Jessie wasn't so sure about that, but the doorbell was ringing already. Well, it wasn't like Ronan hadn't seen her without makeup or in ratty jeans. And he kept coming back. She was going to wear those jeans forever.

"I'd better scoot." With a wink, Paisley sauntered away, her light footfalls almost drowned out by Ronan's much heavier ones. Jessie could recognize him by the sound of his footsteps already. Much scarier, she *craved* the sound of his footsteps.

And she was smiling from ear to ear. Time to tone it down a bit. No need to show how eager she was to see him. She was going to stay in her chair and look nonchalantly at him. Madeline had perfected that look, and it drove men crazy.

He entered the room and lifted a coffee tray and a paper bag that emanated yummy sweet scents. "I come bearing gifts."

She bolted from her seat and wrapped her arms around his neck, breathing in his masculine scent of leather and pine needles. Heat rushed to her cheeks as she scooted back. What was she doing? So much for looking nonchalant. "Um, coffee and desserts deserve a hug."

He'd already removed his coat. The black sweater underneath it stretched over his muscular torso and biceps, offset by his camel-hued scarf and matching cowboy hat. He must wear that cowboy hat year-round.

His deep brown eyes gleamed as he put the tray and the bag on the conference table. "Then I'll make sure I do it every time I come here. Well, I brought enough for everyone, but I wanted to give you the right of first choice."

Huh. The man just scored brownie points with her *and* the girls.

She chuckled. "That was wise." She sipped her coffee. Sweet and warm, touching a spot inside her.

Just like Ronan. She nearly coughed.

He raised a brow, brown eyes searching her face. "Too hot?"

"Just right." She forced herself to draw her gaze away from him to the bag. She found her favorite, a banana bread muffin, rather fast.

He said grace. But she wasn't ready to start thanking God yet. One more reminder about their differences. He'd been brought up a Christian. Jessie's foster parents didn't care to instill faith in the children they'd fostered. But then, they didn't even care much to feed them.

She'd had difficulty comprehending how a kind God could let horrible things happen to them, especially Madeline. And yet, Ronan had experienced loss and pain, too, and still believed. Could she begin to believe again?

She pushed the thought away. Didn't she decide to get Ronan's help and enjoy his presence—and fine, the yummy food she'd started to associate him with—without falling for him? She didn't have to have a good relationship with God to work with a guy.

But with Ronan, the not-falling-for-him part was easier said than done. Warmth spread further inside her, and she couldn't blame it on the coffee. He chose a pumpkin roll for himself, and she committed it to memory. Though she doubted the day would come when she'd start baking, but if he joined her...

"I see Emberlynn's name is circled." His words sobered her up.

"Turns out, Wyatt's ex-wife ran up some large debts recently. She's used to living a grand lifestyle, and the divorce settlement must be running out. It didn't help that she's constantly giving funds to her son and grandson." Jessie gave due to the muffin and flushed it down with coffee. The muffin was soft and yielding, and she wondered if his lips would be, too. Her pulse quickened again.

Seriously! She'd never had difficulty concentrating on a case before, not even when she'd been in love. But then, she'd never met Ronan before. And maybe, just maybe, she hadn't been in love with her fiancé as much as she'd desperately needed someone to love her and stick around. Look how well that had turned out.

She gestured for Ronan to sit down, and they settled in chairs side by side at the conference table while sipping from their cups.

"I've read what's in the file, but can you tell me more about Emberlynn?"

Did he wonder, like she had, whether Emberlynn might be behind the tragic events? If the plane crash wasn't an accident, Emberlynn had a motive to order Mylah's death, as well.

Jessie dug into her memory, fueled by coffee. "She's been dating a lot lately. For the last five months, a prominent doctor."

Lowering his disposable coffee cup after a quick sip, Ronan narrowed his eyes. "What kind of doctor?"

"A cardiologist."

A silent understanding passed between them. Emberlynn would know how to switch pills then, not just placebos, or how to substitute other medicines Wyatt was taking so they'd become incompatible with heart medicine. Of course, she'd need an accomplice in the house. Was her grandson desperate enough for that?

He finished his pumpkin roll and reached for a paper napkin. "I imagine you've checked out the doctor."

"Of course." Jessie absently ran a finger along the conference table's edge, tracing the natural lines of the tree it had been cut from. "So far, his reputation has been impeccable. There's a hiccup. Both she and her boyfriend were out of the country at the time of Wyatt's death."

He took another sip of his coffee, his brows furrowing. "She has a perfect alibi. Unless she paid someone to poison her former husband or convinced her youngest son or grandson that they owed her enough for that."

Tapping her fingers against a knot in the wood, Jessie raised her gaze to the new photo on the whiteboard. "There's something else. Despite her age, Emberlynn's athletic. She's an experienced mountain climber. Though wouldn't it make it all a bit too obvious in Hayden's case?" Jessie placed her empty cup directly over that knot, aligning it as a perfect cover-up.

"Hmm. I have difficulty imagining her turning on her son."

Jessie did, too. But her own mother had abandoned her, so Jessie didn't believe in parental feelings as much as he did. "Maybe he started blackmailing her? Our mole overheard Hayden's conversation with the attorney shortly before his death. Looks like Hayden was going to change his will. In his current one, his mother was his beneficiary. Whatever was left to his soon-to-be ex-wife and his son was merely symbolic. By the way, with Wyatt gone, she wants to come back to the family business. Not that she did much when she was married to him, but that might be because he didn't allow her."

"Hmm." Ronan set his cup aside as well, then leaned toward her, one arm braced on the table, his pine scent embracing her. "Why would she return now after all these years?"

Her body moved toward him, as well. Her memory did her a disservice, bringing up their almost-kiss yesterday. "I believe people around her underestimated her. Overall, she is described as intelligent, strong-willed, and determined."

"Seems like one needs to be to survive in that family."

Jessie eyed the paper bag but decided against another dessert.

He must've caught her gaze. "Help yourself."

"I'd better not. If I get a chance to chase after criminals again, I need to stay in shape. Wish I had an exercise partner. Paisley and Genevieve don't like to exercise. The only person who does show up at the gym here sometimes is Madeline. But she's a picture of misery when she tries to work out. I mean, she doesn't complain much, but her face tells it all. And of course now her wrist is broken, she can't do much."

"I'd be glad to join you in the gym after my shift tomorrow." He smiled.

Her cheeks flushed. "I didn't mean it as a hint." Or did she?

He shrugged. "I could use a workout partner, too."

An image of Ronan in a tight T-shirt, his muscles straining, made heat pool inside her. That was so not a good idea. Their gazes met and held, and she scooted a little further toward him, her blood stirring under his perusal.

Then, through the open doorway, Paisley's distant laughter in the kitchen made Jessie jerk back. She needed to remember why the two of them were in the incident room.

Disappointment flashed in his eyes, but he also moved back. "Tell me about the accident that took Hayden's life."

She rubbed her temples as if to bring some sense into her head. "Right," she squeaked. Squeaked! Just great.

Then she said in a stronger voice, "Hayden seemed to like living on the edge, despite his mother's pleas. He stopped letting anyone know when he'd take off on his latest adventure. He'd done over twenty parachute jumps, gone scuba diving, swimming with the sharks, bungee jumping, and so on.

Thankfully, he did most of it sober, or rather, wasn't allowed to do it drunk. Rock climbing was his latest obsession. After several lessons with an instructor, he decided he could do it alone, drunk, and chose a dangerous spot to boot. The rope slipped, and he plunged to his death."

"Let me guess. There'll be no autopsy, no tox screen, nothing in this case, either."

She grimaced. "No sign of foul play, and the police are overloaded with more obvious murder cases. I'm checking some of the girlfriends he dumped since separating from his wife. And, well, his mother and his rogue son who just inherited a huge fortune. Because it's clear she'd share her inheritance with the grandson she adores."

Ronan stared into her eyes, making her blood rush faster again. "I found a lot of info about Braxton in the file. Lots of partying while in high school, and the partying didn't stop after he joined the family business this year, which seemed to be in name only. From careful interviews of subordinates, it appears he was in the company only by birthright and hadn't contributed much."

"People change." Often for the worse, like her first love had. Or rather, he'd been just an illusion she'd painted for herself because he'd only been kind and attentive to win her trust and gain access to information.

How many illusions had Wyatt's family painted for the world to see, and what really went on between them? Had they ever known how ruthless Wyatt was?

A shudder went through her. After she'd learned what he'd done, she'd almost begged Paisley to find a security breach in his mansion. Or in his office. She didn't know what she would've done once she got in, and it was for the better she hadn't. The girls had talked her out of it, and she'd be forever grateful to them for it.

In the end, she probably wouldn't have been able to do it, anyway. That was the only time she'd ever considered walking on the other side of the law, and it would've killed her. Her insides went cold.

"Are you okay?" His voice filtered through her mental fog. "I've never seen you look like that."

"And I hope you never will again."

Jessie wasn't a murderer. But neither was she a forgiving person, and she feared that was another thing she didn't have in common with Ronan.

Straightforward and honest, he deserved a woman who was just as straightforward and honest.

Not a woman with a murky heritage and an unknown future.

Jessie wiped the perspiration from her forehead as she ran on the treadmill the next day. Agreeing to be Ronan's workout partner was a bad idea indeed.

Sweaty and flushed was just the way she wanted the man she liked to see her. Not!

With her throat parched, she pressed the button to slow the pace and reduce the incline, then brought the treadmill to a complete stop. Her breathing evened out but then went shallow again as she looked at Ronan.

He was lifting weights, his muscles straining. His skin gleaned. His chocolate-brown T-shirt imprinted with a cowboy riding against sunrise stretched, the movement making it look as if the cowboy was galloping. She reached for her water bottle without looking at it and nearly knocked it down.

Just great. She was gawking, ogling him even. Yet she couldn't look away. She'd never understood women who salivated after a man's physique. Until now.

Not that she was salivating. Quite the opposite. Her mouth was dry. She took a hurried sip of water, then splashed a bit on her cheeks. The gym's temperature was low, but she felt like she was in the tropics.

Ronan would look good in the tropics....

Argh. She'd never been this shallow. In her line of work, she'd seen a lot of fit, muscular men. Worked out with them. Trained with them. Granted, when she'd been pushed to the limit in training, she hadn't had any place for other thoughts.

Either way, they'd never affected her as much as Ronan did.

As if he was made to set her on fire.

Meant for her? Was it true that God could've made Ronan specifically for her?

She nearly snorted. She'd believe it if she could believe God cared about people like her and her friends. People who'd been damaged and couldn't work up much forgiveness.

God surely loved people like Ronan and his family. Those people were easy to love. But if even the kind, merciful God Ronan had talked about couldn't love her, how could she expect Ronan to?

Jesus spent His time here with the outcasts of society. What makes you think He couldn't love you?

She ignored the whisper.

Maybe pushing herself to the limit wasn't such a bad idea. Then she could push these thoughts out of her head. She walked to the weights.

He abandoned his and crossed to her. "Let me help you with that." He must have an extremely efficient deodorant because, despite his skin glistening with sweat, he still somehow smelled like pine-forest soap.

She didn't know how she smelled, but it sure wasn't pine forest. With her skin clammy and her T-shirt stained, she could only hope her deodorant held up as well as his did. She told him what bars to add on.

His brow furrowed. "Are you sure?"

She nodded. For the next hour, she pushed herself to the point that every cell in her body begged for mercy and the only thing she wanted to do was to slide to the cold cement floor and stay there.

They talked about their experiences in the police academy as she grunted oh-so unladylike and lifted and pulled. While her muscles protested the strain, sharing that experience with someone who understood, who'd gone through the same thing, felt good, strengthened their shared bond.

There was a reason she'd had to succeed in the police academy so desperately. She'd needed to do well and prove she had the chops to become a cop because people like her didn't get second chances. If she wanted to achieve anything, she had to make a plan early on and stick to it. She'd had to be careful with every penny she'd earned in her part-time jobs. It wasn't like she could come back to her parents and crash in her childhood room. Making mistakes wasn't an option if she wanted to make something out of herself, unlike many foster children who aged out of the system without any support. While growing up, she'd heard about too many who ended up on the wrong side of the law.

Ended up overdosing.

Ended up ended.

Despite her heated and sweating skin, she shuddered, her gut twisting for the people lost behind those heart-wrenching numbers. She'd been determined not to become another statistic and to prevent it from happening to her girls.

None of her foster sisters had the luxury to flounder after school or change their majors while in college, either. Well, except Madeline, who'd changed her specialty while in medical school from surgery to something no one had expected from her but something that made sense to Jessie. A medical examiner.

It had been a miracle Genevieve had been able to study at all after everything that happened to her, even somehow earning a scholarship and becoming an English teacher. Still caring, still loving toward her students instead of turning into a bitter recluse like Jessie probably would have.

Then her thoughts and conversation with Ronan turned to Wyatt's case.

"I don't think the motive in Wyatt's murder, if it was a murder, was revenge," Ronan said.

"I agree." While she'd still worked on the list of people with such motives, she came to the same conclusion. Because then he or she wouldn't have let Wyatt go so peacefully. Unless it was someone very, very patient. Or, maybe, someone who'd once loved him. Regardless, she'd worked through the list diligently, especially on verifying Huxley's alibi. "They'd want him to suffer and remember—really remember—what he'd done."

Ronan gave her a surprised glance. Maybe she'd said it with too much passion.

She continued in a more even voice, except for an occasional grunt when she overestimated how much she could lift. "This looks like he was removed because of being in the way."

Yet Ronan lifted much more than she had. "We talked about the inheritance. How about a business competitor? I saw the two most prominent ones mentioned in the file."

"I'm checking them. But what motive is there to remove the youngest son? To let the inexperienced-in-business ex-wife and troubled grandson enter the picture and destroy the company from within? That wouldn't happen while Marshall is still in charge. He still has a fifty percent stake in the company." Yet the idea of this motive sat much better with her than the idea of the motive being revenge.

Not only because it was more likely but also because she knew all too well which person had that motive simmering in them for many years. Which one had been working in Wyatt's house and had the opportunity. She'd grown up with her.

To distract herself from the thought, she pushed harder with the weights.

Ronan kept up with her and surpassed her, but then his muscle mass was much higher than hers. And every time he leaned over her, changing bars or handing her water, her entire being shifted toward him despite her exhaustion. So unfair.

He tried to stop her, but she only asked him to add more weights as if she wanted to punish herself for needing something—*somebody* who was so close to her and yet unreachable.

"That's enough. Or I'll have to carry you out of here." He handed her a fresh towel.

Her exhausted body perked up. That wouldn't be such a bad idea....

Chapter Eleven

Despite her legs protesting, Jessie managed to get up. Okay, fine, Ronan pulled her up and blotted her face with a towel. The scent of pine forest was fainter now, but still there. Enticing and unfair.

Based on her rivers of sweat, she needed to get into a shower as soon as possible. Even if the steps there seemed insurmountable.

"You might need another towel." He blotted her neck with a new towel gently.

Her nerve endings reacted when his fingers brushed her skin, and awareness cascaded over her heated flesh. She didn't even know she had that many nerve endings until he touched her. Then the words registered, and she suppressed a groan. Time for the shower.

If he ever suggested exercising together again, she'd counter with something like skiing, despite how she was reluctant to be out in the open.

Not... this.

She slid onto the bench and drained the rest of her water bottle, as much to distract herself from her treacherous reaction to him as to stay hydrated. She needed to remind herself that nearly everyone she'd loved had abandoned her, some right after her birth. The thought weighed her down more than her current muscle fatigue, and that was saying something.

"I found my birth mother," she blurted out.

Why... why had she said that? She'd only told her foster sisters. Not even her partner at the force had known.

His gaze, pensive and compassionate, washed over her. "I thought you would." He didn't ask questions, but he sat on the bench and handed her another water bottle.

She took it, as well as his silent offer to share her pain.

For a moment, she was transported to a dingy apartment that smelled like rotten food, mothballs, and human desperation. "She looked gaunt, little more than yellowish skin stretched over bones. I asked about my father. She laughed and said even the faces of the men she'd been with were hazy, much less the names. She didn't sound remorseful. She had to support her habit, after all. When I asked for any relatives, she told me a little about my grandmother, who was a foster kid like me, alone in the world. I asked for my grandmother's things, but Mom didn't have any. The apartment was bare indeed. Just a bunch of mattresses on the floor, empty syringes in sight. I tried to clean up, but she stopped me. I offered to pay for rehab. To rent her a better place. Addiction is a disease, and she was my mother, after all."

She took a few sips as if the water could clean the memory from her. Then she put the cap back on and placed the bottle on the floor.

"That was kind of you." He covered her hand with his, anchoring her to the present instead of the past. Anchoring her to the people who cared about her instead of those who'd hurt her.

"She looked shocked, then asked for money. But I said I'd pay for rehab but wouldn't give her cash. She refused. Then her 'friends' showed up, and I thought I'd better leave. But I kept coming back, making sure she was alone first. She finally agreed to rehab." Jessie closed her eyes, seeing the woman again, feeling her own hope anew. Then the crushing disappointment.

His fingers tightened over her hands. He could probably guess what had happened next. But he didn't say a word, and she was grateful. That support meant more than a bucket of roses. Even more than a bottle of exquisite perfume.

She gathered inner strength. She could still smell rotten food and the stench of bodies that had gone without bathing for days. "She checked herself out the next day and returned to her 'friends.' By then, I verified their background, and it was frightening. I visited her again, and the story repeated. The fourth time, she disappeared after checking herself out of rehab."

Jessie swallowed hard, but she didn't feel the familiar bitterness. "I could've tracked her down. I was a cop, after all."

"But you let go. You did the right thing. You'd done so much for her already. And... you're not like her. You'll never be."

"I'm a foster kid." She pushed the words past her throat.

"All the more admirable what you've accomplished. And you're not alone in the world. You've got your foster sisters. God. And... me. If you allow it, of course."

The thought was as exhilarating as it was frightening. But unlike the water bottle, she couldn't take that offer yet. Not until she'd worked through her issues. And he'd already lost Isla to a dangerous profession. She wouldn't make him risk it again. She couldn't.

Her throat constricted.

"As much as I admire you for it, why *did* you keep going back, trying to help her?" He searched her eyes as if he were trying to understand something about her.

"Something she said stuck with me. That she could've aborted me. Instead, she got clean for me. At that time, she wasn't using that much. I imagine I could've been born with lots of diseases. Well, I was born with issues that required a bunch of surgeries. But I could have been... not born at all. I–I can sound cynical sometimes, but Paisley's optimism rubs off on me. I do try to see the best in people. Even the ones I had to arrest. Maybe it makes me gullible." It probably did, considering she'd believed all the lies her fiancé had told her.

"No. It makes you kind. And it gives you hope." Ronan brought her fingers to his lips and kissed them one by one as if he needed to give her more hope, this time that a relationship between them was possible.

"Well, one of my foster sisters has a... peculiar history. Whatever we know of it. It taught me a lot about redemption. Everyone deserves a chance."

"Including you." The gaze of his brown eyes unnerved her.

So she closed her eyes and leaned against the wall. "I didn't try to find my father. Despite my mother's hazy memory, I could've talked to her neighbors from that time, tracked down her associates, persuaded people to take paternity tests, and so on. But most of her associates at the time were other people who shared her addiction. I couldn't repeat what I'd gone through already with her."

Couldn't risk being rejected and abandoned again. She'd had too much of that in her life already.

For some time, they stayed silent. When she opened her eyes, she found him watching her. Not with pity, but compassion, and so much more lurking beneath the surface. She was used to deciphering clues. But she wasn't sure she was ready to decipher these. Or if she'd ever be.

"We need to go." Yet her muscles seemed to weigh a ton.

"If you're too tired, how about I take you there?" He scooped her up.

Her mouth went dry, but for a different reason than before.

What... just happened?

The workout had already sent her heart into overdrive, and yet being in his arms brought it up a notch. The only time a man had carried her, he'd dropped her. At least, on the carpet, not on hard cement. Still, she'd had back pain for months afterward. But then, to lift and carry someone was way more difficult than in the movies where a guy would pick up a woman easily as if she weighed no more than a feather.

Either way, she wouldn't want anyone to carry her at the police academy or later on the job. She'd needed to project the strength and assurance that she was just as capable as the men she'd trained with and later worked with. Without thinking about it, she'd cut her hair short and kept to her tomboyish clothes as if she needed that image of being capable to fit in, to do the job that made a difference in the world.

But it should be okay to be vulnerable sometimes. She didn't need to prove herself with Ronan. Maybe one day she wouldn't have to hide her wounds from him, either. And she had a feeling he was one man who wouldn't drop her.

So she wrapped her arms around his neck, breathed in his masculine scent, and settled against his broad chest as if it was something she did all the time. A pleasant wave spread through her despite the muscle pain.

Madeline gaped as she met them in the hall. "Maybe I need to start working out, too."

Ronan didn't skip a beat. "I'll suggest Brandon join you in the gym."

Surprisingly, Madeline didn't protest. Instead, she asked, "Do you and your brothers work out a lot?"

"With all the work that needs to be done at the ranch, yes. But this was my first trip to the gym in a while." He marched on toward the bathroom.

So he'd done it for Jessie. Another icicle around her heart chipped off. She couldn't afford to lose too many of them. She stirred in his arms. "I'll take it from here. Thank you."

"My pleasure." His gaze lingered on her as he put her down. That gaze could melt the snow outside, much less her heart. "I hope to see you tomorrow."

"I don't doubt it." Madeline chuckled behind him. "Either one of those statements."

Jessie sent her friend a stern look Madeline promptly ignored. Then Jessie rose to her tiptoes and kissed Ronan on the cheek, tasting salt and hope.

She slipped inside the bathroom and turned the water on. She didn't need to look in the mirror to know her face was flushed and her hair was sticking out in all directions.

She had a lot of things to figure out. The mysteries of Wyatt's family. And the mystery of her own heart that didn't want to accept reality.

"Why are you so dressed up?" Ronan stared at Brandon's crisp white shirt, tie, and ironed black slacks as they were setting the dining table at their parents' house. The air smelled of beef stew and freshly made Irish soda bread, familiar and comforting scents from his childhood.

Brandon glanced toward the kitchen, where their parents were, and whispered, "Can't I dress up for a family dinner?"

What was with the secrecy? But Ronan lowered his tone just in case while he put utensils in their places on the large oak table which had enough space—and chairs near it—to accommodate a family of eight and a few guests. Scratcher weaved between his legs, hoping for a handout, or rather demanding it with loud meows. But then, it was Ronan's own fault. He'd brought the cat too many treats lately. "Right. The last time you dressed up was for our cousin's wedding three years ago. And that was only at Mom's insistence. But even then you didn't wear a tie."

Brandon grimaced, tugging at the collar as he moved napkins around, yes, napkins that were in their place already. "This thing's suffocating me. Like someone put a rope around my neck."

Ronan laughed. "From what I've seen at the lodge, you've been lassoed all right."

Brandon's shoulders bunched like he was about to throw a punch, and Ronan ducked out of habit. But then Mom called from the kitchen to pick up the main dish, and they hurried there, followed by Scratcher, infuriated over being ignored.

Minutes later, Ronan lugged back the steaming beef stew while Brandon brought the salad bowl and bread plate. Scratcher stayed with Mom, who picked him up and, based on the purring, stroked his soft fur. Since that one incident, Scratcher hadn't tried to escape again. On the contrary, he ran away from the cold gust any time the front door opened. Ronan still didn't know what motivated the cat to escape the first time around.

Back in the dining room, Brandon whispered, "I'm *not* lassoed. I'm going to the place *you're* going to every day. We might as well hitch a ride together. Only unlike you, I have a moral obligation to do so."

"If you say so. But why are you whispering?" Ronan needed to go back to the kitchen for the iced tea pitcher, but nagging his oldest brother was more fun.

"Because if Mom finds out how much time I spend with Madeline, she'll hear wedding bells."

"Oooh. You're spending a lot of time at the lodge?" Mom released the cat and rubbed her hands together as she appeared in the doorframe.

Scratcher darted into the dining room, out of curiosity or because of the food aromas.

Brandon muttered toward Ronan, "Aren't you supposed to be a cop? You couldn't hear footsteps?" Much louder, he said toward Mom, "I'm only doing it because she got hurt due to our horse. It's the right thing to do, and you raised us to do the right thing."

"Yep, and a white shirt and a tie is the new uniform to visit a sick person." Ronan grinned.

Scratcher meowed his agreement, and Ronan nodded to his new buddy. Scratcher was worth every scrap of the fancy food Ronan had given him.

Brandon shot Ronan a look.

"Let's eat." His father appeared in the room. "Don't let your mom's food go cold."

They sat down, and Dad said grace.

Mom ladled stew for everyone, and Ronan took a spoonful. "Delicious as always, Mom."

She beamed, but apparently not from the compliment. "We finally might get a chance at grandchildren."

Scratcher stretched on the floor nearby and meowed again as if taking credit for that or at least a part of it.

Ronan and Brandon groaned in unison. "Please don't read too much into it."

"You should invite both lovely girls for dinner here," Dad said.

Ronan swallowed hard. "Dad, you're not helping."

"I'm helping my wife. Just like I should." He smiled at Mom.

Something shifted inside Ronan. He'd nearly given up hope that one day he'd find someone to look at that way. Until Jessie appeared in his life.

His mother smiled back. "Great idea, darling. Maybe the girls could even help me make dinner."

Ronan blinked. Madeline looked like she'd be afraid to break a perfectly painted nail, plus had a broken wrist. And while Ronan had tried to teach Jessie some cooking skills, he'd been happy to do most of the cooking for her so far. Besides, there was an obvious horse—wait, elephant—in the room. "I don't know how long they are going to stay. They act like they might be leaving soon."

Mom clasped the spoon tighter before eating her stew. Noooo, she wasn't letting the chance to get grandbabies slip through her fingers. "Then it's up to you to change their minds. It took a while for your father to win my affection. But if he gave up easily, neither one of you would've existed."

Good point. But Ronan hit his brother's leg with his own under the table. He couldn't be doing the job all by himself. Meanwhile, he enjoyed his stew.

"Seriously, Mom? Didn't you hear anything we said?" Brandon helped himself to more bread.

That was the best he could come up with? One, two, three...

Mom huffed. "Well, whose fault is that? I tried to set you up with a nice local girl, but none of my sons would go for it."

Just what Ronan expected. But as much as he liked Jessie and suspected his brother was getting more and more attracted to Madeline, those women were nothing like his parents would expect. Jessie was ready to bolt at any moment as it was. A family dinner could turn into a total disaster.

Easy.

Chapter Twelve

Jessie read the reports about the private plane crash in the Dominican Republic again. A certain part bothered her. This wasn't right. At all. Why had no one paid attention to such a glaring fact? But what could she do now, years later? She lifted her chin. She wasn't going to give up. Maybe if she could visit the place...

She resisted the urge to grind her teeth as she closed the file and placed it in the incident room safe.

What was she missing?

Ronan.

Okay, that was *who*, not what. But just thinking about him brewed a pleasant feeling inside her.

Argh. She should be concentrating on the investigation and her friends, not her untimely attraction. But did she really, truly want to dig deep into the case? Her stomach clenched. She'd always believed in justice, in searching for truth. Always. Her life and her job centered on it.

Yet, in these circumstances, what if the answer was the one she dreaded?

There should be photos of more people in the Suspects column, though it was way too long already. But how could she suspect someone she knew so well and loved so much?

She rubbed her throbbing temples. Could this be something to ask God? If only she could believe the Lord would answer. A whisper escaped her. *Help me, Lord.*

At least, she didn't have to suspect Paisley, Genevieve, and Madeline. Paisley had the perfect alibi because she'd been camped out on Jessie's couch at the time of Wyatt's death. She'd said she could work from anywhere, Jessie's couch sounded as good a place as any, plus she'd missed Jessie.

Jessie liked to be missed, but she guessed the real reason was that she'd had the blues after losing her fiancé and her job—in that order. And sweet Paisley wanted to be there for her friend. She'd often shown up on the doorstep with a pie and a compassionate smile when one of them had gone through heartache.

Then, at the time of Hayden's accident, all of them apart from Arianna were in the lodge already. Genevieve had been teaching when Wyatt died, and Jessie had double-checked.

Madeline had vacationed in a town in south Florida at the time, and the ticket stubs confirmed it. No way she could make it to Houston and somehow sneak into Wyatt's house.

But a strange feeling nagged Jessie, so she pulled up the map of Texas. Her heart went cold. Was it possible? She tried to remember whether Madeline had said the town was in south Florida or Jessie had assumed it because she'd heard of that town on the ocean shore.

Because there was a town with the same name about an hour's drive away from Houston. By Texas measures, not far. Though Madeline was a former model, not a current one, she was still gorgeous and the type the men in Wyatt's family seemed to favor.

Jessie's heart tumbled with suspicions she didn't want to entertain. Madeline had been the most vocal that Wyatt should be punished for what he'd done. Maybe she'd also been projecting her frustration because her parents' murderers had never been discovered, had never paid for what they'd done.

Then guilt stabbed Jessie. She had to trust her friends. Or was it naïve of her? What was right and what was wrong in this situation?

Madeline's words rang in her ears—"But don't you think it's unfair some people never pay for what they've done?"

Jessie suspected Madeline was talking about her childhood tragedy then, and her heart had gone out to her friend, who'd never gotten closure. Would this be a twisted way to get closure by avenging her friend and making sure Wyatt wouldn't hurt anyone again?

Madeline wouldn't make it look like revenge. She had enough patience for that. As well as enough patience to wait many years. As strange as it was, Genevieve had seemed to come to terms with what had happened, and while she'd surely still be hurting, she'd forgiven Wyatt, partly because of her enormous kindness, partly because they'd gotten Gold from what had happened.

But the rare times Jessie and Madeline had talked about what had happened to Genevieve, Jessie realized Madeline had never forgiven Wyatt. And Madeline believed in a different kind of justice than Jessie did.

Jessie got up with a groan. Then her phone rang.

When she disconnected, she knocked at Madeline's door, nerves getting the best of Jessie. "You and I are invited to a family dinner at the O'Neills. You should receive your invitation soon."

Madeline opened the door and flipped her immaculate chestnut-hued hair back. Even in her injured state, she looked ready to be on a fashion magazine cover in a turquoise-hued knit dress that hugged her body and brightened her blue eyes. "That's good news, no? But why do you look so horrified?"

Jessie leaned against the wall, suddenly weak. She really should be given only one shock at a time to handle, not two in a row. "I might have to cook!"

Jessie hadn't suffered from insomnia since she was fifteen. On the contrary, it had taken her an ocean of coffee not to fall asleep on a stakeout. Even after seeing gruesome crime scenes, she'd usually been so exhausted she'd fallen into oblivion the moment her head hit the pillow.

Not so now.

She'd tossed and turned the entire night, and not only because she'd have to cook the next day. Cooking was far from her strong suit, and she wanted to impress Ronan's mother. Not that Jessie would have a chance to marry into a family so welcoming and warm, so different from what her own family must've been like.

Well, any family would be different from hers for the sheer virtue of existing.

Now, during the family dinner at the O'Neills, a shiver went through her as she managed a shaky smile and a few bites without tasting anything.

Even a trace of unwelcome suspicion about Madeline upended Jessie's world. Her life had been precarious since her conception, but the camaraderie between her foster sisters had infused it with much-needed stability.

They'd had to rely on each other because it was the only way to survive. At least, for Jessie. Growing up, she'd believed her foster sisters would be adopted soon. Beautiful Madeline who could be a child model. Quirky but cute Paisley who had her perennial smile. Tenderhearted Genevieve who oozed kindness. *They* had chances to be adopted. Jessie could never understand why they hadn't been. Maybe something in Madeline's file prevented people from adopting her, like nightmares, screams, and cuttings, in addition to Madeline's heavy, unchildlike stare.

First a guy and then a married couple had tried to adopt Paisley. But after all three of them died in accidents with Paisley barely surviving the last time, new adoption requests had somehow fallen through. Nobody could blame a toddler for a car accident, of course. But people had become... more cautious. When it came to Genevieve, none of the sisters had an idea why she hadn't been adopted, but selfishly, they'd all been glad she'd stayed.

Jessie had learned at a young age not to hope for much. She'd been a sickly infant who'd required several surgeries. Then she'd lost her welcoming smile after a prospective couple chose a more obedient child. Not to mention, she had a history of fights in school, and nobody cared to look into it to discover all those fights had been to defend her friends or newbies against bullies.

Jessie used to be sure she could trust her foster sisters with her life and equally sure they could trust her with theirs. But could they trust her with theirs now? What was she going to do if one of her friends was involved in Wyatt's death as a means to avenge the tragic past?

The right answer would be to go to the police.

Yes, the same police that had caused her to resign.

Unable to stop thinking now at the O'Neills', Jessie tightened her fingers around the fork, and she'd bend it if she wasn't careful. Despite the Finchs' lack of teaching the girls life skills, she was an adult and knew what was right and wrong, and it had guided her life and her conscience. If she'd done something to Wyatt that crazy evening, she'd have turned herself in. But it would be far easier and less painful to cut her limb off than turn in one of her foster sisters.

Madeline had teased sometimes that Jessie saw the world in black and white, while Paisley looked at it through rosy glasses. Madeline had been built differently or had become different once her world had been crushed. Jessie guessed a lot of Madeline's world was colored in red, the color of blood, and Jessie's heart had gone out to her friend.

But if Madeline had done something wrong, Jessie wouldn't cover for her. Well, she hoped she wouldn't.

Catching a concerned glance from Ronan, she straightened her spine and nibbled on her bread. The scents were enticing and the company great, but she'd lost her appetite.

Thankfully, the food prep with Ronan's mother and Madeline seemed to have gone well. Jessie hadn't burned or even dropped anything, and right now, everyone praised the food instead of grimacing. Ronan's mother was straightforward, but sweet, and Jessie couldn't help wondering how much easier her life could've been if she had parents like his, how much less bitterness or brokenness she'd carry then.

He smiled at her, sending awareness shooting through her, but this lovely family dinner only reminded her how much she didn't fit into his world.

Madeline was a whiz in the kitchen as much as Paisley was a computer whiz. After many years of relying on each other, Madeline, seeming to anticipate Jessie's next thoughts, had taken the most difficult parts of cooking on herself despite her wrist being in a cast.

As Jessie looked around the table, her gaze lingered on Madeline the longest. If only she could read Madeline as easily as she could read Mrs. O'Neill! Reading people used to be part of Jessie's job. But she doubted anyone could read Madeline. Jessie winced, curling over a painful jab at her chest. How could she be sitting here, suspecting Madeline? Shouldn't she know better?

"Are you okay?" Ronan touched her hand, and a warm wave sluiced through her arm to her heart.

Solid and honest, *he* wasn't difficult to read, and she craved that certainty more than ever. He made it easier to breathe while suspicions threatened to choke the breath out of her.

She'd rebuilt her life from ruins once, brick by brick. But now those very bricks seemed about to be shattered by not one but several wrecking balls coming from all angles. Her breath lodged in her throat as if she were pitched under ruins already.

She nodded her response because her mouth felt cottony.

Her body shifted toward him, needing that solidity and honesty before she lost the ground under her feet. She could deal with danger to herself, and had done plenty of times as part of her job. But the thought of losing her foster sisters sent her hyperventilating.

The same would happen when she had to leave Ronan. She chased the bitter taste in her mouth with sweet tea.

"Would you like more tea?" He reached for the pitcher.

She nodded again like a puppet whose string was pulled, and he refilled her glass. Being quiet and having tension emanating from her wasn't the best way to impress his parents. She probably even scowled, unlike Madeline, who beamed her megawatt movie-poster-worthy smile. Ronan's parents wouldn't know Jessie's scowl resulted from inner turmoil and most likely would think she didn't like them, their house, or the meal.

Which wasn't true at all. But that was the same thing prospective foster parents had thought before passing her over.

She loved the spacious ranch house with its antique furnishings, motley handwoven rugs, barnwood-framed landscapes where cotton-ball sheep roamed rolling green fields, plaques with inspirational quotes, and a shamrock-green sofa and armchairs with matching four-leaf-clover throw pillows. Though she was unable to eat much, dinner was so awesome that even she hadn't ruined it.

As for Ronan's parents... Dealing with a lot of crimes and disturbances, including domestic violence, she'd gotten used to seeing the ugly side of marriage. She'd been involved in cases where a husband had killed his wife or vice versa. Her foster parents had bickered enough for her to see they'd stayed together more for financial reasons than romantic ones. In the end, she'd stopped believing in a good marriage where two people loved each other because, from what she'd seen, it only happened in the movies.

If even gorgeous Madeline's relationship, which in the beginning had seemed as perfect as she was, had ended with brutal soul wounds and nearly cost Madeline her life, what hope could there be for tomboys like Jessie? Her fiancé's betrayal proved it, and Jessie had been hurt, but not surprised. She'd even kind of expected it.

But when she stole glances at Ronan's parents who still smiled at each other, held hands, and were attentive to one another, even after many years together, a longing stirred her. She looked down so nobody would notice it and helped herself to more bites of the russet potato on her plate.

Thankfully, Madeline kept the conversation going. She rarely made the effort but could be charming if she wanted to, and based on a few tender glances she sent Brandon's way, she very much wanted to appeal at this dinner.

Jessie munched on a gravy-slathered biscuit, hoping the intense longing would disappear, but it only increased, if that were possible. Yes, with her entire being, she wanted what Ronan's parents had, and she already knew the person she wanted it with. He was sitting beside her, her rock in the storm she was going through now.

Was this marriage an exception to the rule? Or was it possible?

Her gaze met Madeline's who was sitting right opposite Jessie, and for a moment, her friend wasn't difficult to read at all.

The same longing mirrored in those gorgeous blue eyes. Their friendship notwithstanding, they'd all become fiercely independent. But now, at this dining table, even Madeline wasn't immune to the happiness thriving in this house. They all wanted different things, but in the end, they wanted to be happy. The girls just doubted it was possible for them, based on experience.

Maybe Madeline had built a sparkling illusion of it with a successful career and designer outfits. And Jessie used to take satisfaction in her job, in serving a purpose, in being part of something bigger than herself.

But so far, personal happiness eluded them. Jessie hadn't realized how much she was missing until she met Ronan and his family.

"We're so glad you two could join us today. Please feel free to come share a meal with us anytime." Ronan's mother's lips widened, making her look younger. Despite her web of wrinkles and gray-streaked hair tucked in a messy bun, she looked more vibrant than a lot of people Jessie knew.

More genuine, too. Though maybe spending so much time with suspects had made Jessie's mind, well, suspicious.

Mrs. O'Neill wore a pretty sweater and jeans, and her husband sported a faded Wrangler's shirt and jeans, an outfit similar to Ronan's. Madeline was overdressed in her spiffy designer outfit with its cream-colored jacket and a long skirt she'd miraculously avoided staining while cooking. But then she was overdressed in many places she'd gone to and seemed to like it. Madeline was like royalty, always poised, always elegant. At this point, Jessie was grateful Madeline didn't show up in an evening gown, though that might've only been due to the cold outside.

"Me, too." Ronan touched her fingers again. "Glad that you're here."

As fleeting as the touch was, Jessie felt it deeply and craved more of it. More... of *this*. Whatever this incredible feeling growing inside her was.

"Thank you. I enjoyed it, too." More than they'd ever know. It was about time she found her voice.

Was it a good idea to come here, though? It was difficult to resist Ronan as it was.

Could Madeline's heart, that by now seemed to be made of the same stainless steel her scalpel was, change after all? Could Jessie's ice-encased heart do the same?

Chapter Thirteen

The next afternoon, Ronan called his father on the hands-free phone halfway from Springfield. He always couldn't wait to get out of this city, but he had more reasons than one to hurry back now. "I picked up those tractor parts. I'll be at the ranch in about half an hour."

"Thanks. See you then." His dad, a man of few words, disconnected.

On the contrary, Ronan's mother had given him an earful this morning. Despite Jessie's gloomy mood, Mom liked Jessie even more than Madeline, much to Brandon's dismay. Some raw authenticity and realness about Jessie made her appeal to people without her even realizing it. And their family respected authenticity. Ronan, eager to please his mother, had even considered asking Jessie to pretend to date him. But fake dating would be unfair to her.

Maybe bringing her to meet his parents wasn't a great idea. Mom already had prayer chains going for Jessie to regain her faith and for this "non-dating" to end in marriage.

Ronan smiled. As much as he enjoyed time with his parents, the sooner he delivered the tractor parts, the sooner he'd be able to go to the lodge. His pulse sped up together with his vehicle in anticipation of seeing her soon. It was getting dark, but in his mind, the lodge's welcoming lights were becoming a beacon to him.

Yes, he was getting in way too deep.

He squared his shoulders as he passed a navy-blue van. Well, despite what Brandon had said, this time Ronan would see Jessie on official business. His former boss, Garcia, had retired to the Dominican Republic, but he was back in Springfield to spend part of the winter with his grandchildren. Thankfully, Ronan had remained in touch with Garcia and the latter had asked Ronan to stop by anytime while he was just an hour away. Ronan was going to relay their conversation to Jessie.

So he pressed on the accelerator and passed another slowpoke, then moved into his lane. His gaze scoped out the fields covered in a white blanket. Who was he kidding? While he'd wanted to help Jessie with the cold case—not just cold, frozen like the fields right now—he was far more eager to see her. Her mere presence did something to his nerve endings, made them come alive like these fields and hills would come alive in spring.

He didn't want to think that one day soon she might leave the lodge. It wouldn't be easy with a blemish on her record, but she'd find a way to return to the force somewhere. Just like him, she was a cop at heart. Every time she'd talked about her time on the force, her face lit up. Or she might become a security officer, though she'd probably like it way less. She was a born protector with an affinity for justice and truth.

Was he a sucker for punishment then? He might pay with a lot of heartache later, but for now, he couldn't resist the pull, couldn't abandon her while she needed him. No matter how much his heart ached already at the mere thought of losing her.

Once he parked near the garage, he rushed inside despite carrying the heavy tractor parts.

He found his father working on one of the tractors. Unlike the two larger-scale ranches down the road, theirs was a small operation, and they cut costs wherever they could. Mom had slowed down from the days she'd taken care of the herd. But she still cooked for their ranch hands, helped with tagging cows, bottle-fed the calves rejected by their moms, and did a myriad of other things Dad insisted she stop doing.

Mom was stubborn. Just like Jessie. Warmth spread through Ronan at the thought.

Then guilt wormed in over him choosing to be a cop rather than continuing the family tradition of cowboys and ranchers. Sure, he'd helped whenever he could. But if he'd worked on the ranch full time, maybe his parents could retire to somewhere warm year-round, like his boss had.

He placed the parts in their designated space, then walked to Dad, breathing in the familiar smell of metal and faint gasoline. Something shifted in Ronan at the sight of his father's more stooped frame now. "Dad, I can take it to the mechanic. Or to our neighbor."

One of the guys who co-owned the nearby ranch did repairs and never refused to help a neighbor. While Ronan had learned lots of needed ranch skills from his father, he'd never gotten the repairing bug.

"I've got it." His father wiped his hands on a rag. "I need to talk to you about Jessie."

Ronan stiffened. Jessie was nothing like the cowgirls his mother had tried to play matchmaker for—with Dad's silent approval. But none of them had Ronan's heart beating fast like Jessie did.

He shoved his hands into his jacket pockets. "Yes, sir."

"Have you seen her today?"

"I'll be going that way after I talk to Mom."

His father nodded. "Good."

Good? Ronan blinked.

His father examined the parts Ronan brought and nodded once again, this time to himself. "Yesterday, Jessie looked as if she needed a hug. She needed to be held."

That stung. Ronan *should* have done more. "I tried to talk to her, but she wouldn't tell me what upset her. And I feared she might bite my head off if I hugged her. She's strong and independent." Qualities Ronan admired, but ones that also made it more difficult to approach her.

His father picked up another tool and returned to the tractor he'd been working on. "Even strong and independent women need to be held. Even more than others, because they get hugged so rarely."

"Is this the secret to your marriage?" Ronan was willing to learn as he followed his father. If he wanted his relationship with Jessie to last... Whoa, he was getting ahead of himself again.

"There's no secret. Love God above all. Love your wife. Oh, and do your best to say yes to anything she asks for and hold her even when she doesn't ask for it. Now, scoot and go to your girl. I'm praying for her, and for you."

Ronan gave his father a man hug. Dad hadn't graduated from university, but Ronan had never stopped learning from him, never stopped admiring him. On the contrary, Jessie had grown up without parents, and Ronan's rib cage constricted. He couldn't imagine his life without the supportive presence of his parents.

He said a quiet prayer for his father's health, then for Jessie's healing—emotional and spiritual.

"She's not my girl." The words pinged something inside him.

"That's a shame," his father seemed to mutter, but Ronan couldn't be sure because he closed the garage door.

Blood rushed faster in his veins. He'd be seeing Jessie soon. He brought a few staples his mother had wanted from the big city into the house and left the kitchen carrying her Irish barmbrack.

Minutes later, he was on the lodge's porch. The door opened before he had a chance to ring the bell. Clearly, they'd watched the road and the surroundings. He brushed off the unnerving feeling the same way he brushed snowflakes from his shoulders.

"Come on in." Genevieve waved him inside. "Paisley will let Jessie know you're here."

He obliged, though disappointed Jessie hadn't met him. He took off his cowboy boots and coat fast to keep from letting snow melt on the hardwood floor.

"I brought a barmbrack." He handed her the covered dish. "It's a fruitcake."

"Thank you." Genevieve was wearing a canary-yellow cardigan thrown over sweatpants, and everything about her, from the hue of her clothes to her posture to her eyes emanated warmth and kindness.

But Ronan looked closely enough to sense brokenness in her, too.

Of Jessie's small group, he'd seen Genevieve the least, and he had an uneasy feeling that was on purpose. Was she just hiding from him, or from everyone?

She led him to the living room where a fireplace, larger than in his parents' house, greeted him. A few classics with gilded letters filled the built-in shelves, and he suspected those belonged to Genevieve, who had a Master's in English, according to Jessie. His gaze stopped on one of the titles. He had such difficulty keeping up with this small group's dynamics that he felt like going down the rabbit hole himself. He was fascinated, but weirded out, as well.

Hmm. The room was occupied already.

Madeline was sitting, staring at the fire, motionless like a beautiful statue. Her German shepherd, Rusty, stretched out beside her on the navy sofa, occupying nearly all of it, his front paws and jaw on her lap. Her left hand was rubbing the dog behind his ear, but she seemed to be doing it absentmindedly. Her right hand rested on the sofa's arm, still in a cast.

Rusty lifted his head when Ronan stepped into the room but didn't bark or growl, and Ronan took satisfaction in that. Rusty seemed to acknowledge Ronan as one of their pack.

Then premonition squeezed his heart. Something wasn't right, especially when Rusty gave out a pitiful whine, so uncharacteristic of the dog.

When one of the fire tongues lit Madeline's face, Ronan winced. While not a muscle moved on that marble-like pose, her eyes harbored the most profound sadness he'd ever seen. He'd better call Brandon because she also looked like someone who could use a hug and a friendly ear, even if she might refuse it at first.

Ronan stepped forward but stopped himself. He didn't want to send the wrong message by hugging her.

Concern flashed in Genevieve's eyes. "Let's go, Madeline."

The statue didn't move, didn't even blink. Well, she was here first.

He started, "It's okay. I—"

Genevieve stopped him with a shake of her head, then touched Madeline's shoulder. "Help me make some tea. Ronan brought some of his mom's fruitcake."

Madeline flinched, then looked up at him. "Oh. Hello, Ronan. That was sweet of you. Literally."

Had he ever heard a voice so void? What had happened to her? And how could he help?

Genevieve must've read his thoughts because she shook her head almost imperceptibly and led Madeline away like someone would lead a small child. Rusty jumped from the sofa and padded after them, nudging her uninjured hand with his nose as if trying to comfort her.

Jessie appeared a moment later, and the same concern etched her features. Then her face lit up as she looked at him, and he had to make a physical effort not to take her into his arms and kiss her senseless.

She gestured him to the plush sofa decorated with throw pillows the colors of Paisley's hair, respectively. In the dimly lit room, Jessie looked even lovelier than usual, and he told her as much.

Chuckling, she sat down. "So what you're saying is that in bright lights you can see all my blemishes."

Heat rose at his faux pas. He joined her, breathing the slight scent of her citrusy perfume. "I didn't mean that."

Still chuckling, she waved a hand. "I'm just giving you a hard time."

He itched to touch her, to run his fingers along the outline of her face, to press his lips to her birthmark and move to her mouth. His pulse spiked. He cleared his throat, exhibiting remarkable self-control. "You looked worried yesterday. Can I help you with something?"

She averted her gaze, suddenly fascinated by the books on the shelf. "It's not my secret."

How many times would he hear that phrase from her? His teeth set on edge. But how could he begrudge her loyalty to her friends?

The issue was—just how dangerous were those secrets? His job taught him that when people had to hide something, it was rarely something good. And sometimes it could even be deadly.

But he let it go. For now. Instead, he reached for her hands and cradled them in his, something akin to an electrical current going through him at the simple touch.

Jessie didn't make it easy for him. But there must be a reason God had led Ronan to her. And why God had led Brandon to Madeline.

"Is Madeline okay?" A stupid question since she clearly wasn't.

"No." The misery in Jessie's eyes tugged at him.

So much that he drew her close and wrapped his arms around her slim frame. He thought he could feel her heart beating against his in the same rapid rhythm. She stilled, and he feared she'd struggle out of his embrace. Instead, she settled against him as if she always belonged there. Attraction and tenderness coalesced into a living thing inside him, and he didn't want to let her go.

Not now.

Probably not ever.

However, she had other ideas because she eased out of his embrace.

"Mom loved you. Dad, too. She's giving me a hard time when I say technically we're not dating." He swallowed hard. Maybe he shouldn't have said that.

"You have awesome parents. How about making it easier for them? Tell them *we are* dating."

He stared at her. "Are you serious?" Could he believe that...

"Well, people fake date sometimes. And when I leave, you can tell them we broke up."

His heart dropped. *When*, not *if.*

What if he didn't want to *fake* date? What if he wanted the real deal? Besides, he disliked anything fake, and he thought she did, too. But maybe, just maybe, he could let her adjust to the idea slowly. In her own time. Mom had a point. He couldn't give up, and he had to take what Jessie would give him.

"Okay." He nodded.

"Okay." She settled into his embrace again.

Now, the road from fake dating to real dating could be a long one, and he didn't even know how to start.

He'd ponder that thought later. Right now, he just enjoyed having her in his arms. He placed a kiss atop her head, breathing her citrusy perfume again. But then she looked up, and so much longing clouded her stormy eyes that all rational thought fled him. He might die if he didn't kiss her the next moment.

His breathing became shallow. *Her* breathing went faster as if in rhythm with him. Excitement spread through him as he claimed her lips with his, and every cell in his body came alive. An incredibly pleasant wave washed over him, sweeping him away in euphoria.

Then the clanking of utensils registered, and Jessie pulled back. She had the same dazzlement in her eyes that was intoxicating him.

"Sorry to, um, interrupt." Genevieve placed a tray with a teapot, creamer, cups, and slices of barmbrack on the coffee table.

"We were just talking." Jessie blushed endearingly like a schoolgirl.

Genevieve's lips curved up. "I'll leave. So you can continue to, you know, *talk.*"

Jessie shifted away from him on the sofa, and disappointment ripped through him. Then she poured tea into delicate cups with purple flowers as if it were the most important thing in the world.

Did she regret their kiss already? That was thin ice he didn't want to step on, so he didn't ask.

Maybe he'd let his attraction carry him away and pushed her too far. His entire being ached to feel her heart beat against him again, to taste her lips, to hold her close. But he should have more willpower than that. Besides, he'd come here with information she might find valuable.

"Creamer?" she asked, a little breathless.

Yes! Breathless. Good. He could take some satisfaction in the latter. "I've never had hot tea with cream, but now is as good a time as any to try."

Jessie's kissable mouth twitched at the edges. "English literature isn't the only English thing Genevieve is fond of. She introduced us all to the tradition of drinking hot tea, and it stuck."

Well, if she was going to avoid the elephant in the room, he'd better, too. He swallowed a bitter thought that the kiss might've meant much more to him than to her. Then he took a careful sip of mint-flavored tea and helped himself to some barmbrack while he told her about meeting with Garcia. "He's going to try his contacts and see if he can discover more about the plane crash."

Wisps of her short hair feathered over her cheeks as she nodded, making him itch to brush them away. "I appreciate that. Meanwhile, I was digging into Candy's story. Candy is that stunning blonde, Wyatt's daughter-in-law, his youngest son's estranged wife. If Wyatt disinherited Hayden or even kicked him out of the company, Candy would lose a lot, too. And she seems to be used to a flashy lifestyle. Arianna, our mole, made friends with one of Candy's close friends. Candy confided to her on several occasions that Wyatt lived way too long. She also thought Wyatt treated her husband and son unfairly. That they rebelled because he always preferred his oldest son. According to the household help, Wyatt wasn't too fond of his daughter-in-law, either."

That seemed like a plausible idea, except for an important detail. "But since she's currently separated from her husband, she didn't live in the house with him, so she'd have to pay someone to switch pills."

Speaking of switching, how could Jessie switch from passionate to businesslike so fast and so effortlessly?

"She is well liked by the household staff, just like Wyatt's former wife. Wyatt pays well, but he treats his help like robots while Candy was attentive to them. She gave them gifts for their birthdays and their children."

Despite the whirlwind of emotions Jessie created in him, Ronan did his best to concentrate on the case. "She has a motive. And by removing her husband before they divorced, she inherits a lot and helps her son avoid a disaster. Plus, she might feel he owed her for her giving up on a great career. Is she athletic? Could she climb the mountain her late husband did?"

She waved a hand. "It's all circumstantial again, but yes, Candy is athletic. She stayed in shape by running and rock climbing."

"What about the private plane crash? How could she be connected to that?"

Setting her tea aside, Jessie moved toward him again along the sofa. "That's what I hope your boss can help us with."

Us.

Did "us" exist when it came to romantic feelings, or only when it came to the investigation? His heart shifted. He clasped her hand on her lap. "I hope so, too."

"You need to know something about Madeline. It's public knowledge, anyway, so I don't think she'll be mad at me for telling you." Her fingers trembled in his hands.

He stroked her fingers, then laced his through hers to stop the trembling. "What's that?"

"Her parents were murdered when she was little. That was how she ended up in foster care. But that's not all."

His heart constricted. Based on the pain in Jessie's eyes, he wasn't sure he wanted to know the rest.

She looked away. "Madeline was the one who found them."

Before the entire horror of the situation registered, Rusty started barking in Madeline's room. Then a loud banging on the door made Ronan jump and bolt into the hall, his protective instincts on high alert.

"Open up!" Brandon yelled from outside.

Jessie's jaw dropped. Ronan's almost did, too. He'd never heard his calm, reserved brother yelling.

"Your brother knows we have the doorbell, doesn't he?" She followed him into the hall.

Rusty growled in Madeline's room, then barked again. Madeline issued a command, and Rusty stopped barking. But Ronan could still hear a low growl.

Paisley stepped into the hall without her usual smile. "I let Brandon through the gates. Maybe I shouldn't have."

Jessie's eyes narrowed. "That's fine. Don't worry." She opened the front door, and a gust of cold air stormed inside with Brandon.

Ronan stepped forward, ready to diffuse the situation. "Bro, what happened?"

Brandon's eyes were frantic. "Madeline broke up with me on the phone. And I need to know why."

Chapter Fourteen

Jessie was still reeling. One look at the desolation on Brandon's face yesterday wounded her heart, but Madeline remained as cold as an ice statue. She'd refused to talk to Brandon or leave her room. Ronan had nearly pushed his brother out of their lodge and driven him home while Brandon probably kept demanding answers.

Would Ronan think Jessie would break up with him in the same way? Would he withdraw from her now? She winced. Of all the selfish thoughts…

But after they'd shared a kiss yesterday—sadly interrupted— something changed inside her. She'd changed. Their relationship had changed. And she had no clue what to do about that.

Madeline stayed in her room most of the day with the German shepherd. But she appeared by dinnertime, her eyes not swollen, but empty, her makeup immaculate. Rusty trudged nearby, looking lost and bewildered while usually he was the model of strength and confidence. Jessie had no clue what Madeline had done in that time, except for sulking. When Jessie or one of the other girls knocked on the door, Madeline yelled at them to go away. She'd only stepped outside her room to walk Rusty, feed him, and give him water. The girls nearly had to force Madeline to eat something.

During their time at the lodge, Paisley had worked on designing software and troubleshooting for her customers. Genevieve had read and continued working on her PhD thesis. Jessie had been going through files and reports about Wyatt's family. But Madeline couldn't do her work long-distance. So what was she doing in her room for weeks?

Of course, now bigger questions demanded Jessie's attention. So when Madeline joined them for dinner in the evening and Rusty stretched on the floor in the hall, always on guard, Jessie blurted out, "Why did you break up with Brandon?"

"I didn't 'break up' because we weren't dating. I can manage on my own now. I don't need his help." Madeline's mouth thinned. "And… he started liking me."

"And that would be bad, how?" Jessie poured hot tea from the teapot for herself, then topped up Paisley's cup. Then she poured tea for Madeline and pushed the creamer toward her.

"You know my story. He's better off without me." Madeline stared ahead of her, her food and her drink untouched.

"That's not true," Genevieve spoke quietly.

Jessie's stomach clenched, and she hugged her friend. Then everyone else did the same. A dreadful thought entered her mind. Would it be more humane to Ronan and herself to end their relationship now, like Madeline had, whatever that relationship was?

Jessie shuddered, her gut wrenching even at imagining it. She was in too deep already. She'd even suggested fake dating him, as ridiculous as that idea was, just to spend more time with him. And, well, she'd liked the feeling of being part of his family, even for a short time.

Madeline finally reached for a biscuit, and some color returned to her pale face. "I wanted to make things clear before they got... they got too complicated." The heaviness of long-lashed eyes contradicted her indifferent tone.

So Brandon had gotten under Madeline's skin. Jessie hadn't met Ronan's entire family, but from what she'd seen so far, one would have to be made out of stone not to like them.

Yet she had to resist. The wise thing would be for her to sever ties with Ronan. Her heart squeezed. She told herself she needed his help in the investigation, fully knowing it was an excuse not to let him go. And if he already told his parents he was dating her, how could she hurt those nice people's feelings?

Later, after she took care of the dishes since she hadn't been the one to cook, she retreated to her room. Her phone rang, and she fished it out of her pocket. While her heart jumped at his name on the screen, she swiped the screen to answer. "Hello, Ronan."

"Are you up for a late dinner tonight?"

"Sure." Her heart jumped again, and she scolded herself. There was no reason for such a strong reaction.

And probably best not to tell him she already had dinner or she was *always* up for dinner with him. She didn't care whether it was cardboard from a pizza box as long as she shared it with him.

So far, nothing sinister had happened, so it should be okay to go to a restaurant again. Especially if she carried her weapon. Besides, if he'd told his family they were dating now, they needed to show up together in public.

"Great. I got some information from Garcia, though not much. I'll pick you up in about forty minutes, okay?"

"Sure." She swallowed past a hard lump. *That* was the reason he'd wanted to see her?

Would he ever ask her on a proper date? Not a fake one?

She didn't have time to untangle her emotions. She'd dwell on them later, or on how much she craved his presence, his lopsided smile, his scent of pine needles, his strong arms around her, and the slightly rough feel of his five-o'clock shadow when he'd *finally* kissed her. Yes, she craved his presence more than she craved food and soon more than she'd be craving air.

Huh. She needed to prepare for her fake date.

A knock on her room door prompted her to rush there. Madeline walked in, the same stony expression on her face, but a stylish white coat in her hands. Jessie suspected the coat cost more than her own monthly salary—what *used to be* her monthly salary. Rusty, like Madeline's shadow, followed her inside and sat near the chair.

"Getting ready for your *fake* date with Ronan?"

Was Madeline eavesdropping? Jessie bristled.

Madeline must've read her thoughts because she continued. "I heard you on the phone. It's not difficult to guess. I wondered if you'd like to wear my coat. I also have a collection of scarves. You're welcome to choose from them and to wear my earrings."

It wasn't uncommon for them to lend each other things while growing up. But they hadn't done it recently, living in different places in Houston.

"Why?"

Madeline gave her a weak smile. "Ronan is as much of a catch as Brandon, maybe even more so. And you deserve to be happy. Ronan already likes you for who you are, but beautiful clothes give me a boost of confidence."

Who knew Madeline could need a confidence boost?

Madeline had an hourglass figure, and Jessie, well, didn't. But as Madeline adjusted the belt, the coat fit, though it was much longer on Jessie than on Madeline, who wasn't just slimmer, but taller. And Jessie easily found a scarf and earrings she liked from Madeline's vast—and expensive—collection.

"If you like Brandon—and he obviously cares about you or he wouldn't be this upset over losing you—maybe you should give him a chance," Jessie suggested.

Madeline stiffened, then blinked fast as if to keep tears at bay. "Too late for that. He must hate me now and with good reason."

Jessie hadn't cried on the job, but after seeing horrible things happen to innocent people, she'd cried sometimes when she'd gotten home. She'd held Genevieve, Paisley, and even Arianna when they'd cried. But she'd never seen Madeline cry, and that wasn't normal.

Yet there was so much hurt in Madeline's blue eyes that she'd never allowed to spill. Ouch. She didn't break up with Brandon because she didn't care about him, but because she started caring too much.

Those weren't the eyes of a killer. Or was Jessie naïve to believe that?

Decades ago...

The apartment Genevieve rented was small and furnished with pieces found at garage sales and on roadsides, but Jessie had a warm feeling every time she entered it.

It was home now.

She was years away from going to the police academy and one year away from graduating high school. Unlike Genevieve, Arianna, and Madeline, she hadn't aged out of the foster care system yet and would still be living with their foster parents if not for Paisley.

No matter how much Jessie couldn't stand the idea of separating from her foster sisters, no way would she be able to complete the emancipation process on her own. Even for a brainiac like Paisley, it wasn't so easy, but Paisley was determined to do it for herself and Jessie.

By then, Paisley had been doing computer work for friends' parents, neighbors, and most likely people around the world. Their foster parents had demanded she give them all her earnings and work at their family café. Or they'd punish one of her foster sisters since they'd learned they could make Paisley comply much faster by threatening her friends.

Paisley and Jessie, and the others before they left, had been free domestic labor since Mrs. Finch couldn't be bothered to cook or clean. They were also falling off their feet after waitressing and cleaning dishes in the café Mr. Finch ran.

Jessie's blood had boiled at all the injustice. Genevieve, who worked as a maid for rich people now, said she'd take them in if they didn't mind living in a cramped apartment. Paisley's earnings from computer work she'd squirreled away paid for the deposit. The Finchs had found the rest of Paisley's stash and taken it away. Madeline, studying pre-med and living in the second bedroom of the tiny apartment, had encouraged them, as well as Arianna, who'd slept on the floor in Madeline's room.

But what had persuaded Jessie to go through the emancipation process was that, after Genevieve had left, Mr. Finch began lingering near Paisley's room, and Jessie could only live on a little sleep for so long.

Today, as she entered the scratched mustard-hued front door of Genevieve's apartment, the mouthwatering scent of liver and onions greeted her. Paisley or Genevieve must've gotten paid because they all usually ate something simpler—and way cheaper. Jessie suppressed a wince as she dropped her backpack and marched to the only bathroom in the apartment. That place had seen a queue of girls every morning. Good thing Jessie didn't use any makeup because the counter with one large crack and a web of small ones was filled to the brim with Madeline's eyeshadows, lipsticks, and lotions.

Somehow, Madeline managed to scrounge free samples often. She'd gotten a full scholarship to the university, like everyone had expected, so she contributed her earnings from modeling gigs to the household fund and her clothes fund. She hated modeling, but she loved her friends and hiding behind pretty clothes, though not to the same degree. Beautifully built, Madeline could probably make a fortune if she moved to LA or New York and loosened up her standards, but she'd stayed here and refused to be photographed other than fully clothed.

Most of the time Madeline spent with her nose in a textbook. She studied when she ate, jogged, or cooked, and a textbook was the last thing she saw before going to bed. Paper sheets where she wrote things she needed to memorize for the next exam wallpapered her room, desk, floor, and bed. Madeline even studied when she baked, and Jessie was shocked they didn't end up with salty pies or with cakes decorated with utensils—or at least notes of disgusting medical information.

Yet people who met Madeline for the first time still assumed she was going to coast through life on her looks.

This time, Madeline was sitting over a book at the breakfast nook, her legs crisscrossed on a wooden bench Genevieve and Paisley had rescued from the roadside, sanded, polished, and painted in Paisley's favorite azure blue. Scraped wooden furniture was considered a good find. But the girls had learned fast that anything cushioned like sofas and armchairs was best left on the roadside because they might already contain tiny inhabitants they didn't want to be neighbors with.

Madeline was mixing a Greek salad where she sat. Jessie was grateful Madeline wasn't cutting vegetables, or they might have a fingertip for dinner. Then Madeline stirred her tea. Jessie watched her for a minute before placing Madeline's fingers around the glass.

"Thanks." Madeline took a sip, her gaze never wavering from the page.

Genevieve greeted Jessie with a smile and a spatula, and Jessie returned the smile. She wasn't offended by Madeline ignoring her. This lack of attention wasn't because Madeline was arrogant—she wasn't—but because her studies consumed her. When she wasn't reading, she was memorizing, which often gave her the distant look photographers loved.

Even among the food scents, Jessie distinguished a faint scent of a new perfume. While she didn't care for makeup or fancy clothes, perfumes with citrusy scents fascinated her. Maybe because they brought distant memories of her childhood, of her grandmother baking something with a lemon zest. Then the memory of the foster mother who considered adopting her. When Jessie hugged the woman's legs, she'd smelled a slight perfume.

Since then, light citrusy perfumes smelled like hope.

Growing up with the Finchs, Jessie couldn't afford perfumes. It was still a luxury item, so she wouldn't even think to buy it for herself. But the girls had asked for empty perfume bottles from their friends' parents once they'd learned what Jessie considered her weakness. Later, they'd pooled their money to buy her tiny bottles with gentle citrusy aromas. Madeline had passed samples to her, or when her suitors gifted her perfumes, she'd always given them to Jessie while using cheap deodorants she shared with others. Lavender-scented ones were her current favorite.

This time, Madeline reached into the pocket of her cream-colored pants without looking up and handed Jessie a delicate bottle with golden lettering.

"I signed up for commercials for this perfume," she told her book.

Jessie opened the glass top of a bottle that seemed to emanate a soft glow and breathed in. This citrusy scent was even lighter than the others and created the images of a breeze moving the curtain at a beachfront house and a tall glass with refreshing lemonade on the table.

"Thank you." She capped the lid on both the elegant bottle and her unclear desires. She was a practical girl. Allowing the girls to indulge her with expensive scents was her only luxury, and she treasured every tiny drop.

She turned to Genevieve. "Do you need any help?"

Genevieve stirred pieces of liver smothered beneath rings of caramelized onions, then pointed at the Greek salad on the table. "No, I'm good."

Jessie grinned. "I hoped you were going to say that."

The grin wavered because, again, she couldn't bring as much to the table, in many senses, as the other girls had. As a waitress, Jessie wasn't earning much, and she wasn't a good cook. She compensated for it by pitching in more with the cleaning, but still.

Paisley waltzed into the kitchen carrying a scrappy chair. She'd spiked her azure-blue hair with gel, leaving it sticking out around the daisy tucked behind her ear while a headband with two balls on long wire bobbed over said hair. With her black-and-yellow striped T-shirt and knee-length skirt, where cerulean blue and vivid crimson flowed into each other, she looked like a weird combo of a bumblebee and a butterfly with a personal flower.

"Look what I found!" She hefted the thing missing one of its legs, thankfully far enough from the stove.

Jessie sure hoped Paisley had wiped that chair down.

Even Genevieve looked skeptical as her eyebrows moved closer to each other. "We already have enough furniture."

"But nothing like this." Paisley put down the chair reverently as if it were a throne. "It has lots of potential." That was the thing about Paisley. Despite the difficulties in her life, she still saw the best in people and things.

Jessie did her best to learn from that.

Genevieve's mouth twitched up. "Fine. I'll help you repair it. But now, everyone, wash your hands and help me set the table."

Paisley grinned and sauntered away with the chair that seemed to squeak in gratitude for being adopted after losing all hope.

Jessie's heart swelled. Though she wasn't as optimistic as Paisley and knew they'd have lots of challenges in life, right now, she could believe happiness was possible. They all were getting somewhere in life in their own way.

Even Arianna, who'd missed years of school but was now pursuing her GED when she wasn't waitressing. Genevieve was tutoring Arianna in English and history, Paisley in math, and Madeline in chemistry. Plus, Arianna was taking free classes at a community center in the evening, where she was studying now. Genevieve would make sure there were enough leftovers for her to eat later, when she came home. She always had.

Now, they had food on the table other than the bags of popcorn they'd had to live on at the beginning of moving to the apartment, and even those had to be rationed. They didn't have to sleep on the floor any longer. Not that they *could* sleep then because the neighbors liked to party all the time. Those same neighbors had rarely bothered to take out the trash, which meant hordes of roaches roamed the entire building, including their place. Thankfully, those guys had moved out, and a quiet and more sanitary family moved in. The roaches left.

And most importantly, Jessie was among people who cared about her, and in her pocket, she had a dreamy bottle of perfume.

Little did she know this evening would mark the end of their way of living, full of hopes for the future. That the next evening, Genevieve wouldn't come home. Or that several months down the road, all of them would make a decision they'd have to live with for the rest of their lives.

Present time...

Ronan had done what he could, but Brandon was still sulky. Not that Ronan blamed him. His gut twisted at the thought of Jessie walking away from him. That might happen sometime soon, anyway.

Brandon seemed to prefer to spend time with their father or their horses, not Ronan, maybe because Ronan reminded him of Jessie and that, in turn, reminded him of Madeline and his heartache.

So after mucking the stable in silence and making sure the horses had enough hay and water, Ronan marched outside. Fresh frosty air met him, and he breathed in a lungful and let his steamy breath fog out. He said a fervent prayer for Brandon, then the rest of his family, and then Jessie as he gazed at the crisp blue sky.

While he'd prayed for his family all the time, he'd rarely prayed for a woman other than his mother and Isla when she'd been alive. His heart shifted. It was… it was as if Jessie was a part of his family already.

Lord, what should I do?

He started walking to his parents' house, and the snow crunched under his cowboy boots. He wanted to ask her for dinner. But he didn't just want to date her, much less fake date. His heart started beating faster.

He wasn't one to play dating games. He wanted a serious relationship that would result in marriage. A real relationship, not a fake one. The issue was, with every fiber of his being, he felt Jessie wasn't ready for that. Wasn't even ready to tell him her secrets. Would she ever be?

He gave the ranch house where he'd grown up a loving look, longing to fill his own house with the same happiness and love. He'd gradually have to show her that he was the real deal, that happiness and faith were possible.

Lord, please give me patience.

She also needed closure. He didn't understand how she and her friends were connected to the mystery surrounding that wealthy Texan family, so susceptible to accidents or murders, but he intended to find out. He just hoped he wouldn't lose her in the process.

Garcia was flying back to his retirement villa soon and invited Ronan and a plus-one to come, too. Ronan had a lot of vacation time saved up. Normally, he'd use his vacation time to work on the ranch. This time, however, he wanted a vacation with Jessie.

Would she agree to join him? As much as he carried respect for her friends—well, for Madeline, he had mostly resentment because of his brother—being around them pressed into Jessie's subconscious all the reasons marriages didn't work. Taking her away to a new place would allow him to show her that a relationship *could* work and be wonderful instead of painful.

His pulse picked up speed. Was this the answer to his prayers? He even had something he could use to persuade her. They could go to the crash site and do research on location. Yes, it was years too late, but still better than mere speculations. Garcia had also promised to get them the report of the investigation the local police conducted.

Minutes later, with his father's approval and his mother's—and even Scratcher's—enthusiastic support, he drove the short distance to the lodge. It was dark by then, but the many windows lit up inside surrounded the place in a glow easily visible, even behind the tall fence.

As he pressed the code Jessie had given him for the gate, he wondered whether he was heading on the path God had chosen for him. Or was he a moth flying to the flame, only to get burned like his brother had?

This time, Jessie met him on the porch. "It's a beautiful night. How about we stay outside?"

"Sure." Though worried she might get cold, he selfishly wanted to be the one to keep her warm.

He swiped snow from the porch swing's cushions, and they settled on it. She looked cute in a white knit hat and a cream-colored coat with a large belt that cinched a slightly big-for-her coat. Her signature citrusy scent never failed to spike his pulse.

Since he'd always been a straightforward guy, he told her about the invitation to the villa in the Dominican Republic right away. "We'd have separate rooms, of course."

She smiled and leaned toward him, giving him hope, but then she stiffened. "I don't want to leave the girls. You know, just in case... And I need to continue the investigation."

He could understand her loyalty. He really could. And he didn't want to grit his teeth at all. Well, maybe a little.

"So far, everything you've done has been long distance. There's internet at the villa. You can continue doing it all there, but on the other hand, you can visit the plane crash site. Search for parts that were most likely missed. Interview the locals. Read the report. As for leaving your friends just in case..." He still didn't have a clear idea just in case of *what* exactly, only guesses, and all the half-said sentences irked him. People in his environment said things as they were. "Nothing's happened since you've been here."

"*You* happened," she said, ducking her head.

"You happened to me, too." His heart soared. "The most amazing thing in my life." That seemed unfair to his first love, and he winced as the thought sliced him. What he'd had with her was amazing, too, but he'd made a mess of things he'd never forgive himself for, would never be able to ask her for forgiveness. Grief combined with guilt was a double-edged sword.

Jessie lifted her head, her eyes bright. "Considering how great your family is, that's saying a lot."

"I do love my family. But... I want some time for it to be only God, you, and me."

Her lips curved up. "And your retired boss."

"Garcia takes lots of naps and fishes the rest of the time. With the villa so large, he said we likely won't see him much during the vacation, if at all." And Ronan was selfishly grateful for that.

He needed to make peace with his past mistakes and take the opportunity to persuade Jessie to open her heart to God and to a real relationship, not a pretend one. And she needed answers to her questions.

Chapter Fifteen

A week later, as Jessie walked hand in hand with Ronan along the majestic beach, she could hardly believe it. It was like a door opened into a magical new world, and she'd stepped inside.

They'd left behind the cold white fields of yet unwritten beginnings and stepped into the sunshine, warmth, and vibrant colors of turquoise and emerald-green possibilities. Even her clothes were different from her usual jeans and dull sweaters. Now her pink flip-flops with funky flowers, Paisley's gift, slapped against her heels. Loose linen pants flowed around her ankles beneath a Hawaiian shirt with hibiscuses all over it, also Paisley's gift but from ages ago. Jessie never had an occasion to wear it. She wasn't changing herself for Ronan. It just... seemed like a different and exciting era in her life.

She lifted her face to the sun, relieved not to look over her shoulder every second. She was still aware of her surroundings, and she knew he was, as well. But for the first time since the tragedy happened, she could breathe... more fully.

She'd been right, after all. The girls should've chosen a warmer place as their hideout—which was why she'd packed the Hawaiian shirt for the lodge. But then she wouldn't have met Ronan if they hadn't gone there. Things like that made her wonder if she could believe God cared.

Her heart squeezed, and her fingers followed, squeezing his fingers. He responded to her gesture with a smile that rivaled the Caribbean sunshine. When he looked at her like that, her heart trembled like a flower in the wind. She wanted to say how much he meant to her.

Instead, she said, "So weird that the temperature can be in the high seventies in February here. And it's all so... green and beautiful." That was deep. Not!

"Because of all the rain during the wet season, the place is still lush. This is a good time to visit the Dominican Republic, drier but without the extreme heat of summer. But then, any place and any time is good when I'm with you."

Her insides warmed, and not only because of the comfortable weather. "You're flattering me. And I like it."

She moved closer. Stepping from winter into summer melted something inside her, made her put down her guard, and she surprised herself by going with it. Whatever happened next, at least they'd have the Dominican Republic. Even if happiness slipped through her fingers like sand, as it always did.

"Is this the first time you've seen the ocean?" Dressed in cargo shorts and a T-shirt with a cowboy riding across it stretched over his chest, he looked as relaxed as she felt. It was the first time she saw him without cowboy boots, too, but she was right before. He looked great in the tropics.

"I've seen it, but that's not the same. I've driven from Houston to the coast, but this is different... feels more tropical. *And* this beach is so private." She must be acting like an amateur, gawking at the ocean and the fruity drinks Garcia had served them this morning on the terrace. She also had a huge goofy smile. But the smile wasn't just because of the novelty of the ocean. It was because of being with Ronan.

"I love that you look at everything with awe," he said.

She shielded her face from the sun with her free hand and stared at the ocean, hoping to see dolphins. "Our foster parents didn't take us for vacations. At first on my own, I never had the funds for a beach vacation, not even a day trip down to the coast. Then I lived and breathed my job, and while I went once or twice, I was too focused on work and seldom took time to drive there. I even dreamed about my job."

Now her dreams featured him, and she didn't mind in the least.

"You deserve an ocean of joy." He paused as if he said too much. "Frankly, it's my first time outside the state. Two of my brothers traveled the world. But I was always content in my hometown. And, well, while I don't work at the ranch full-time, I help out." His voice roughened. "My parents are getting on in age. Though when I tell them to slow down, they don't listen."

She squeezed his fingers again, this time to show support. "You're doing everything you can. And from what I've seen, you're doing a fantastic job. You're a great son and brother."

And one day he'd make a great husband and father. Her rib cage constricted because she wouldn't be the woman he'd marry.

Besides them living in different worlds, he clearly wouldn't leave his parents' ranch, and she didn't want to be far from her foster sisters. It was bad enough she'd left them for several days. Added to that, the way he'd talked about his late fiancée showed his grief. Their moral obligations anchored them to others, not to each other.

Her chest tightened painfully.

As Genevieve always said, they could only deal with one thing at a time. But right now, Jessie didn't want to deal with anything. She wanted to cherish the precious gift of this time alone with him in this gorgeous place.

"I'm glad we came here at a good time. Garcia says that back in November, the soil was so saturated the roads were barely drivable. And in many places, probably not drivable at all."

She stopped. "Hold on. The plane crash was in November." She pulled the phone out of her pants pocket and checked online. Yes, that month and year had heavy rains. "What if rain and landslides affected the roads then, too? The authorities wouldn't be able to access the site fast, right?"

"Okay. Do you think something was staged by the time they arrived?"

"I don't know." She rubbed her temples under Paisley's wide-brimmed straw hat that, of course, boasted an annoying *gigantic* pink flower. Jessie should've taken her gray baseball cap. "Or maybe some things were removed. Too much information is missing from the file Garcia gave you. It doesn't sit right."

"Nothing about it sits right," he said.

She couldn't agree more. And as much as she loved this idyllic environment, they were here on a mission, not a vacation. Early tomorrow morning, they'd start their search. They already had the guide lined up.

Her heart shifted. Would she find the answers? The chances were slim to none. And she wasn't even sure she wanted to.

The next morning, Ronan slowed, breathing in air heavy and humid. Thick vegetation alive with bird calls crushed in around them as it took a guide, special boots, and a lot of patience on his and Jessie's parts to access the remote location, first by a souped-up Jeep, then by foot. They still had to keep hiking. At least, he'd insisted on carrying the larger backpack despite her protests. Even with her carrying the smaller pack, sweat glistened on her pale forehead and bare arms. He'd never imagined khaki pants and clunky low-heeled boots could look so lovely.

He shook his head and swatted at a giant mosquito stalking him despite the repellant they'd doused themselves in. He was on a mission, and that mission wasn't to keep his attention glued to Jessie.

A flock of something green and bright—parakeets?—took flight as Jessie paused for several sips from a water bottle, and their gazes met. His eyes narrowed.

Yesterday, his former chief had introduced them to several locals, including those who'd been living here during the time of the crash. But they'd all claimed they didn't know anything.

Maybe they didn't. But something about the way they avoided his gaze had told him otherwise.

This trip had a hopeless goal, but he didn't mind because he got all this time alone with Jessie.

On the plane, then yesterday during their walk on the beach, she'd opened up about her childhood. Her stories, said so matter-of-factly, made him shudder, as well as appreciate his modest but comfortable upbringing.

"*Estamos aqui*," the guide said, then walked away as if to give them privacy.

"We're here," she whispered, lifting onto her toes to crane around.

Thankfully, she spoke Spanish. The foster sibling he hadn't met had Hispanic heritage, so she'd studied Spanish. Jessie had done the same to help her friend. Considering Houston's diversity, it must've helped Jessie later in her job. It was invaluable now.

She made it sound like being bilingual wasn't a big deal, but he loved her modesty and her consideration for other people. On the contrary, he only spoke a few words of Gaelic, despite his Irish heritage.

He looked around, and his eyebrows shot up. Where were the remains of the plane? Under a thick canopy of undulating branches—West Indian cedar, calabash, and of course, a variety of tropical palms, and at this elevation, even Creole pines—he couldn't see anything in the tall undergrowth.

So. Much. Vegetation. The jungle didn't need long to take over again.

If any parts of the plane remained, it had succumbed to rain or the plant life or something else. He resisted the urge to grind his teeth.

Even though years had passed since the crash and heavy rains could have washed away some parts, this was strange. Could it be that they'd done a thorough cleanup?

"Could there have been survivors from that crash?" Jessie asked.

"Only two people were on that plane. Both, um, bodies were accounted for."

Her eyes narrowed. "How do we *know*—for sure—there were only two people?"

Good point. "We don't." He removed his backpack, unzipped it, and handed her one of the two metal detectors. "What we know is that Mylah was going with the pilot to Wyatt's villa on the Dominican Republic coast. And that burned remains of two people were found at the crash site and the remains matched the pilot and Mylah's descriptions. The guy wore a uniform and was later identified based on dental records. The woman was the same height and build as Mylah and wore her clothes and shoes and the unique pendant Wyatt gave her. She was photographed wearing those clothes and that pendant before. The remains of her wallet with half-burned IDs were found nearby."

"Mylah's sister recognized the pendant." Jessie sipped more, then replaced her water bottle in her backpack. She fiddled with the metal detector. "See, this is a remote difficult-to-access location. The report your former chief obtained said there was an explosion and everything burned. Despite it being the rainy season, it didn't rain that day. I read the report he got us. I read it several times. By the time authorities made it here, the bodies were not only burned but mauled by animals and unrecognizable. Especially Mylah's body."

He frowned. That fact had bothered him before, and now Jessie spelled it out. "Why weren't dental records used to identify her body?"

"Exactly. The investigation started late and then wrapped up fast." She searched the ground with a metal detector. "Wyatt didn't request any additional probe into the case. Instead, he arranged and paid for large funerals for both the pilot and Mylah. Then Mylah's family received a generous payout."

Another thing that didn't sit well with Ronan at all. He concentrated on searching the ground parallel to Jessie, far enough away so they wouldn't overlap but close enough they could talk. He didn't want to let her out of his sight. The place was beautiful, but... but somewhat creepy, and not only because of its history.

"Sadly, the local authorities who conducted the investigation died, from what I could see, of natural causes two and three years later. At least, I hope they were natural causes, as people claimed," he said. There'd been too many deaths for him to completely believe that.

Then the cutest bird he'd ever seen—a cross between a hummingbird and a kingfisher—landed on a nearby branch and inspected him.

She looked up from her search, holding her breath as she gazed at it, too. "Ooh. That's a tody. Isn't it precious?"

The little fella cocked its emerald head, looking between them, then flew away, exposing geranium pink and white underparts, and she sighed and resumed her conversation. "Don't ask me how Paisley found out the next part. But the person investigating the crash at the time started building a veeeeeery nice house shortly after the investigation concluded. Nothing in Wyatt's records indicates he made a payment here, but even if he did, he most certainly wouldn't do it himself."

His frown deepened. "Do you think he paid to falsify documents?"

"No. I think he paid to speed up the closing of the investigation. He also might've had someone organize the cleanup to avoid any later probes. Plane parts don't disappear by themselves. Of course, there's a chance the investigator's sudden access to substantial funds had nothing to do with all this."

Her metal detector beeped in the tall grass, and he crouched to help her. They inspected a metallic burned part that could've belonged to a plane.

About half an hour later, she picked up a small metal clasp.

He frowned. "That doesn't look like part of a plane."

She rolled her eyes. "Thank you for your astute observation. This might've once been part of a purse. Or not."

He realized the implication. "Mylah's purse was found close to her body, according to the report."

"Conveniently, with her wallet and IDs in it, and not burned up like everything else. Okay, this might not be connected to the crash at all. Maybe it was left by some random tourist." But Jessie's pinched-together brows expressed her doubt. "Of course, finding an ID would be super helpful."

But no matter how hard they'd tried, it was all they found that day, and as dusk wove through the jungle and yellow warblers called their good nights, they returned to Garcia's vacation place.

She didn't complain once on the long hike back, and he admired that.

"Do you think several deaths could've been prevented if someone properly conducted the investigation back then?" Her voice was pensive.

He handed her the remaining water bottle as he drained his, since his throat was parched.

"Thanks. I'm thirsty. But I'm even thirstier for answers." She gulped some down.

And he was thirsty for *her*.

He had to remind himself of her question. "We might never know for sure. But we'll do our best to find out."

They spent two more days at the crash site, this time without the guide. He agreed to set up tents to overnight there, so they wouldn't have to borrow transportation from Garcia, then hike back and forth in the evening and morning. Guarding her sleep in the nearby tent, he got little of his own.

With the time saved by not needing to travel to the site, they expanded the search.

At the end of the third day, they found a gold earring with a tiny red stone like a blood drop.

Jessie's eyes narrowed. "I believe it's a red sapphire. I saw similar earrings in one of Mylah's photos."

In the late evening, Jessie looked up at the lit lanterns strewn on the terrace overlooking an ocean basked in moonlight. Cicadas sang into the night, and the soft waves washed the shore. Something fragrant and sweet complemented the salty tang in the air until she wanted to bottle the fragrance and add it to her collection back home.

Her heart squeezed. She'd never thought Garcia, a retired police chief, would play matchmaker, but something had been done to the décor because the mood *was* romantic. Or Jessie could almost imagine it was God's doing.

A light breeze ruffled her short hair, and she welcomed its gentle touch. But even more, she welcomed Ronan's gentle gaze. She'd never received much male attention, and whatever she'd received, she hadn't welcomed. She'd wanted male cops to see another cop in her rather than a woman, and had worked hard for it.

Now her heart fluttered like her lavender-hued silk scarf—Madeline's gift—in the wind. She lapped up Ronan's attention with an eagerness she didn't expect. Her muscles hummed from tiredness after days of hiking and searching, but she stayed on the terrace with him. After a leisurely dinner of seafood, rice, and local vegetables, she sipped her freshly made mango juice in a funky glass with an umbrella and didn't want these moments to end.

They were a generous gift she'd never take for granted. She'd been able to relax and enjoy herself without being on guard. And with the beauty of the stars reflecting on the ocean, the sweetness of his company and the drink, the soft lantern light basking them in a golden glow, and the bright tropical flowers offering their poignant aroma on the wicker table, the evening was... magical? As practical as she was, she could treasure it just as much as Madeline would've with her taste for fine arts and beauty.

Guilt stung. She missed the girls and felt responsible for their safety. But she hadn't realized how much she'd needed this respite and how much she'd craved time alone with Ronan.

Okay, maybe she'd realized the latter but didn't want to admit it. Such vulnerability would make her weak, and a Defender couldn't be weak.

For here and now, though, it all could be forgotten. She could forget about her responsibilities and feel more feminine than she'd ever felt before. She could be... a woman? An admired one at that. It was a new feeling and a welcome one.

She smiled and took another sip of sweet juice as they shared a companionable silence with no words needed.

Then he reached out and brushed her face with the back of his hand, a simple gesture making her pulse skyrocket. "You look beautiful tonight." Then he seemed to catch himself. "No, I'm wrong."

She winced. So much for the compliment. "Excuse me?"

"I wanted to say, you're *always* beautiful."

She chuckled. "Nice save."

"I mean it. You have no idea how much I'm attracted to you, do you?"

A pleasant wave swept her up, carried her like sea-foam. "Give me a few hints."

"Oh boy. How about I show you instead?" He walked around the table and leaned in for a kiss.

Mesmerized, she rose to meet him halfway. Her heartbeat went into overdrive. By the time she lowered herself back into her chair, she was weak in her knees and as light as that sea-foam on the ocean. Everything in her begged for more, and she wanted to lose herself in the wonderful sensations once again.

As wonderful as this was, though, she had to tell him about Gold. Even though it concerned Genevieve the most, the story was such a big part of all their lives and always would be. She took a deep breath of air saturated with that salty-ocean and tropical-flower aroma.

Before the trip, the girls had given their permission to share the story with Ronan, which signified they understood how important he was to her. Over a decade later, he'd be the first person outside their circle to hear about it. She hadn't even told her fiancé. Her foster sisters had kept it from their significant others, even Madeline from her husband, and Madeline had loved that waste of a human being with passion.

Her heart started beating even faster for several reasons.

"You should know the secret we girls have carried for many years. You'll be the first person outside of our circle to know."

He studied her, his expression unreadable in the light of lanterns. "You or they didn't do something illegal, right?"

"No. We didn't." At least, not that Jessie knew of.

"I trust you. I don't need to know about your past—or the past of your friends. Your willingness to share already tells me everything I need to know. I'm honored that you trust me that much."

Something shifted. If she was ready to share someone else's secret, could she share her own?

Then she revealed the truth she and her foster-sisters hid. How they protected Gold, a child born of rape, now a teen. A teen who was also heir to Wyatt's fortune.

His eyes were wide when she finished. "I'm so sorry that happened to all of you, especially to Gold's mother. I'll pray for you and the girls."

She didn't know what to say to that, apart from "Thank you." She stared at the ocean because it was easier to say this without looking into his eyes. "I'm scared of being weak. Of feeling helpless again."

"Trusting someone or trusting God doesn't make you weak. It has the opposite effect. If you trust someone as much as yourself, you double your strength."

The scar where she'd taken the bullet from the man who'd once professed to love her nagged at her. "What if that trust gets betrayed?"

"Then it's a reflection on that person, not on you. It might be difficult for you to believe this now on a subconscious level because of what happened to you in the past. But I'm not going to betray you. I'm not going to abandon you."

She pondered that. Could she believe this time around things could be different? "You're not that kind of person."

"That, and I care too much about you."

Her heart made a strange movement in her chest, and before she knew it, she ran around the table and hugged him. "I care about you, too. More than you'll ever know. Probably more than I know myself."

He hugged her back, making her heart dance like the light over the water, then looked in her eyes as he got up. "Care enough not to walk away when all this is over?"

She stumbled, her joy ebbing like the outgoing tide. "I don't know."

His face fell. "Well, thank you for your honesty."

Did she let her past define her without noticing? *Hold on.* Her ideas about this case might be far-fetched, but what she saw in the Dominican Republic so far confirmed them. It wouldn't hurt to look at it all from a different angle. Then she'd have to let Arianna know her suspicions.

Jessie felt lighter as she slipped her hand into Ronan's, letting herself lean into him as they walked the shore. There were several reasons for her euphoria. First, if her wild hypothesis proved true, they wouldn't have to worry about Gold. At least, not now. Every one of them could continue living as they pleased, instead of guarding Gold.

Which meant Jessie might be able to pursue a real relationship with Ronan, not the fake dating she'd suggested, and just the thought made her dizzy.

She wasn't there yet to trust her own heart, even if she'd started trusting his. A lifetime of abandonment couldn't be corrected with a simple talk. Words could be erased like their footprints in the sand.

But the way she felt right now... That would be etched in the corners of her heart forever.

Chapter Sixteen

"Well, that was useless." Jessie grimaced at the end of the next day as they left another house without any results. Only one house left to visit in this village, set a bit apart from the rest. Several people didn't open the doors for them at all, and she bottled up her frustration. She could understand people being wary of strangers.

He glanced at her. "I wouldn't say that. Every minute spent with you is useful and amazing to me."

Embarrassed, she ducked her head as heat tingled up her neck, but a healthy dose of delight warmed her, too. "I–I didn't mean it the way it sounded. And... same here."

No matter the result of the investigation, the trip was everything she'd dreamed it could be, and more. The beauty of nature, the friendliness of the locals, but most of all, the company of one man... She'd never forget this time with Ronan.

She wanted to slip her hand into his to remind herself this wasn't just a dream, to have a tangible connection, but they were already passing some goats along a muddy path to the next house.

Thinking people would be less afraid of a woman than a man, Jessie was usually the one to knock on the door. She did so this time, as well.

Nobody answered, but she distinguished movement inside. She put on her friendliest smile. "*Necesitamos ayuda, por favor.*" By now, Ronan would know she said they were looking for help, so she didn't translate for him.

"*Por favor,*" she said again when nothing happened. *Please.*

The door opened a smidge. One brown eye of a young female face showed in the crack, and the scent of herbs drifted to them. "*No sé nada.*"

Jessie was used to such an answer. Word must have traveled on what she was seeking help for. Still, with Ronan's broad back covering her in case the neighbors were watching, she lifted the Ziploc bag with the earring and several banknotes of Dominican pesos. Then she gave in Spanish the approximate timeline and the description of the woman they were looking for, a woman who might've been wearing the same earring.

The door opened a crack wider, revealing a young woman. Long dark hair covered her shoulders, and a little child with pigtails cowered near her legs. The woman repeated that she didn't know anything. But her pupils dilated slightly when she saw the earring.

Jessie tensed and glanced at Ronan. He must've seen the telltale sign, too, because he gave a curt nod.

Since childhood, Jessie knew that to gain something one must offer something. She glanced at the kid goats gamboling in the yard below the children's clothes swaying on a clothesline. Boys' and girls' clothes.

Jessie added more banknotes and hinted the woman could buy food for the children and more baby goats.

The woman hesitated. "*No se mucho. Fue mi madre que ayudó a la mujer extranjera. La mujer pagó con eso. Nunca vi a la mujer.*" She gestured at the earring.

So she hadn't seen the foreign woman with the identical earring, but her mother had. The woman paid for helping her with an earring.

In Spanish, Jessie offered to pay for any information and asked to speak to the woman's mother.

The woman shook her head. "*Ella murió el año pasado.*" Then she glanced at the kid goats, her expression wistful. She must need that payment.

Jessie's heart sank. She told Ronan her mother, who'd helped the foreign woman, died last year. Jessie asked the woman if her mother mentioned anything at all about the foreign woman. Maybe the color of hair or eyes?

The woman brightened. "*Sí. Tenía los ojos espectaculares. Ojos verdes.*"

Jessie's pulse picked up. That fit Mylah's description. "The foreign woman had green eyes," she said for Ronan's benefit. Which was a rare trait, with only about 2 percent of people having green eyes.

"*¿Qué dijo su madre sobre esta mujer?*" She handed the young woman the money.

The latter snatched it and swallowed hard. "*Fue quemada. Muy quemada.*"

When Paisley's name lit up Jessie's phone screen that evening, she swiped it to answer. One—it was always a joy to bask in the sunshine of such a cheerful person as Paisley. Two—that morning, Jessie had told her friend about her findings and asked Paisley to research whether any woman Mylah knew had disappeared around the crash time.

Jessie plopped on the guest room bed to be more comfortable and angled her body toward the open window where lazy white curtains billowing in the breeze framed an ocean of endless dazzling blue. Lemonade on the white side desk emanated a citrusy aroma, just like in her dream. "Any news?"

Paisley laughed. "Glad to talk to you, too."

Jessie cleared her throat. "Oh, oops. I didn't mean—"

"I know. I'm just teasing you. Okay, here it goes. Mylah volunteered at the women's shelter, as well as donated to it. I did a teleconference interview, and spoke to the director. She praised Mylah's efforts, and said they missed her at the shelter after her death. Mylah did get especially close to one woman her age. She even promised to take her on a vacation to some exotic country so the poor woman could escape her troubles for a while. Now listen to this. After the vacation, that woman never appeared at the shelter again."

Jessie kept silent, mulling over the implications. She'd read all the information Paisley had dug up on Mylah and studied the pictures. Dating beautiful models seemed to be a family tradition, and Mylah was one. But she didn't fit the usual mold of women in that family. She didn't just attend charity galas—she also volunteered at the women's shelter and spent time talking to women and serving them food. Her dating history included guys who weren't famous or rich. And unlike the other trophy women, Mylah didn't come from a prominent family.

Her family was poor, with a single mother struggling to raise two daughters on a waitress salary in a neighborhood where parked cars often lost their tires. Once Mylah's modeling career had taken off, she'd bought houses in a great neighborhood for her mother and sister, even provided cars or anything else they needed.

Of course, she shouldn't have dated a married man, but Jessie felt there was much more to Mylah than unscrupulous intentions.

"Did you manage to track the disappeared woman down?" Jessie finally asked.

"I tried. The identity the woman gave the shelter didn't exist. My guess is she was running away from an abusive husband and covering her tracks. I do have a description from the director's words. Blonde, about the same height and build as Mylah."

And knowing what it was to be poor, Mylah had probably given her clothes, a purse, and shoes. Jessie nodded as if her friend could see her. "Thank you. This helps a lot."

"You're welcome. I'll keep searching. Do you want me to tell Arianna to ask for vacation time and join us?"

Jessie pondered it, then exhaled a slow breath. "Tell the girls what we found out. Vote on it. But my vote is yes. We might be getting close, and it's too dangerous for her to stay there."

"Okay. Do me a favor, though."

She didn't hesitate. "Sure."

"Stop trying so hard not to fall in love with Ronan." Paisley knew her well. Maybe a little too well.

"I'm not, but you know how much divides us." Then something about Paisley's voice attracted Jessie's attention. "What happened?"

"Nothing." Paisley's voice strained. Not a good sign.

"What happened?"

"Cormac is coming back to the States for his leave."

Jessie placed the name fast. "Your army pen pal? The one you've been talking to online for years? Though you never met?"

"Yeah. And... his family lives near Cowboy Crossing."

"Waaaaait a moment. You did say one of your online friends lived near there. That was the reason you chose that lodge. Is that him?"

"Yep. And he wants to meet me."

Jessie did her best to wrap her mind around the news. "Well, shouldn't you be excited? You've been gushing about him for a long time." That made Jessie believe the guy was too good to be true, especially after her boyfriend had put a bullet in her. But after meeting Ronan's family, she'd started believing good guys *did* exist.

Hmm, the pause stretched too long. She even glanced at the screen to make sure she didn't lose the connection. "Are you there?"

"Yes. Well, a pen pal relationship is easy. I like to live in an online world. Way less disappointment than in the real one. If... if he meets me, what if he gets disappointed?"

"I can't imagine that happening. Everyone loves you. You're a true sunshine. I'm a grouch compared to you."

Paisley chuckled, but it was a nervous chuckle. "You can be a grouch not even compared to me."

"Ouch."

"I mean, why spoil a good thing? Why meet in person? We have a great thing going right now."

Hmm, usually, Jessie worried, and Paisley talked her out of it. Now when the roles were reversed, Jessie didn't know what to say. "Does he want to meet you?" Which technically should be a good sign.

A sigh traveled down the line. Apparently, Paisley didn't think that way. "Yeah. He says he can't wait."

"That's wonderful. If he wasn't smitten before, he'll be smitten after spending a minute in your company."

"Here's the thing. He wanted to see my photo, and I sent him one with you, me, and Madeline. He... he assumed I was Madeline."

Jessie groaned. She looked out the window at the gorgeous view of the ocean and sand to calm herself. "You corrected him, right?"

No answer.

"Right? I mean, you're so sweet and pretty. And *honest.*"

"I should've told him the truth. I know. I tried to, several times, but... I didn't think we'd ever meet in person. And... It felt so nice to be admired. To be told I'm the most gorgeous girl on earth."

"But you are! Just the way you are."

Another sigh huffed through the speakers, so uncharacteristic of Paisley. "Right. I mean, I like the way I look. But a lot of guys find it weird. Pink and blue hair and all. And I'm short and kind of plump."

"You're petite. And perfect!" Jessie nearly yelled. "You haven't been self-conscious before. So why..." Then it dawned on her. "You cyber met Cormac right after your ex broke up with you."

Jessie didn't bother to mention the name of the ex. The guy wasn't worth it. He'd dumped their wonderful, sweet Paisley just because she didn't fit into the snooty circle of his friends and family. His mother had been clutching her pearls when he'd brought Paisley to dinner, in all her pink-blue hair and bumblebee-outfit glory. Then Paisley had no idea how to use most of the cutlery. And she'd been so nervous she spilled the fine red wine on their precious damask tablecloth. Then there had been the fact that she was a foster child with no clue who her parents were in a place where pedigree had been valued. Somehow, the guy had made her feel less worthy before breaking up with her.

Jessie suppressed the desire to choke him with his tie. Argh.

Well, Genevieve would say they had a classic literature example here. Cyrano de Ber... something. "You're going to tell Cormac everything before you meet him, right? And you *are* going to meet him. From what you told me, you had a real connection."

Paisley's voice dropped. "He and *Madeline* had a real connection."

"No, no, no! It was *you* he liked. Okay, once I'm back, I'll talk some sense into you. It's rare to find that special person in your life. You can't let it go because of a mishap."

"That applies to you, as well. The rare special person in your life. I hope it works out between you and Ronan."

Jessie perked up at the footfalls in the hall. "I've got to go. Please think about what I said. Come clean to Cormac. Or you might regret it for the rest of your life."

She met Ronan in the hall. Just the sight of him and his smile made her run to him and hug him and keep him close. Paisley was right. What Ronan and Jessie had was beyond precious, and she knew it. Just as she knew that, after all this was over, she might be the one walking away.

For now, she held him, and he held her. Close enough for her to hear his heartbeat.

Once he let her go, he looked into her eyes. "Have I told you lately how wonderful you are?"

Her heart warmed. "Not in the last five minutes."

He laughed. "Well, *you're* wonderful. And I can't wait to introduce you to more of my family. Soon, my brother is coming back from deployment for his leave."

Jessie blinked, then blinked again. Right. Cormac. No wonder Paisley was smitten.

Jessie didn't want to think it was their last day in the Dominican Republic. She wanted to do so much more here with Ronan, but she settled for a trip to the capital. As beautiful as the city was, her heart was hurting already.

"I read up on the Dominican Republic," she said as they strolled the streets, hand in hand. "Before the Europeans arrived, the native Taíno people inhabited the island of Hispaniola. Christopher Columbus landed here and claimed it as a Spanish colony. And so it became the first permanent European settlement in the Americas. Over three hundred years later, it became the independent Dominican Republic."

She tipped her face toward the blue sky, the air warm and soft as it caressed her and rustled palm fronds. So beautiful. So peaceful, and yet… "But in 1822, they were annexed to Haiti by force. There is so much beauty and at the same time such tragic history here." Her throat constricted, and she kept silent for a few seconds. It was difficult to believe pain and violence once ruled this idyllic place. "Twenty-two years later, they won true independence. Then came civil wars, invasions from their neighbor, even a brief return to colonial status, and so on."

"That's one of many things that amaze me about you. You always look deeper than other people."

Heat rose. "I just happen to have a curious mind. Which helped me a lot in my profession. Genevieve is a real history buff. Especially anything concerning England."

"You're humble, too."

Unnerved and pleased by his admiring gaze, she ducked her head and muttered, "Thanks. I don't look at myself as humble, though."

"Humble people usually don't."

She chuckled. "To look on the bright side, today the Dominican Republic is considered the largest economy in the Caribbean and Central America and the most visited place in the Caribbean."

"I'm not surprised. It's a gorgeous place." Then he added in a quieter voice, "A perfect place to fall in love, too."

She agreed, way too much. Her heart fluttered. She needed to change the direction of her thoughts—and fast. She gestured to a colorful tourist shop in an aquamarine-colored building sandwiched in between pastel yellow and glorious pink buildings. Vivid orange balconies jutted from the floors above. Paisley would've loved it here.

All the color brightened up Jessie's heart, contrasting her drab existence, and she wanted to buy something to remember the place by as well as bring souvenirs for the girls. "Care to stop by?"

"Sure." He opened the door for her.

It looked more like an art gallery than a tourist shop, with paintings as vibrant and bright as the island's nature. Art was more Madeline's territory, though the love of it had nearly gotten her killed. Madeline's brain combined an affinity for science and an appreciation of paintings, but then she was a whirlwind of contrasts. From visits to Madeline's house, Jessie had learned—not entirely of her own free will—a few characteristics of different art movements.

So here, she could discern the elements of romanticism, realism, and impressionism. She chose a still life with orange and yellow fruits for Madeline. Madeline could use some sunshine colors in her life, whether she wanted it or not. For free-spirited Paisley, Jessie settled on a smaller painting with butterflies and tropical birds with azure-blue feathers.

Despite her protests, Ronan paid for the paintings. Then he chose another painting of the ocean sparkling in the sun's rays, the sky turquoise and breathtaking, painted with thick strokes, in impressionist style. "This will always remind me of this place. The way I feel here." He opened the door for her as they left the shop and added so quietly she wasn't sure she heard him correctly, "The way *you* make me feel."

Something changed inside her. Something she wasn't ready to admit, even to herself.

So she channeled her thoughts to a different topic as they strolled the capital's streets. "This city is known for having the first monastery, cathedral, castle, and fortress in the Americas." Again, thanks to Madeline, she could say the ornate buildings around her belonged to the baroque style, which was one of Madeline's favorites. Genevieve's, too, for that matter.

Jessie preferred the small houses and furniture influenced by the Taíno people. Dragging a mahogany table and chairs back on a flight didn't seem like a great idea, so yesterday, she settled on a hand-carved mahogany jewelry box, bought in a gift shop. Since she didn't have much jewelry to put inside, she'd dedicate it as a memory box.

She only hoped that, after this trip, she'd have more than just memories.

Large modern buildings on this street rose with angular corners, huge windows, and a luxurious feel. Somehow, this blend of different cultures and times not only worked but also seemed fully embraced here.

They stopped at a cozy café for lunch. La Bandera, translated as The Flag. She knew by now lunch would be white rice, red beans, meat, and a salad, plus freshly squeezed juice. Those were abundant here. When Ronan gave thanks for the food, her amen was more than a muttered pretense.

For dessert, she had a snow cone, which here was called *frio frio*, meaning literally *cold cold*. Then they visited museums and tourist shops until Ronan carried too many packages.

After delivering the packages to the house, they returned for an evening out. She wore a dress for the first time she could remember. A long, flowy sundress with bright-yellow tropical flowers that she'd bought at a local shop swirled about her calves. At first, her stomach squeezed with discomfort. Then Ronan's admiring gaze chased the tension from her muscles and opened her heart to joy.

Without discussing it, they settled for the outdoor café where a band played merengue. Or was it bachata? She read both were popular here, but she'd never heard either one to know the difference. With so many firsts for her today, she hadn't understood the expression "made my heart dance" until now.

While they were waiting for their food, delicious scents of meat and vegetables swirling around them, he got up and gave her his hand. "Would you honor me with this dance?"

She swallowed hard. "I—I'm not a great dancer. In fact, I'm not *any* kind of dancer. I'm worried for your feet."

His gaze didn't waver. "I'm not. Please. Or should I say *por favor*?"

She squared her shoulders and took his hand. "Well, you do it at your own risk."

Once he held her and led carefully, he whispered to her shoulder. "Deep inside, I knew I'd risk my heart once I met you."

She nearly melted like frio frio in the Dominican Republic's sun as she swayed with the romantic music. But would he feel this way once they returned to their everyday lives? Would she allow herself to continue to feel this way? What about when she applied to be a police officer again? In Houston, where her foster sisters would surely return after the investigation was over and Gold was safe again?

No man had ever stayed with Jessie, be it her father or any romantic relationship. Why would Ronan be any different? She'd had to toughen up because it was the only way to survive. She couldn't become weak now.

But for now, she stayed close to Ronan, her hand in his, so very trusting, and let merengue—or was it bachata?—carry her away.

Chapter Seventeen

With gentle waves lapping the sand beside them and time standing still, the last evening on the island lingered in bittersweet farewell. Well, Ronan looked forward to going back to the ranch and his family, to returning to his work. He did, really. But part of his heart would always stay here, among the whisper of the ocean and the romantic merengue, among the vibrant colors and the diverse history.

Because this was where he realized his world was so much bigger than the ranch and the small town he grew up in and Jessie wasn't just an important part of that world. She was an essential one.

This wasn't the time or place to say goodbye to the love he'd lost and embrace the love he'd found. Because deep inside, he'd already said goodbye to Isla when he'd started falling for Jessie. At first, liking Jessie had enveloped him in guilty betrayal. *Layers* of guilt because he didn't feel he'd done right by Isla and their last fight had weighed heavily on him.

When he'd opened up about it at the café, something Jessie said stuck with him. If God forgave him and Isla would've forgiven him if she were alive, then Ronan could forgive himself.

Could let go.

Could grow and become a better man from it.

Yes, Jessie spoke of God as if she knew Him, a huge answer to prayer that left him giddy with relief and hope.

Maybe away from the tragedy, it was easier to embrace the future, but he started feeling that way now. It might be gut-wrenching at first, but he'd support Jessie if she decided to work as a cop again, instead of berating her for being in a dangerous profession and asking her to quit like he'd done with Isla. No matter how much worry for her was going to cut through him, right? Because even some time with Jessie would be far better than a lifetime without her. One couldn't and shouldn't make demands on the person they loved, even out of the best intentions.

Loved? Yes. Because he loved Jessie.

Without beautiful words and grand gestures.

With his entire being, he simply longed to be with her forever. He'd have taken a bullet for her before, but now that took on a new meaning.

Where that left him, he didn't know.

Lord, what now?

As they wandered along the beach, moonlight painting a silver path on dark waters, he wanted to tell her how he felt. But something stopped him. Was he cautious that she didn't return his feelings?

In some ways, it was easier for him to fall in love than for her. While there'd been plenty of sibling rivalry and occasional punches and bruises, he'd grown up with a lot of affection and care. Work was abundant, but so was love and food. He'd never gone hungry or had to look over his shoulder or worry about survival. Unlike Jessie, he'd never experienced betrayal and abandonment while she'd gone through it many times.

He could understand why she guarded her heart. He'd guarded his for years since losing Isla. Jessie had taught him to look beyond the past, to expand his horizon, and not only because he'd traveled to the Dominican Republic because of her.

Oh how much he wanted her to let him in.

She stopped and gazed at the horizon or maybe beyond it. "We've done our job here, and I'm grateful. But is it bad that I want to stay longer?"

"I love my work and family and the ranch, but... I want to stay longer, too. We can, you know."

She kept quiet, then shivered despite the warm night. "I have to see this through to the end. And I need to warn Arianna—our other foster sister, our mole in Wyatt's mansion. I have a gut feeling she needs to leave. Her life might be in more danger than we realized. I'm sorry."

Wow. She put her friend's well-being above her own. But then, he didn't expect anything else from her.

Lord, please help me... not scare her away.

"When we're back, I"—he swallowed hard to release the clogged-up words—"I don't want this to be over. Even if you return to Houston. I want to make this work. And I want a real relationship. Not a pretend one for Mom's sake."

"A long-distance relationship?" She looked him in the eyes as the breeze lifted her lavender-hued silk scarf. "It works for Paisley. Or... not exactly. She's kind of in a predicament right now. But what if it's not enough for us? I mean, I know it's not going to be enough."

His heart sank into the nearby waters. Did she think she'd meet someone else? Someone who would be enough?

She stepped closer, her eyes burning into his. "I mean, I want to be able to see you." She traced his bare forearm with her fingertips, igniting a road of fire. "I want to feel your skin under my fingers."

"Yes. Me, too." His voice grew husky as he embraced her. "I want to hear your laughter, the timbre of your voice when you simply tell me good morning. The citrusy scent of your perfume drives me crazy. I crave the taste of your lips more than I need my next breath."

She lifted on her tiptoes and brushed her lips against his but withdrew way too soon. Giggling, she ran away, splashing water.

His heart beating fast, he chased her, then lifted her in his arms, treasuring the feeling, making her spin, making his head spin. "Got you."

"I'm afraid you do." Laughter disappeared from her lips.

She was afraid of it? He set her down but slid his hands to her hands and kept hers in his. His heart shifted when she didn't try to remove them.

He wouldn't try to compete with her loyalty to her friends or to her profession, but in this place where they were alone on this stretch of beach, with the clear sky and the clear ocean, he needed to make his intentions just as clear. At least, as much as he could.

"I need you in my life." So much so it scared him.

"I need you, too. It terrifies me how much I need you." Her voice was quiet.

"You know I wouldn't abandon or betray you."

She squeezed his hands. "But you have a dangerous profession. I get your passion for justice. I do. I share it. But in one form or another, no man has stuck around for me. Or for my friends, for that matter." She looked away, wisps of dark hair caressing her face. "I don't know a single happy ending to a romance. Well, other than those in a book or a movie."

Was he losing her already? He freed one hand from hers, touched her chin, and turned her face toward him, making her look at him, letting those silky breeze-tousled wisps of hair kiss his hand. "Then why don't you make your own story the first one?"

Her eyes widened, and the vulnerability in her beautiful moonlit gray eyes tugged on him.

This was it. He wanted to marry her. Full commitment.

Such tremendous joy and peace filled him when he stood by her side that he knew she was the one God had meant for him. He'd once asked his father how he'd figured out that Mom would be the one for him. His father had said he just knew.

Now Ronan *just knew*.

But he also knew if he said something about commitment now, she'd flee. Instinct told him she wasn't ready yet. Would she ever be?

"Care to have one more dance?" Maybe it was an excuse to keep her close for now, but so be it.

Her eyes widened. "Without music?"

"We'll dance to the music of our hearts."

And so they did.

"I'm back!" With their careful surveillance system, Jessie probably didn't need to announce that when she arrived home late the next evening. Already, the girls squealed and rushed to hug her. She dropped her bags on the hardwood floor. Ronan had wanted to bring them inside, but she'd spared him and his eardrums the girls' assault. And the dog's frantic barking.

Genevieve paused for a second before joining a group hug. But as soon as the girls released Jessie, Genevieve leaned in for another hug and whispered into Jessie's ear. "And you're in love."

Heat tingled through Jessie. Was it that noticeable? "I've got gifts for you and some new information."

Her friends sobered up.

"Good or bad?" Paisley asked.

Genevieve raised her hand. "First, Jessie needs to eat. We all do. Well, I don't *need* to but I want to."

Jessie chuckled. She'd missed her friends, though an important part of her longed to be with Ronan again already, never mind that she'd seen him minutes ago. "You say we're amazing the way we are. The same applies to you."

Rusty bolted into the room with Madeline. His tail was wagging, and at Madeline's nod, he placed his front paws on Jessie, making her harrumph and stagger, then covered her with drool.

Madeline issued another command, and the dog stepped down. "Sorry. I didn't mean for him to do that."

Sure, she hadn't. Rolling her eyes, Jessie grinned. "Oh, please. It's great to be greeted so enthusiastically."

Something flashed in Madeline's eyes. Of all the girls, she seemed the least affectionate, but Jessie suspected it was due to an enormous restraint. They'd all reacted differently to trauma, and Madeline's way was to keep everything hidden and all emotions contained. She'd even earned the nickname of Ice Queen in school for her icy demeanor and cold blue eyes—or maybe she'd earned it for showing people only a small part of the iceberg.

Jessie's heart constricted. She guessed Madeline was far from an Ice Queen. That a lot of fire simmered beneath her aloof and collected demeanor. And one day, she wouldn't be able to contain it all inside. The results of such an explosion could create lots of damage and shatter everyone around. Which must be why she'd broken up with Brandon.

True to her carefully created persona, her hug was light and fleeting. But this time, Jessie held on a tad longer. Though perfect on the outside, Madeline was more miserable inside than ever, and Jessie ached to do something to change that.

But all in due time.

The girls—and her nose—led her to the dining room where the table was already set. She breathed in the enticing aromas of roasted chicken and russet potatoes with green beans and bacon bits. Genevieve must've added more herbs than usual because it also smelled like thyme and parsley.

"Sorry, Gold already ate and is asleep, she couldn't wait up till you arrived," Genevieve said, as she poured tea into their mismatched cups. Though they had good china by now, everyone had their favorite cup or mug and kept using it. Except for the ones dropped, and even then, unless shattered, they kept using the chipped ones. Probably because those pieces were so much like their own lives.

Paisley's favorite drinking container was a funky pink mug with a blue butterfly on it. Madeline's cup had to be replaced since even she couldn't glue together the shattered one's tiny pieces, but she stayed with the same style, white with elegant golden trim and a golden handle.

Genevieve's cup, also porcelain and white, displayed a drawing of a Regency couple. One of their neighbors, an elderly lady Genevieve had brought homemade food and read historical romances to from time to time, had gifted it to her, saying it passed through several generations in her family. None of the girls had their own history, so Genevieve had probably needed to borrow others'.

Jessie's container for tea and coffee was a no-nonsense mug that held a lot of coffee but also fit in the car's cup holder. Cops ran on coffee.

She was okay with hot tea for now, though. As much as she missed Ronan already, warmth pooled in her belly at seeing her girls again. Invisible ties bound her foster sisters, and severing them would be like severing her own aorta. One of the many reasons she needed to clear her suspicions. Well, Madeline would know better what that important vein or artery was.

The tea soured in Jessie's stomach, but she covered it by digging into Genevieve's yummy food. When her friends left the lodge in the future, she'd have to go with them, no matter how difficult it was going to be. It was her duty, and she took her duty seriously. Besides, the investigation showed her how much she missed being a cop. That was one thing she needed to do. She'd even consider it was in her blood. But without knowing her ancestors' history, it was difficult to say.

The girls peppered her with questions about the trip and added light teasing about Ronan. Then the conversation switched to her discovery, and the mood sobered up.

"Arianna is on her way." Genevieve poured more tea. This time, it was mango and passion fruit flavor.

"Does she have an idea who it might be?" Jessie straightened her back and pushed away her empty plate. Good thing Gold wasn't eating with them. She wouldn't want the girl hearing this conversation.

"She'll bring the list of people working at the house, but she's got a gut feeling about one of the other maids."

Jessie's fingers tapped on the table. "That's what I was afraid of. But even if we figure it out, getting proof is going to be much more difficult."

Madeline's fingers tightened around her delicate cup, a sign that she was going to say something the others might not like. "Do we need proof? The main thing is for our Gold to be safe. If what you suspect is true, the murder has nothing to do with what happened to Genevieve."

Jessie's tap on the table quickened. "What about justice? And remember, there was a second murder. That means there can be a third."

Madeline leaned back, her relaxed posture deceiving. "I forgot your constant quest for justice."

Heat flared through Jessie, then dissipated. Madeline's parents had never gotten justice.

Paisley tilted her head, ever the peacemaker, while she loaded her fork with green beans, then pointed it at Jessie. "I think what Madeline is concerned about is that, if the culprit suspects we're onto her, she'll come after us. That is, assuming it's the person Arianna is concerned about."

Jessie resisted the urge to grind her teeth. In her desire to find the truth, she didn't want to put others in danger. She drained more of her tea as if it could help her bitterness. "Murder probably gets easier after the first time. And what if she already suspects us? That's why I wanted Arianna out of there. I can better protect her if she's at the lodge than miles away."

Genevieve waved in the air. "Let's wait for Arianna and regroup, okay?"

When Genevieve said something, the rest of them listened. Just like they had that horrible day Genevieve told them not to go to the police. Genevieve had never gotten her justice, either.

It had gone against everything inside Jessie, but it had been Genevieve's decision to make. It had been their decision to support her.

Could they put the past behind them, or would it haunt them the rest of their days?

They all nodded agreement to Genevieve's words.

When Jessie started collecting empty dishes, Paisley shook her head. "You must be tired after your trip. I'll do it."

Jessie's bones did hum from tiredness, but not so much from the flight as from walking and dancing on the beach with Ronan until sunrise. Yes, she was athletic, but even athletic people needed to sleep and rest. Yet she didn't regret a single precious moment spent in his company.

She shook her head, eager to talk to Paisley. "How about we do it together?" They'd done cleanup so many times, first in the Finchs' house and café, then at Genevieve's apartment, so they worked easily in tandem.

"Sure." After a few minutes, Paisley nudged Jessie as she kept loading the dishes. "You want to ask me about Cormac, don't you?"

They knew each other well. "Yup."

Paisley grimaced. "I didn't tell him yet. I–I don't want to lose him before I lose him."

"Who says you're going to lose him?" Jessie placed dirty dishes in the dishwasher.

Paisley wiped down the table. "A man who expects a Ferrari won't be happy with a Beetle."

An unusual comparison for a woman who wasn't into cars.

"Just tell him."

Paisley visibly swallowed. "I... I'll figure something out."

Jessie didn't like the sound of that. She didn't like the sound of it at all. She didn't have much time to think about it, though, because Genevieve announced Arianna's arrival.

Chapter Eighteen

Ronan had done his best to give Jessie some space. He really had. She was back with her three foster sisters and the fourth one had joined them yesterday. But the void of not seeing her grew too much inside him.

So by the evening, he gave up and invited her to dinner at their local restaurant. He'd learned the hard way that every moment was precious. And moments spent apart from her seemed wasted.

Not that he didn't love his family or his job, because he did. Argh. All these feelings were so confusing.

But nothing was confusing about the way her face lit up when he picked her up for their date—a real one and not a fake one this time around. Nothing was confusing about the way his entire being responded to her hug, either. He knew where his heart was, and it was with Jessie.

He'd done the right thing by going to Springfield with two of his brothers and choosing an engagement ring. Even if it took years for Jessie to get to the place where he was already, she was worth the wait.

She introduced him to Arianna, a slim woman with long, straight brown hair, who studied him as if evaluating him. As much as Jessie was protective of her friends, they were protective of her. He wanted to say he'd never hurt Jessie like her ex had, but... it seemed too forward. And really, how comforting was it to say he wouldn't *shoot* her?

The rest of Jessie's friends and Rusty greeted him like an old friend, warming him. They mattered to her and, therefore, mattered to him. Arianna nodded to herself as if making a decision and smiled at him. He felt lighter having passed the test, though he could sense a large part of Arianna remained guarded.

He didn't have much time to think about that as he and Jessie were already on their way to the restaurant. His joy of seeing her again was tempered by a sense of... what, premonition? He tried to shake off the feeling as he checked the rearview mirror, partly out of habit, partly because of that premonition.

No tail. Good.

He squared his shoulders as he glanced at her, then returned his attention to the road and turned to the street leading to the restaurant. It didn't take long to get anywhere in Cowboy Crossing. He was going on a date with the woman he loved, and he was determined to enjoy every minute of it.

Warmth pooled in the pit of his stomach as he reached for her hand. Who'd think such a simple gesture as holding a woman's hand could send pleasure jolting straight to his heart?

Her fingers laced through his, sending another jolt. He didn't want to think that she might leave town once she felt danger passed, taking his heart with her. Or that she might get a job as a police officer again and risk her life every day. He winced at the thought as he parked.

Right here, right now, she was with him, and he had to concentrate on that. This time, this moment was all they had. Isla used to say that, but he only understood and embraced it now. Because of Jessie.

Thoughts about Isla didn't bring heart-wrenching pain and guilt any longer, only lingering sadness. He'd never forget her, would never stop being grateful for her being in his life, however unfairly short that time was. But it was time to move on with his life now.

Yesterday, he'd gone to the cemetery, put flowers on her grave, and talked to her as if she were there. Tears had streamed down his face at the end of that one-sided conversation, but his heart didn't weigh like a tombstone any longer.

He could live in the here and now again. Did already.

He surveyed the parking lot, then walked around the vehicle and opened the door for Jessie. She slipped out of the car and smiled as she looked up at him, and for this evening, everything was right in the world. Not just right. Great, actually.

He shielded her from the wind and assault, even if the latter was unlikely, as they walked to the restaurant. He opened the front door and followed her inside, greeted by warm air and enticing aromas of barbecue and potatoes.

Thankfully, a table was available at the end where he could see both exits, and based on Jessie's satisfied nod, she liked that, too. It was incredible how he could already guess what she was thinking. He'd never been this attuned to anybody else.

He greeted people he passed, their eyes curious. He'd heard lots of speculation already and endured some gentle and not-so-gentle teasing.

It so happened that Makenzie worked again tonight. With a smirk on blue-lipsticked lips, the teen brought them menus and took their drink orders.

Five earrings gleamed in her ear as he and Jessie went for coffee. He was used to drinking gallons of it at work, and his system craved the liquid.

Not as much as he craved Jessie, though. This was real. Not pretend. Not fake. Very much real.

Was she simply addicted to coffee, or was she missing being on the force? Despite his decision, everything inside him rebelled against the idea of her being in the path of danger. He tensed just thinking about it. He'd barely survived losing Isla. But if he'd known Isla would eventually die on duty, because of her need to protect others and her heightened sense of duty, would he have done anything differently? Would he have preferred to walk away from her, to never have what they'd had? He'd wished so much he could protect her, but he couldn't.

His heart seemed to turn over in his chest as he couldn't take his focus off another stubborn, courageous woman with an innate need to serve and protect, no matter the danger to her own life.

The answer was a resounding no. As much as he'd hurt to lose Isla, he'd never regret the wonderful time they'd shared. He'd never been as happy as when he'd been with her. Well, not until he'd met Jessie.

He might've been crazy to do what he'd done today, and he wasn't talking about buying the engagement ring. He didn't have connections in the Houston Police Department. But he had connections in Springfield PD and had left a good impression there. He'd put out feelers today for any vacancies.

And that wasn't just because he was desperate for her to stay in the area. Her eyes sparkled when she'd talked about her work, and he wanted her to be happy more than he wanted to be happy himself.

If he didn't, what he felt for her wouldn't be love.

He'd spent months after Isla's death stewing in resentment before that emotion hardened into guilt. If only she'd listened to him when he'd asked her to find a different field where she wouldn't be risking her life. If only she'd agreed to his suggestion. She'd be alive, and they'd be getting married. Maybe starting a family later on.

He ducked his head, wincing. Not once had Isla pointed out that he was in a dangerous field, as well. When she'd told him how much she'd worried about him, he'd dismissed her concerns. How could he have been so selfish?

Jessie was right that last evening of their vacation, what she'd said in the café. He was a different man now. Well, at least he hoped he was.

Her mere presence, her dedication and wholesomeness despite everything she'd gone through, had been healing him with every light touch of her fingertips, with every taste of her lips, with every rare smile beaming from her heart.

Just like now when she smiled over the top of her coffee cup.

"Ahem." Having brought their drinks, Makenzie now stood poised beside them in his peripheral vision, her fingers with black fingernails expectant over a notepad. Since he'd been in this place so many times, he didn't need to read the menu because he knew what he wanted.

It wasn't just about the barbecue. He wanted a lifetime with Jessie. And if she gave him a chance, he wouldn't spend that precious time arguing and trying to persuade her to leave the dangerous job she loved. He'd support her in it and everything else. Just like he knew she'd support him.

That healed part of him might be ripped apart later if she walked away or if something happened to her. Yet he'd take that risk. She didn't even realize how much she meant to him.

Gratitude warmed him that Jessie simply existed, though he'd be way more grateful if she remained existing somewhere close to him.

But he wouldn't try to tuck her into a safe place and call it love. Yes, he'd worry about her, but he wouldn't change who she was.

Just like Isla, Jessie was fiercely independent and thrived on protecting others. It was something to admire, not to berate her for as he'd berated Isla. He took another hurried sip of coffee to chase away the bile over how he'd acted, appreciating the sweetness of the drink nearly as much as the sweetness of Jessie's smile.

Makenzie smirked again as she wrote Jessie's order and hustled away.

Maybe it was a good thing he hadn't met Jessie earlier in his life. It wouldn't have worked out between them because he wouldn't have been ready to be the man she needed and deserved.

God, I hope I'm that man now.

Jessie seemed to have changed, as well, and not only because she wore more feminine clothes now. She made his heart race whether she was in a sweater and jeans like when he'd met her or the spectacular flowing dress with yellow tropical flowers she'd worn in the Dominican Republic. But she seemed softer around the edges and more trusting, and he was thankful for the latter. Calmer, less intense, less hurt.

More willing to trust both him, and he hoped, God. He'd keep praying for that.

"How is Scratcher doing?" Her question threw him for a loop.

Then he grinned and took a sip of his hot, flavorful coffee. "Getting spoiled. I bring him treats all the time now. After all, thanks to him, I met you."

She laughed. "I think you would've met me anyway. But yes, Scratcher helped." Then she leaned forward and whispered, "Do you feel like we're being... watched?"

He winced. He was supposed to pay attention to his surroundings instead of staring at her and delving into his past. He glanced around.

True, a lot of people kept glancing in their direction. But he knew them, and most likely, it was curiosity about the new couple in town. However, he didn't recognize a few people, and a shiver of premonition ran down his spine again.

He'd had the same premonition the night before Isla died, when they'd had their biggest fight and he'd said all those harsh words he wished he could take back.

Was that it? After all, he'd been dwelling on the past ironically just when he was ready to move on. Or was something more going on?

"I think so, yes. Though the majority of these people just wonder about us." All the same, he didn't want Jessie to be uncomfortable even if his stomach rumbled in its demand for food. "Do you want to leave?"

She shook her head. "No, it's fine. Maybe I'm just paranoid."

Maybe he was, as well. While he didn't engage in reckless behavior, his safety worried him way less than hers. There wasn't even a comparison. Could he spend a lifetime worrying about her?

The quickened beat of his heart gave him the answer. Yes, if that meant he was going to be *with* her.

However, the mystery about the plane crash and possible murders following it wasn't over yet. He and Jessie had suspicions, and she was working through the list of household help Arianna had brought. They'd zeroed in on the female staff, especially the one Arianna had an odd feeling about. But they still had no proof.

He did a quick sweep of the room again, which wasn't easy because he'd let her take the chair with her back to the wall. Three people put him on guard. Two bearded biker guys and a woman in a hoodie who kept her head down at a nearby table.

When he turned back to Jessie, he caught her looking in the same direction. Then Makenzie walked to them with a tray emanating enticing aromas of barbecue and fries and obstructed the view.

After she left, he said grace. His heart sang when Jessie said a strong amen.

He told his heart not to make too much out of it. He wanted to ask questions, but he didn't. So they ate in silence.

Then she said, "I thought a lot about what you said about God. But what affected me the most isn't what you said, but the way you are. Even after your fiancée's death, you didn't become jaded and bitter. You're kind to people and animals, and yes, Rusty is a good judge of character. I'm sure Scratcher is, too. The way your parents are. You and your family and the way you treat people... The fact that I met you... That showed me the possibility God does care about me." She lifted her hand when he lit up and wanted to run around the table to scoop her in a hug. "This is just the beginning. But I'm open to trusting God again. I'm willing to pray and spend time getting to know Jesus the way you do."

Heat seared the backs of his eyes, and he sent up a prayer of thanks. "You have no idea how happy it makes me to hear it."

"I want to tell you something else." She paused to sip her coffee or maybe to gather her thoughts. "And I'll understand if you won't want to see me again."

His heart dropped to the floor.

Was she breaking up with him? *No, no, please no.* He held his breath, food forgotten.

"I needed a break away from work. It was good for me. Good for my friends. But as I spent time thinking about what else I want to do in my life..." She paused again. "Well, I don't. I mean, I don't want to do anything else. The chief who didn't like me is retiring soon. One of my buddies is rumored to become the new chief. I want to apply for the job again and take my chances. I know what happened with Isla. If that's too much for you—"

He raised a hand to stop her. He didn't even need to think. "I'll stand by you."

She blinked. "You... you will?"

He cringed. So many people had abandoned her that she'd expected it from him, too. Though in this case, he'd given her a good reason, considering his history.

He covered her hand with his, wishing he could be a human shield for her from her doubts and regrets and later from the danger in her job, too. But spouses couldn't be partners on the force. Besides, she wouldn't let him defend her at work, and he could learn to be all right with that. Even admire it.

Her courage and inner strength were some of the main features that attracted him to her in the first place. Well, besides those stormy eyes and the tiny birthmark above her upper lip that still drove him crazy even after he'd kissed it several times.

Warmth spread through him just at the memory, making his heart beat faster. "I'll always stand by you. I'll support you, including in your career. And I'll always be very, very proud of you. Actually, I already am."

She blinked fast as if struggling with tears. "I–I didn't know such things were possible. But why?"

He reached out and swiped an escaping tear from her cheek, his heart full even if his stomach wasn't yet. "Because you deserve it. And because I love you."

Her eyes went huge. "What?"

Argh. He shouldn't have said it. It was too soon. He busied himself with barbecue ribs though he could barely taste them. "You don't have to say anything. In fact, please don't say anything." He polished off a yummy rib, but it might as well have been cardboard.

What had he done?

"Please, please don't feel obligated to say anything back." His fingers tightened around the fork.

Regret bit into his insides. She wasn't ready for commitment, and he might've pushed her over the edge. Based on her half-full plate, he'd probably ruined dinner for her, too.

She rubbed her forehead. "I need to process it. I mean... Are you sure?"

He dropped the fork with a clatter against the plate. "Excuse me?"

"Right." She forked a potato, then placed the fork back. "But… I'm stubborn. I'm set in my ways. I can't cook to save my life. I'm not good at all this domestic bliss. My mother was a junkie, and who knows who my father is. And—"

He leaned over and pressed a finger to her lips before she'd find any faults with herself. "None of that matters. I find your stubbornness endearing. And I can cook. Though I'd happily live on turkey sandwiches all my life if it meant I'd be sharing them with you. What matters is that I can't imagine my life without you." His gaze fell on the salt and pepper shakers. This table had ones shaped like all-white and all-black horse heads. He fiddled with the all-white one. "And I'm willing to wait as long as it takes if there's even a grain-of-salt-size chance you'll ever feel the same way about me."

Her jaw slackened. "You suffered enough with Isla. Do you want to risk going through that again?"

He drained his coffee. "That's the thing. I didn't suffer with Isla. I was happy with her, despite our bickering over her work. I know better now. And I want to do my best to make you as happy as you make me. That said, I can't make you feel something you don't."

Everything inside him tensed. He couldn't be mistaken about the attraction between them. But there was a long way from attraction to love. And considering Jessie's tragic childhood, obstacles barricaded that road.

Enough obstacles for her to turn back and run.

Jessie's mind was reeling as they drove from the restaurant, his car filled with his signature pine-forest scent. Was it possible he truly loved her?

From what she knew about him, he wouldn't have said it if he didn't mean it. Her heart swelled, leaving her dizzy.

Then she deflated.

He'd gone through so much after Isla died. While Jessie didn't have a death wish, she knew the realities of her profession, and so did he. How could she be selfish enough to risk putting him in the same gut-wrenching situation again?

She stole a glance at his handsome profile, her entire being aching for him already, and she hadn't even left yet. His scent of pine needles filled her nostrils again, wreaking havoc on her senses.

Or did these thoughts stem from her own issues? It didn't take a psychology degree to figure out that neither she nor her foster sisters could form attachments easily, if at all.

Ronan deserved someone warm and affectionate, two things she wasn't. Yet he created a whirlwind of emotions in her that pulled her to him with an incredible force, to his quiet strength, reliability, realness, and yes, to his clear admiration of her.

Her feelings for him ran deep, but she couldn't separate all the undercurrents, much less label them.

Well, she might not know many things, but she knew she didn't want to be away from him.

She glanced out the window, partly to distract herself and partly to check on the rearview mirror. Then she tensed. Two vehicles behind them, a navy-blue SUV with tinted windows attracted her attention. When Ronan turned, one of the cars went straight, but the SUV turned, too. And was it a coincidence that snow covered its license plate?

She took a deep breath. It might not mean anything. Even after the SUV merged behind them onto the road leading to the ranch. But when she looked at Ronan, his frown confirmed her suspicions.

"You're wondering about the SUV." He seemed to speed up.

"Yes. It was in the restaurant parking lot. Okay, a lot of cars were there, but still..."

Her pulse spiked. It wasn't the best time to think about it, but things clicked in the face of danger, as if adrenaline wiped some fog in her brain. She'd been so sure men would abandon her like her parents had that she'd reinforced it by picking the wrong guys. In reality, her father had never abandoned her because he had no clue about her existence. Her foster sisters had stuck around.

God had never abandoned her. *She'd* turned her back on Him.

And Ronan had meant what he'd said. He'd stand by her. Even if she went back to Houston. Geographic distance didn't matter as much as distance in one's heart.

At the hint of imminent danger, all the reasons she couldn't let herself love Ronan didn't matter any longer. If he could have the courage to love her, even after what had happened to his fiancée, Jessie should meet him halfway. She should admit what deep inside she already knew.

"I love you, too," she said as she watched the approaching vehicle.

She couldn't risk shooting at it in case her assessment was wrong. Innocent people could just happen to travel on the same road they did. And while she could aim at targets and she was a decent shot, hitting tires easily only happened in the movies.

"What?" His voice was incredulous.

Well, her confession of love was going about as well as his had. She cringed even as she felt so much lighter believing there might be a chance for them, after all.

The SUV drew closer in the rearview mirror. She should've chosen another time for this conversation. But they both learned the hard way that sometimes there wasn't another time.

She took her weapon off safety, and everything tensed inside her. The navy-blue SUV drove around them while Ronan pressed on the brakes. Then it disappeared ahead. Air left her lungs in a sigh of relief, and she holstered her gun.

"I love you," she said again. "I have no clue how things are going to work out between us. But I also have no doubt about the way I feel."

A truck pulled from the country road as they passed it, then it practically rode their bumper. Premonition curdled her blood at the sight of the ravine ahead.

Guilt slammed into her even as the truck slammed into his car. She'd distracted Ronan, so he didn't have time to react. The screech of metal on metal assaulted her ears.

She took her weapon off safety and rolled down the window, but it was too late. Their car careened on the side of the road.

Ronan lost control of the vehicle as it slipped downhill on the snow. He couldn't do anything to stop the fall. A scream lodged in her throat, then escaped as his car skidded down the ravine.

She didn't want to die! This wasn't how it all was going to end for her and Ronan. She couldn't lose him. She loved him too much. Horror chilled every cell in her body, crystallized her blood to ice.

Her foot moved as if she were the one pumping on the brakes. Of course, he was doing everything to stop their fall. Including praying.

Lord, please.

It was half a prayer, half a scream.

Then an airbag exploded, and so did the pain inside her. Everything seemed to disappear.

Chapter Nineteen

By the time Ronan opened his eyes, blinked, and everything came into focus—okay, everything was still slightly blurry—the car had stopped moving. The latter was a good sign. The pain in his chest and the blood running from his nostrils weren't.

It smelled like smoke, and he wasn't sure whether it was from a deployed airbag or... Well, if he could smell something, his nose wasn't broken, despite the blood dripping. He was also alive.

Thank You, Lord.

He wiggled his toes and fingers and nothing seemed to be broken, which earned a careful sigh of relief as his chest still hurt.

Aware of his surroundings, he glanced out the window in case whoever had driven them off the road had arrived to finish the job. It was difficult to say for sure, but he couldn't see anyone so far.

"Jessie!" Worry slammed into him. How selfish to think only about himself. Did he say her name loudly, or did he whisper it?

With noise in his ears, he couldn't be sure. "Jessie! Are you okay?" he said louder, or so he thought.

Still no answer.

Shivery things coiled in his gut. She must be unconscious. Or... He went cold all over. No, he wouldn't think that. He couldn't.

He also couldn't see much because of the airbag, so he called out her name again and again in vain. His stomach roiled. He turned his head slowly, doing his best to deflate the airbag.

Then he gasped. Blood covered Jessie's face, and she wasn't moving.

No, no, no!

Everything inside him shuddered. He reached out and touched her forearm, to zero effect.

Lord, please, please, please!

He had to think. To keep his composure. He'd been in dangerous situations before, including being shot at or helping people in accidents. Only those situations didn't include the woman he loved covered in blood and unconscious. He needed to call for the ambulance, and...

Was the car in danger of exploding?

He needed to get them both out of the car. He couldn't be sure, but he suspected he distinguished a gasoline odor. The thought urged him to click his seat belt open and half fall, half climb out of the vehicle. So many places in him hurt and protested, but he didn't stop to assess it or even pay attention.

He hoped someone on the road had seen them getting driven off and called the ambulance, but he couldn't see any passersby. Well, that also meant their attacker hadn't shown up masquerading as a concerned citizen.

With shaking fingers, Ronan fished his cell phone from his pocket and called 911 and put them on speakerphone as he circled the car. He'd explain the situation while he tried to help her.

Panic gripped his throat with ghastly fingers as he pulled the passenger door and it wouldn't budge. He tried again to the same result, shaking the car. Stuck!

He picked up a branch and broke the window, then managed to open the door from the inside. The sight of Jessie injured and motionless nearly undid him. But he couldn't let himself fall apart. He'd been trained for situations like this, and he needed his training to take over.

He placed his fingers on her neck.

Please, Lord, please!

He nearly wept when he distinguished a weak pulse. She was alive! He relayed the information to the dispatcher and disconnected, despite the dispatcher's protest.

His heart thudded, going between despair and hope and back. "Jessie, can you hear me? Please answer me, darling."

No answer.

It wouldn't be recommended to move Jessie's body due to possible back injuries. Normally, he'd wait for paramedics to make the assessment and move her. Unless there was a danger of the car setting on fire. He shuddered at the scents of gasoline and smoke. Besides, there was the added danger that the person who had driven them off the road might show up.

He needed to get her out of the car to a safer location.

Adrenaline pumping in his blood, he leaned over to unbuckle her seat belt. It didn't budge. Seriously? Did everything have to be *stuck* today?

He took a deep breath of air tinted with even more smoke now. Getting angry never helped anyone. Ask him how he knew.

Thankfully, he carried a pocket knife. His brothers called it paranoid, and he called it cautious. Right now, cautious was good. He retrieved the knife from his pocket, clicked it open, and snipped the belt.

Jessie groaned but didn't open her eyes.

"It's going to be okay. It's going to be okay. It's going to be okay," he said it more for his benefit than hers. Well, hers, too, because he had to believe she could hear him. "I've got you. I promise."

He lifted her from the seat, doing his best to disturb her as little as possible in case of injuries. Then he walked away from the vehicle as fast as he could, carrying his precious cargo.

Minutes later, the explosion shattered the earth, assaulting his eardrums and nearly rocking him to his knees. He staggered as a heat wave hit him in the back with a wild force, and it was a miracle he stayed on his feet. He shielded Jessie with his body from shards flying in their direction.

Thank You, Lord, for saving us.

Then a movement behind a tree ahead caught his attention. He'd reach for his gun, but then he'd have to drop Jessie.

A blonde woman dressed in a leather blazer and dark jeans stepped from around the tree, a gun in her hands. "You just refuse to die, don't you?"

Was this Mylah? She didn't look like her photos, but then plastic surgeries after facial burns could alter her appearance to the point of being unrecognizable. Even by people who'd once known her closely, like Wyatt.

Ronan's every muscle tightened. How could he be this careless and not pay attention to his surroundings like he'd been trained? Yes, he was occupied with helping Jessie, but that was no excuse. He placed her on the snow gently. Then his hand flew to his holster. "Hello, Mylah."

Her eyes narrowed. "I wouldn't pull that gun on me, you know. I have a few precious seconds on you, and I intend to use them. Lift your hands so I can see them. If you do anything else, anything at all, I'm going to shoot Jessie."

Ronan grunted but did as Mylah commanded.

Remorse stung. Some cop he was. That's what he got for ignoring his surroundings. Mylah had somehow made it down the ravine, and preoccupied with getting Jessie from his car, he'd had no clue. The ringing in his ears after the accident and the explosion must've prevented him from hearing her. Well, no time for regrets.

Lord, please help me. Guide me through this situation so Jessie stays alive. Please save her. Please!

Where were the police and ambulance? If he could stall long enough, maybe he and Jessie had a chance for survival. Maybe.

He had to keep Mylah talking.

"I understand why you killed Wyatt," he said. "He caused the plane crash to kill you. You were left burned and disfigured, well, at least until surgery repaired your face. And I guess his youngest son died because he discovered your secret. But why follow us? Why try to murder us?"

"Because you put your nose where it didn't belong!" She snarled. "I overheard Arianna on the phone, saying she suspected one of the other maids. And I knew you'd been to the Dominican Republic, asking people about me. Someone might have talked. The friend who helped me get a new identity and a new face told me you'd been persistent. He also told me where you lived."

"We had no proof at all that you survived the plane crash. Only guesses and one of your earrings." He could try to run, duck, and roll, but that would leave Jessie exposed. He didn't doubt Mylah would make good on her promise to shoot Jessie. He shivered in his sweater and stayed where he was, shielding her as much as he could.

Mylah's face crumpled. Then she shook her head. "No proof? Doesn't matter at this point. I've started a new life with a new identity before and I can do it again. I already have the papers for another fake ID."

Where were the police? And would they figure out not to arrive with sirens blazing? Sirens would be a sure cue for Mylah to shoot.

He had to keep her talking. And pray. "Why did you wait years to kill Wyatt? And why didn't you leave the house after you killed him? You'd had your revenge."

"Something about crawling through jungles half alive in pain and agony taught me to be patient. And the plastic surgery took some time." She shrugged, but the gun in her hands didn't falter.

"Or maybe you didn't want to kill. But the danger of Hayden being disinherited gave you another motive. You had a soft spot for him, didn't you?"

"Hayden was the son I never had a chance to have. I adore him. Since what Wyatt did to me, I couldn't get close to a man again. Not that I'd want a man to see my scarred body, anyway," she whispered. "Plastic surgeries couldn't correct everything."

Ronan's heart constricted. He'd feel compassion for the woman if she wasn't holding him and Jessie at gunpoint. Why was it taking the paramedics and police so long? Jessie needed help. He sent up another fervent prayer.

After hiding her secret and anger for years, Mylah obviously wanted to talk, to make someone see her side. And he intended to use that to his advantage.

"Weren't you afraid Wyatt or someone else who saw you before would recognize you?" Was that faint sound the police sirens?

Hope unraveled. Sirens. This was far from over. It would be difficult for the police officers to appear unnoticed, and he didn't look forward to being taken hostage. Better him than Jessie, though.

Mylah's mirthless laugh made him cringe. "After all I've been through, even *I* can't recognize myself. Besides, he treats his house staff like an extension of his furniture. He wouldn't pay much attention to a lowly maid." Her hand wobbled. "Despite what his family thought when I was involved with him, *I* wasn't there for his fortune. I loved the man. Okay, I didn't mind him giving me expensive gifts or including me in his will, but who would?"

"Are you sure it's *him* who gave the order to arrange a plane crash? He could've just broken up with you. No need to take such drastic measures." Ronan ached to get to Jessie. He might've heard a muffled groan, but he wasn't sure. After the explosion, he had to strain to hear Mylah, and his ears might've played tricks on him. His gut tightened, and he shuddered in the cold.

Jessie had to be okay.

She had to!

"I found out Wyatt thought I'd cheated on him, which wasn't true. He was a ruthless man who wouldn't hesitate to get revenge. But he didn't count on me taking a friend along for the trip. He wouldn't have been happy with her joining us, but I figured he loved me enough to forgive me. How naïve I was. I just wanted to give her a nice vacation after she escaped from an abusive marriage. Instead, I led her to her death." The weapon shook in her grip.

He waited for the opportunity to attack, but there wasn't any. Not without exposing Jessie to danger. Everything shattered inside him.

"She was an innocent person who didn't deserve to die. Oh, and Wyatt didn't care about the pilot, either. After I survived the crash and realized the others were dead, I crawled back to her body with the chain and pendant he gave me, as well as my purse. She was already wearing my shoes and my clothes as a gift, though most of them were burned by then. I was right to be cautious. My friend told me large sums were paid to prevent an in-depth investigation into the crash." Her eyes became haunted. "I don't know why I'm even telling you all this. Anyway, your time is up."

His insides went cold. Well, he was already cold, but now several shudders racked his body. He tensed, preparing to throw himself onto the snow and roll, then fire. Still, his chances of survival were minimal. And he couldn't risk Jessie's life. "Wait! You don't have to do it."

Sadness shadowed Mylah's green eyes. "Unfortunately, I do."

"Police! Freeze!" Shouts from the top of the ravine made her glance back.

Using the distraction, Ronan fired, then covered Jessie with his body.

Bullets grazed where he'd stood. His heart thudded. Bullets could still go through him and wound her.

"Lord, please don't let the bullets hit Jessie. Please don't let the bullets hit Jessie."

Once the gunfire stopped, he identified himself loudly.

"Drop the gun and stand up with your hands where I can see them!" The command from the police rang clear.

He'd used those words himself many times before. They mustn't be close enough to recognize him. Was the threat neutralized? Mylah was slumped on the ground, not moving. And everything in him ached. After what she'd endured, he couldn't wish this woman ill, though after the standoff he didn't have warm feelings for her, either.

Praying Jessie was okay, he scrambled to his feet and lifted his hands, palms up. He did it slowly, without any jerky movements.

Guilt flashed in his buddy George's eyes as he approached Ronan. George was a stickler for rules, especially now that he was nearing retirement. He also looked ashen for not only having to discharge his weapon but also possibly killing a person. "I'm just following procedure. Oh, man. The chief will want tons of reports for this shootout. Considering we have a dead civilian now. You'll have to go with us to the station. What on earth happened here?"

Ronan cringed. He didn't have time for tons of reports. He had to know Jessie was going to make it and be okay. His heart ached for her. "You saved my life and the life of someone I love." His words made his buddy perk up a little and stand taller. "I'll give you my statement now and file the report later."

George shook his head. "The chief will have a coronary."

"I have to be with the woman I love." Ronan swallowed hard. "She's a former police officer with the Houston PD. She was badly injured in the accident." He desperately searched Jessie with his gaze. She was still on the snow, but... Did she move? Or were his eyes now playing tricks on him?

His heartbeat went into overdrive, and it was already working at high speed. George waved for the paramedics to approach.

Ronan said more desperate prayers as he gave his statement as fast as he could. No lies, yet without revealing anything he knew Jessie wouldn't want told. Mylah's new fake ID could be a blessing—nothing in the report would link her to the Wyatt family. He could simply say she was the suspect in a case Jessie had worked on, who'd decided to eliminate Jessie.

Meanwhile, paramedics checked Jessie's vital signs, then loaded her on a stretcher. He jerked in their direction, aching to go with them.

By then, he was nearly numb with cold and worry. Yet, as he answered numerous questions from his fellow officers, the same thoughts whirled in his head. Jessie had to be okay. She had to be okay. She had to be okay.

And if she was... The investigation was over. Her time in Cowboy Crossing might be over.

Was it going to be over between them, too?

Chapter Twenty

"Do you need me to fluff your pillow? Or do you want some water?"

Jessie half grunted and half chuckled in the hospital bed. "Ronan, you don't need to fuss over me." Despite her protest, she enjoyed it. No man had ever fussed over her.

Even more, she enjoyed seeing him alive and healthy. And not in danger. Danger she'd put him in. She shuddered at what could've happened.

He lowered himself onto the plastic chair near the bed. "Humor me. I like the excuse to touch you and know for sure you're okay."

"You don't need that excuse." She craved to hug and kiss him, but being hooked up to IVs in her right arm and with her left arm encased in a plaster cast, it wasn't easy. Her throat was parched. "I could use some water, please."

He leaned over her, giving her that clean pine-needle scent she'd grown to love, and brought a cup with a straw to her lips. She'd prefer his lips close to her instead of the straw, but she did need to stay hydrated. She took a few hurried sips of cold water, letting it soothe her throat.

"Besides, you're the one with a concussion, two broken ribs, and a broken arm." His face scrunched. "I should've prevented it from happening."

She'd been in excruciating pain before and surely would be later, but right now, the painkillers swimming in her bloodstream numbed it. "I don't see how. And if not for you, I wouldn't be alive. You saved my life three times yesterday. First, when you kept the car from flipping. Next, when you got me out of the car about to explode. And finally, when you didn't let Mylah shoot me."

They kept silent, grieving a life cut short. Ronan's bullet hadn't killed her, but George's had. After his initial worry, George was touted as a hero and now rethinking his retirement. He'd taken Jessie's statement in the hospital and given Ronan lots of teasing.

Mylah's death, though, was so heartbreaking.

Despite all the tragedy and injuries, Jessie felt relieved. Wyatt's death had nothing to do with any of the girls. They'd always be on the lookout and keep their secret, so Gold would never be endangered by Wyatt's family, but Jessie and her foster sisters could breathe more freely for now.

Though it wasn't all over yet. While Mylah was sure Wyatt was behind the plane crash, Jessie wasn't. His wife had a much bigger motive, and to think about it, his sons, as well.

But for now, Jessie would let it go, along with the resentment she'd felt for the man. In Mylah, Jessie had seen firsthand what stewing in past resentment for years could do to a person. God said that vengeance was best left up to Him, and now, she agreed. She could put her future in His hands.

And turn back to her beautiful present staring her in the eyes.

Ronan touched her cheek with the back of his hand, causing her to lean into his touch. "I might've done it for selfish reasons. I can't imagine my life without you. Frankly, I don't want to."

Her heart lodged in her throat. Was he saying... Or were the painkillers causing hallucinations? She did feel funny, a bit bubbly and light-headed. Could she be imagining things?

She didn't have a chance to ask as she tensed at footfalls in the hall. Ronan got up and shielded her as if ready to protect her again.

But then her girls filed into the room, and his shoulders relaxed while he stepped aside.

"Don't ever do something like that again." Madeline positioned a bouquet of elegant white roses perfectly centered on the side table and wheeled it closer.

"I agree. You scared us to death!" Genevieve added a paper bag emanating an enticing aroma to the same table. Food was always her love language.

Without any words, Paisley simply hugged Jessie, mindful of the IVs. Arianna wasn't here, so she must be the one left behind with Gold. Even if the peril seemed to be past, it was too early to lessen their precautions.

Jessie rolled her eyes. "Nah. Next time, I'll deliberately put myself into danger just to worry you."

Madeline pursed her well-outlined lips covered in shiny lip gloss. "Not funny."

"Thank you for keeping our girl alive." Genevieve gave Ronan a bear hug.

Madeline, who wasn't the hugging type, shook his hand with the same words of gratitude.

"Don't mention it." Ronan's ears pinked. "Jessie is my world."

Genevieve looked from Jessie to Ronan and then to Jessie again. Then she touched the sleeve of Madeline's white coat. "Now that we made it all clear to Jessie, we should stop by the cafeteria and see what they have."

"You always think about food." Then Madeline's hand flew to her mouth as if she realized her faux pas. "Oh, oops. Of course, we should stop by the cafeteria. What a great idea. We should go to the gift shop, too, now that I think about it."

Paisley laughed. "We sure should. The décor in this room is too bland. It could use a few bright get-well balloons. Pink ones."

"Thank you for visiting." Jessie smiled.

She loved her friends. She really did. But she appreciated Genevieve and Paisley's tactful and Madeline's less-tactful intentions to leave her alone with Ronan. She ached to know what he was going to say before being interrupted. Spending a lifetime with her... Did that sound like the beginning of a proposal?

Or was it wishful thinking?

Huh. She, who was so afraid of commitment, actually hoped he'd propose someday. Must be the result of a concussion. Or the way she'd changed.

Once her friends left the room, he sat again and reached for her free hand—the one not covered by a cast—careful around the IVs. "It's probably not the best time. And you don't have to answer right away..."

New footfalls followed, and she tensed. A nurse entered the room and checked Jessie's vital signs. Of course, the woman was just doing her job of keeping Jessie alive, and Jessie was grateful for it. Still, she was even more grateful when she was alone with him after the nurse left.

His eyes searched hers as he took her hand again. "I have to ask you..."

Voices in the hall made him fall silent. She suppressed a grimace at another interruption and smiled instead.

His parents and Brandon entered the small room, crowding it. Yet a warm feeling spread inside her. It was wonderful to have people care about her as if... as if she were their family. Of course, she could live without the concussion, broken ribs, and broken arm to show for it. But those would heal.

Genuine worry etched their faces, and she hurried to say that it could be much worse. "I'm alive thanks to your son and brother. He's truly a hero."

His ears pinked again. "Please, don't say things like that. I'm no hero."

His father chuckled. "Eventually, son, you'll learn not to argue with a woman. Especially if she praises you."

Jessie winked back at the man.

His mother stepped forward, holding the bright get-well balloons Paisley had talked about. "You'll come to our house to recover. We take care of our own."

Wait a minute. Did... did they consider Jessie their own? Like... like family? Really? She wished her head was clearer because some things took longer to comprehend right now.

Yet she didn't want to be a burden. She'd learned to be self-sufficient, though granted she didn't have a few bones broken at the time. "That's very sweet. And thank you. But I'm sure my foster sisters will take care of me."

"Nonsense. I don't want to hear any arguments. We've got plenty of room. Oh, Madeline and any of your friends will be welcome at our place to visit and help you anytime."

Brandon groaned at Madeline's name, and Ronan threw him a stern glance.

Once Jessie didn't have fog in her brain, she was going to talk to Madeline. See if she had feelings for Brandon. Because if she did...

Mrs. O'Neill patted Jessie on the hand that wasn't in a cast, avoiding the IV. "I'm so sorry this happened to you. I'm praying you'll be up and running soon so we don't have to prolong the wait for your wedding."

Jessie's eyes went wide. Good thing she was lying down, or she'd slide to the floor. "My what?"

His father shook his head as if in disbelief. "Are you telling me this son of mine hasn't proposed yet?"

Ronan harrumphed. "Well, how am I supposed to do that if I keep getting interrupted?"

His father tsked. "You shouldn't have let it stop you."

Was this happening? She closed her eyes, then opened them. Yes, Ronan was still there, this time on his knee. A solitaire ring sparkled around the neck of the most beautiful perfume bottle she'd ever seen. The girls must've blurted out her weakness.

Joy flooded her. But doubt wedged in, too. Such things didn't happen to people like her.

"You don't have to be blackmailed into proposing to me," she whispered.

His face fell. "You don't love me any longer? Was that only adrenaline talking?"

She wished she could hug him, but she didn't want to pull out any IVs. "I do love you. Though right now, some *painkillers* might be talking." Seeing his widened eyes, she chuckled. She didn't dare to laugh because broken ribs might react despite the meds. "If there's one thing I'm going to be sure about today, tomorrow, the day after tomorrow, and twenty and forty years from now—or however long I'll live—it's that I love you."

He grinned. "And I love you. Now and forever. Will you make me the happiest man alive and marry me?"

Her eyes misted. "I'm a woman without a job, without a house, without a family, without traditions—"

"You're the woman I love, courageous, compassionate, and fiercely loyal to those who are blessed to be close to you. I couldn't find a better person if I lived a hundred years. And I'd be honored to share my family, my home, our traditions, and everything that I have and everything that I am and ever will be with you."

How had she found such a man? Even more incredible was that he wanted to share himself and the rest of his life with her.

His mother cleared her throat. "The family part. You want to share us... It's not because we overwhelm you, is it?"

Ronan hesitated, then said, "That, too."

His mother nodded. "Just checking."

"As for the job, I just heard from my connections in the Springfield Police Department. There's a vacancy. I'll put in a good word for you if you want the job."

She brightened. "Really?"

"Really." Ronan paused, a shadow cast on his handsome face. "Not that I'd want to take you away from your foster sisters."

"I already had this conversation with my girls. Paisley is staying at the lodge for a while. She can do her job from anywhere, and the lodge fits her just fine. Ahem, especially now that a special someone is going to return to Cowboy Crossing for a month. Madeline decided to do some medical research, and solitude suits her. Plus, the big yard suits her dog. We'll miss the others, but they'll come visit as often as they can."

"And they all will be welcome to join us for dinners." This time, Ronan's father cleared his throat. "But aren't you forgetting something?"

She blinked. She was usually more attentive, but she wasn't usually drugged up. "What?"

"To say yes!" Paisley called from the hall.

Then the girls filed in, giggling like teenagers. By now, it was standing room only in the small hospital room. Still, Madeline managed to stay as far away from Brandon as possible.

Jessie better give Ronan another chance to escape. "I'm not an easy person to be around."

He grinned. "That's fine. Neither am I."

"Yes!" She returned the grin. "I'll be thrilled to marry you. Especially if you cook more of those yummy Irish dishes."

"I second that." Paisley high-fived Madeline.

Jessie stumbled. "Not that... that's the only reason."

"I know." He got up and opened the bottle, which filled the room with the most delightful citrus scent she'd ever smelled. He recapped the lid and gave her the bottle, and her fingers tightened around its smooth surface. Then he slipped the ring on her finger, which was good because otherwise tomorrow she might think she'd dreamed of his proposal.

Well, she'd had dreams of him proposing to her, but now it was a reality.

He kissed her, but even that gentle kiss sent butterflies dancing in her tummy the same way they danced on Paisley's skirt.

Congratulations erupted, then hushed when the nurse told them to keep it quiet.

Her eyes still misty, Jessie breathed in deeply, savoring the citrusy smell of hope once again. Here she was, broken into many pieces, with long months of recovery ahead, and she'd never been so happy. "I can't wait to spend the rest of my life with you. I'll even learn to cook."

"If that's not a declaration of love, I don't know what is," Madeline mumbled.

Jessie agreed with her. She just prayed and hoped one day her girls would find their happiness, as well.

Two weeks later...

Ronan had never seen anything this beautiful before. His breath hitched as Jessie walked down the aisle to him. As he'd expected, her dress was simple and elegant, without any lace, tulle, or shimmery adornments. She still wore a cast on her arm but carried a muff to cover it. Still, his heart squeezed from compassion.

Because it was winter, she had to wear boots and a cover, but he'd be thrilled to marry her even if she wore overalls and sneakers, and he'd told her as much.

In a whirlwind of preparation, they'd decided they didn't want to waste any time and would marry in two weeks. He'd felt guilty at first because it might put more pressure on his mother. But she told him she'd been preparing for it for years.

Since Jessie's only family were her foster sisters, they'd decided on a small private wedding, with close family only. That made it safe for Gold to attend. The shy, pretty teen joined in as an extra bridesmaid.

But he couldn't take his gaze off Jessie, her radiant smile. His father had offered to give her away, and she'd had tears in her eyes when she'd gratefully declined. Genevieve was walking her down the aisle now. Ronan still didn't understand all the dynamics in the small group, but he guessed Genevieve was a maternal figure for the rest of them, despite being only a few years older.

Jessie grinned as she took her place near him, and everything inside him melted. He'd waited so long for this day without even knowing it.

He only wished Brandon could be as happy. Right now, his best man looked like a storm cloud on his other side. Brandon had to interact with Madeline, who was one of the bridesmaids, and it looked like smoke was about to come out of his usually even-tempered brother. Ronan stole a glance to the left.

On the contrary, Madeline was calm like the ocean without a cloud in sight. Too calm, and that might mean plenty was going on under the surface. Maybe he had started to understand some of this group's dynamics, after all.

Despite all the fuming or maybe because of it, Brandon threw glances—or was it daggers?—Madeline's way. Like the other bridesmaids, she wore a silver-hued dress that suited her so much that she looked like a silver statuette. The dresses' hues reminded him with tenderness of the moonlight touching the ocean in the Dominican Republic, and he wondered whether Jessie chose the color because of that memory.

Paisley was the maid of honor, but unlike the others, she wore a bright pink dress that matched her hair—well, half of it.

Ronan said a prayer for Jessie and her friends and his brother. Cormac hadn't made it to the wedding from his army deployment as he couldn't change his leave to an earlier date. But Ronan was shocked to find that Cormac and one of Jessie's foster-sisters communicated as online pals.

Was this God's intention?

Then Ronan's gaze wavered only between Jessie and the priest, as all his attention concentrated on his gorgeous bride.

Ronan loved her so much. His chest swelled. He'd received far more blessings in life than he could wish for.

Epilogue

Paisley knew this was the weirdest idea she'd come up with. That was saying something because if weirdness was a country, she'd be its president.

Her friend Madeline stared at her, hugging her delicate porcelain cup in her elegant long fingers. "Good thing I wasn't drinking coffee when you asked me this. Or I'd spew it all over you."

Madeline was always so cool and composed. Paisley doubted her friend ever spilled any drink on anyone. Maybe that aloofness together with high cheekbones and symmetrical features was what made men search Madeline out. Including the guy who made Paisley's heart beat faster. But the latter was her own fault.

She adjusted her bumblebee headband as she leaned against the marbled counter. There was a first for everything, so she moved away from her gorgeous friend, just to be on the safe side if some coffee would fly her way.

She clutched the counter's edges. "It's not as crazy as it sounds." Maybe she was trying to convince herself more than Madeline. "I've been communicating with this guy online for years. And now he thinks I'm you. Or, well, you're me." Okay, it did sound a little crazy. Paisley twirled a strand of her pink hair around her finger.

"Why would he do that?" Madeline pinned her with a gaze from those blue eyes that made men lose their minds. Paisley had never mastered anything similar.

She squirmed. Her friend meant well, but she didn't like feeling like a bug under a microscope. "I sent him a group photo of me and my friends, including you. He jumped to the conclusion that I was, well, you."

Because any man's attention moved straight to Madeline wherever she went.

Paisley's heart skipped a beat as she thought about *his* photos, and warmth pooled in her belly, spreading gingerly. His hair was cut short, military style, and he filled out the uniform nicely. But it went beyond the uniform, and she didn't mean his biceps. It was much more about the way he treated her. The way she wanted to be treated. In real life, guys dismissed her as a geek or weirdo, and if they didn't, it didn't end well, anyway.

How could she have that much of the proverbial spark with someone she'd never met? Yet it wasn't just a spark. It was already a fire burning inside.

"What were you thinking, sending that photo?" Madeline voiced Paisley's thoughts as she sipped her coffee. If Madeline had been born in different times, she'd be born a duchess. Or a queen, maybe. No wonder her nickname was Ice Queen in high school.

Paisley peeled herself from the counter. "I know! And you're not helping."

"Okay. What can I do to help?" Madeline's expression softened. Finally! Then those blue eyes narrowed, and she clattered the cup onto the counter. "Oh no. No, no, no."

That's what Paisley liked about their friendship. She didn't have to spell it out for her foster sisters. They understood her without words, though for some of them it took longer than others.

"Yes." Paisley nodded, making the bumblebee construction on her head bob. "All you have to do is meet with him as me and introduce me as your friend." Of course, the chance that his attention would switch from gorgeous Madeline to Paisley was slim to none, but she had to try.

"No. And wouldn't it seem weird we have the same names?" Madeline shook her head. "You should've told him the truth from the get-go."

Paisley rolled her eyes. "Don't you think I know that?"

Madeline studied her, her eyes unreadable, as always. "You really like this guy, don't you?"

Did she have to say it? Paisley swallowed hard and twirled a strand of azure blue hair this time. Then she lifted puppy eyes at her friend. Even Madeline couldn't be immune to puppy eyes. "Please? If you don't do this, I can't meet him. And I *want* to meet him." Wasn't that the truth?

"Okay." Before Paisley had a chance to exhale, Madeline continued, "But you're going to tell him the truth."

"Eventually," Paisley muttered, and this time she did exhale fully.

A lazy smile tipped Madeline's expertly outlined lips. Uh-oh. She was up to something. But it wasn't like Paisley could back out at this point.

Okay, one disaster averted somewhat. Relieved, she poured herself a glass of orange juice and walked to her room. She opened her laptop covered in butterfly stickers. Usually, working on her laptop uplifted her. But this time, heaviness weighed on her shoulders.

She stared at the screen. Could she do this? Or would it be better not to know?

She'd lived decades without knowing who her parents were or anything about her birth siblings, if they even existed. Why this sudden desire to track them down?

Was it because Cormac had talked so much about his brothers? He didn't mean to be insensitive, but it created a longing in her for what she didn't have. Yes, she had foster sisters whom she adored, though some of them—ahem, Madeline—didn't always make it easy.

But Paisley wanted something more. Deeper. Different. She couldn't name it yet.

And if she could ever have a chance with Cormac, which she doubted at this point, she needed to know about any genetic diseases. Her exes broke up with her partly because they didn't want a wife who "could be a genetic bomb about to explode."

She took a deep breath. She was a whiz at digging up information. And knew which ancestry websites she could look at. Of course, there were no guarantees.

On the other hand, ignorance was bliss. What if she discovered something about her parents that crushed her? She was the optimistic one of the foster sisters, but she'd learned to be realistic. Her fingers hovered over the keyboard. Then she started typing.

Her phone pinged an incoming message. Her heart fluttered like the butterfly wings on her laptop at Cormac's name on the phone screen.

I look forward to seeing you.

Madeline's words rang in her ears.

Just tell him.

Easy for Madeline to say. Men fell at her feet right and left. Paisley wasn't ready for another rejection. It was bad enough that her parents had rejected her, then the boys she'd liked because she didn't fit into their idea of a girlfriend. Only her foster sisters stood by her.

But there should be a way out of this sticky situation. She just hadn't figured it out yet.

She typed, "Can't wait to see you."

THE END

From Alexa. Did you enjoy reading Ronan and Jessie's story? Would you like to read Cormac and Paisley's romance in *No Mistaken Identity for a Cowboy*? If so, please click here[1]. Thank you very much for reading my books!

---

1.   https://books2read.com/u/3G5JvO

Other books by Alexa Verde

To see an updated list of all my other books or subscribe to my weekly reader newsletter (and get a free ebook as your welcome gift!) click here[1].

---

1. https://www.subscribepage.com/alexaverdepublishedbooks

Acknowledgments

First of all, thank You to God for putting up with me, and for all the blessings!

A million thanks to you, my readers, for reading my books, for sending me encouragement, and for supporting me.

For naming the cat, thanks to Lana H, Cathy, Sharon, and Rose.

For naming the horse, thanks to Nancy H and Jeanne

For naming the heroine, thanks to Stephanie, Jan, Susan, and Karen.

Many thanks to my street team, Alexa's Amazing Readers, and to my beta readers, whom I love to pieces. Special thanks to Terry, MaryEllen, Gail, Carol, Susan, Margaret, Trudy, Kim, Nati, and Julie for their feedback and help with typo-spotting!

Heartfelt thanks to author Jessie Gussman for coming up with the idea for the Cowboy Crossing series and for helping me so much on the way. Jessie, you make me laugh, you make me smile, and you make the world a better place.

I also thank my wonderful editor, Deirdre, for coming through for me every time.